# AYLA FOX & THE MIRROR OF SOULS

Dean Crawford

© 2018 Dean Crawford
Published: 24th February 2018
Publisher: Fictum Ltd

The right of Dean Crawford to be identified as author of this Work has been asserted by him in accordance with sections 77 and 78 of the Copyright, Designs and Patents Act 1988.
All rights reserved.

www.deancrawfordbooks.com

# One

**The Storm**

The first storm arrived in the late afternoon, just as school was coming to an end.

Nobody was really prepared for just how bad it would get, even though the television stations had been forecasting torrential downpours and heavy thunderstorms for the past two days. Ayla Fox had listened that morning to the broadcasters as they discussed the dramatic nature of the storm cells marching across the Atlantic Ocean, all with furrowed brows and lots of sombre nodding as experts warned of worse to come.

*'The weather we're seeing is some of the most dramatic evidence yet that our world is changing for the worse, and we're not doing enough to try to prevent it.'*

Although there had been little spoken about it at school during the day, Ayla and her school friends busy with maths and English and P.E in the afternoon sunshine, the horizon to the west had finally caught their attention toward the end of a particularly close–run game of rounders. Gary Schwarz was almost at the end of a home run, the third of that afternoon, sprinting as though his life depended on it as the girls in the class clapped him on. Ayla had been clapping too, but her eyes had been drawn to a dark line that had appeared along the horizon, as though some unseen giant had scrawled with deep grey crayon behind distant hills.

Gary Schwarz crossed into the safe zone a moment before the ball landed in the hands of a member of the opposite team. Too slow to hit the pad, the catcher was forced to watch as Schwarz casually slowed down and high–fived one of the other batsmen, his floppy blond hair catching the sunlight and his smile bright. A shrill voice reached out across the playing field.

'Okay, last team's turn and then we're done here! Give it your best effort!'

Mrs Fattimer was a rotund woman whom Ayla suspected had probably not given her best effort at anything physical for some years, although of course nobody said anything about that. Stern and unforgiving, with a shock of spiky grey hair and round spectacles, she ruled Year Four with an iron fist and a high–pitched voice.

'Best effort,' Ayla's best friend, Rose Trent, uttered bleakly.

Rose was a skinny waif of a girl with thickly curled blonde hair, gangly legs and round–rimmed spectacles that she never, ever removed. The lenses made her eyes look bigger and rounder than they really were, and had earned her the nickname Bug. She hated sports, preferring to spend hours in the library rather than running about on a rounders pitch.

'Nearly over now,' Ayla offered. 'A few more minutes and school's out.'

Ayla gestured with a nod to the clock built into the wall of the main building. A quarter to three. The lesson would finish in five minutes, they would then change back into their uniforms and would be out of the school gates about one billionth of a second after that.

'Then you'll see everyone run with effort,' Rose smiled in reply as she picked up the bat handed to her by Gary Schwarz.

'Try not to screw it up,' he sneered without looking directly at her.

For someone so effortlessly handsome, Ayla found it strange that he was so needlessly cruel to people. Schwarz was taller, faster and better looking than anyone else in the school, yet he acted as though the entire world was against him.

'I'll try,' Rose replied.

'Well, that's all we can expect,' Schwarz uttered as he breezed past them without another glance, loudly enough that the rest of the class sniggered.

Ayla pretended in her mind that they weren't there as she watched Rose walk out to the stump and face the pitcher. The voice of Tamsin Crittall sneered from somewhere behind Ayla.

'Rose walks like she's got an apple up her ar…'

'Aren't you supposed to be supporting her?' snapped a boy from nearby, 'she's on our team.'

Tamsin was a chubby, angry girl with flame red hair pulled back into tight dreadlocks that to Ayla looked like streaks of red carrot pouring from her head. Tamsin reached out to the offending boy and grabbed his collar in one thick fist.

'You got a problem with me, Burton?'

Burton shook his head, his eyes wide with surprise at the sudden aggression. Tamsin glared at him for a moment longer and then shoved him off the bench onto his back in the grass. The other boys behind Ayla rolled their eyes but said nothing. Tamsin glanced at Ayla but did not acknowledge her in any way but for a brief sneer. Ayla sighed. Most of the other kids looked past her like that, Ayla neither interesting to them nor offensive. Someone had once described her as a "hole in the air", which had both hurt her and encouraged her. She liked nothing more than being on her own, and she hated change of any kind.

A rising series of cheers broke Ayla's reverie and she saw the pitcher fire the ball at Rose as though he was attempting to decapitate her with a single blow. Rose squealed pathetically and ducked as the ball rocketed over her head and was caught by the catcher behind her.

'One!' Mrs Fattimer snapped, raising a finger in the air.

'Ton,' whispered a boy behind Ayla, to a ripple of delighted chuckles.

The pitcher fired again and Rose swung wildly. The bat connected with the ball but only just, clipping it and sending it off at an awkward angle. The bizarre trajectory fooled the catcher and the ball sailed past him as Rose dropped the bat and made it to first base in her gangling gait, a feeble ripple of applause following her.

Ayla got up and dragged herself to the stump. She heard a couple of shouts of encouragement from the class, although she knew none of it was done in a friendly manner. They just wanted to win, not to see Ayla send the ball out of the park. Ayla picked up the bat and saw the pitcher glare at her with a steely eye. Mark Wressler, a thick set, spiky haired kid who apparently liked nothing more than to jump his BMX over rows of smaller children, none of whom had ever volunteered for the task. Nobody had forgotten what had happened to poor Timothy Elliot's ankles last summer.

Wressler rolled his arm back, brought his leg up without ever taking his gaze off Ayla, and then the ball left his hand and shot toward her like a cannonball. Ayla knew without a shadow of a doubt that she could not hope to hit the ball by skill, so instead she kept her eyes on Wressler and swung the bat as though attempting to knock his head off instead.

The bat quivered as it struck the ball and to Ayla's amazement she saw the ball rocket up and away from her just as fast as it had come in. It soared into the hard–blue sky as though trying to escape earth's gravity. She stared at it in wonder, and then she saw the approaching storm again. The line of grey cloud had moved startlingly close in a very short space of time, sweeping across the horizon as though the night were advancing in a wave toward them. She had never seen such a dark, threatening storm, capped as it was by high cloud tops that glowed brilliant white in the sunlight. Even as she looked at it she felt something strange, the hairs on her arms and the back of her neck rising up and tingling as though alive.

'Fox, run you idiot!'

Schwarz's yelling provoked her legs to start moving and she sprinted after Rose, who had already started running and had crossed second base. Ayla ran as hard as she could, saw the ball still arcing high above the pitch and two fielders running to catch it, swerving as they tried to judge where it would land. Ayla got her head down and then she really started to move, her legs and arms flying, and she began overhauling Rose as she tore around the pitch to the rising cheers of her team mates.

If Ayla Fox was one thing, it was fast. *Very* fast. *Quick as a fox*, her old P.E. teacher Mr Mathesson used to say with some pride before he retired. She reached full speed and tore past Rose as though she were standing still, years of free–running through the warren of streets and estates around her home building her physical fitness to its peak for her age.

Ayla rocketed past third base and made for the line, heard more cheers as she saw Rose crossing third base behind her and heading toward safety. Ayla put the storm out of her mind and pushed hard for the line and a moment later she crossed it. She slowed gently, knowing from past experience not to try to slow down too quickly and hurt herself, and she turned to see Rose cross fourth base even as she heard the fielder catch the ball just too late to put her out.

The class erupted into shouts and cheers and even Schwarz seemed impressed, watching her with his arms folded and a raised eyebrow above his smile. Ayla caught her breath and walked again to the plate.

Wressler caught the ball and glared at her, true malice in his eyes now as he tossed the ball up and down in one hand and looked at her as though deciding which part of her to target next.

Ayla picked up the bat and swung it over in her hand as she prepared to take the pitcher on again. Above her she could see bruised clouds drifting over the sun but she ignored them now, ready to test Wressler one more time. Her limbs tingled with a strange energy and she felt something humming through her as she raised the bat to show Wressler that she was ready.

Wressler pulled his arm back, his leg came up, and with an audible grunt of effort he launched the ball as fast as he could throw it. The ball arced toward her at what seemed like supersonic speed, and then Ayla looked Wressler in the eye and swung for his face.

The bat swung around and she felt the ball connect, and then there was a crash of thunder so loud that Ayla leaped out of her skin as the world around her turned blue and white. She let go of the bat as she felt a fearsome heat all around her, and then everything vanished into blackness.

***

# Two

'Ayla, can you hear me?'

Ayla heard the voice call her as though from far away, drawing her in. She felt as though she were floating in a great darkness but she knew that she must open her eyes. She blinked herself awake and focussed on a threatening sky and half a dozen faces all staring down at her.

She was lying on her back and could feel the grass poking through the fabric of her sports shirt.

'Can you hear me? Are you okay, Ayla?'

Mrs Fattimer sounded both relieved and horrified as Ayla nodded. With an effort and Rose's help, she managed to haul herself up into a sitting position and rubbed her eyes as though to awaken herself further.

'What happened?' she asked, confused.

'Your bat got hit by lightning and you're out, you dunce,' Schwarz uttered. 'You lost us the game.'

'Be quiet!' Mrs Fattimer snapped, and then looked back at Ayla. 'Are you sure you're okay?'

'I think so,' Ayla said as she got unsteadily to her feet.

'Wow, you're lucky,' said Graham Holt, a small boy with chubby cheeks and a perma–smile that never seemed to wear off. 'I read about lightning striking a tree once in a farmer's field. There were fourteen cows hiding beneath the tree, and the lighting fried each and every one of them. Instant barbeque, right there.'

Ayla wriggled her arms and legs. Despite a strange numbness and tingling sensation, she felt fine. Then she saw the bat, the hard wood split down the middle and the entire bat charred black and smouldering.

'I'm okay,' she replied, 'no barbeque here.'

Mrs Fattimer's flabby shoulders sagged in relief and she glanced up at the sky.

Ayla looked up also and saw that the clouds were a lot lower now, the air cooling fast as shadows crossed the land and the sun began to be eclipsed by the immense storm clouds. A flash of lighting from somewhere nearby lit up the sky and was followed by a tremendous crash of thunder that made the other children leap in shock. Even Schwarz looked worried.

'I think that we should all get inside,' Mrs Fattimer said. 'Come along, hurry now!'

Ayla followed the other children into the school building and they began getting changed quickly. She knew that the storms would bring heavy rain. The reporters on the television had said that there were yellow warnings for severe weather across the south east, and she had no desire to get drenched on the short walk from the bus stop to her home.

As soon as her uniform was on, Ayla grabbed her coat and hurried with Rose from the changing rooms and out to the school's main gates. The sky above was dark now, almost like night time except that to the east there was a bright line of clear sky like a river of molten metal sweeping across the horizon. The light caused nearby objects like houses and trees to be oddly illuminated against the darkness behind, making the storm seem even more threatening.

Ayla walked with Rose to the gates and was about to say goodbye when she saw the knot of girls waiting for the bus nearby. As ever, Tamsin Crittall and her Minions were there, waiting for trouble.

'Why don't you come to mine instead?' Rose suggested, seeing Tamsin and her crew. 'You could go home later once the storm's gone through?'

Ayla shook her head. 'Mum needs me at home, there's too much for her to do on her own now that…'

Ayla didn't say any more and Rose nodded. She alone among Ayla's friends knew what had happened at home all those years before. She hugged Ayla tightly before she turned away, her own home only a few hundred yards down the road from the school.

'Call me when you're home safe!' Rose called as she hurried off.

'Will do!'

Ayla turned and walked slowly toward the bus stop. A crowd of children were there already, and Ayla purposefully aimed for a spot as far away from Tamsin as she could manage. It made little difference. Within a moment or two of turning up, Tamsin and her friends were shoving their way toward her.

Tamsin lived near the estate where Ayla had grown up. Although the same age, Tamsin stood several inches taller than Ayla and threw her weight about just as much as she could. Her podgy face and red dreadlocks surrounded two thin black eyes patched with so much make up that she looked like a panda with its hair set on fire.

'Oh look, it's Ailing Socks!' Tamsin snarled as she came to stand right in front of Ayla and glared down at her. 'I saw that bolt of lightning earlier. Shame it didn't finish the job.'

Ayla stood her ground, but her legs felt weak and rubbery. A flash of lightning forked across the turbulent skies above and seemed to frame Tamsin's head like a hellish halo of white fire.

'What do you want, Tamsin?'

'What do I want?' Tamsin echoed as she rolled her eyes upward and thought for a moment. 'Well, I'd love a manicure and a massage and all of my homework done for me by the morning.'

Ayla had heard this line a hundred times from Tamsin, who routinely recruited others to do her work for her. This often created hilarious results as one heroic victim or another purposefully wrote down ridiculous answers in order to gain a short–lived revenge.

'I'm not going to do that,' Ayla replied.

'Oh, but you are,' Tamsin snapped as she jabbed one fat finger into Ayla's chest.

'You can't make me.'

Tamsin swung a bunched fist into Ayla's nose. The world tilted crazily as Ayla fell and smacked down onto the cold pavement, her bags and books flying everywhere. A cackle of laughter from Tamsin's crew was joined by cheers and jeering as the rest of the children waiting for the bus sensed the start of a fight and began crowding around.

Ayla blurted out a shameful cry of despair, pain and humiliation as she tried to get back to her feet. Her face felt as though it was blowing up like a balloon. She didn't want to show weakness in front of the other children but the grief spilled from her of its own accord. Tamsin lifted one shoe and with it pinned Ayla to the ground, grinding it down on her chest like a vice. She then pulled a maths book from her bag and dropped it onto Ayla's face.

'By the morning, or I'll make that punch look like cosmetic surgery.'

Tamsin lifted her boot off Ayla's chest, turned and shoved her way through the crowd as the sound of the school bus rattled toward them. Ayla crawled to her knees and reached out for her books as fat droplets of rain began falling from the sullen sky above.

Before she could rescue her own maths book another hand reached in, and she turned to see Josh Ryan pick it up for her and slip it into her bag. Ayla smiled her thanks and tried not to blush as Josh took hold of her arm and helped her up.

Josh was a year older than Ayla and one of the school prefects. He wasn't brash and loud like Schwarz, nor was he a bully or a coward. Josh was one of those kids who somehow managed to tread the insanely fine line between cool and dork and come out the other side without a scratch. His hair was neatly parted but not fashionably cut and yet it looked absolutely normal. His eyes were blue, his smile genuine and his quiet voice soothing.

'Ignore her, she only does all this because she's ugly and knows she won't ever get away from that.'

Ayla sniggered in delight as they stepped onto the bus. Tamsin's voice shrieked at them from the back seats as soon as they were aboard.

'Found a friend, Ryan?'

'One more than you,' Josh murmured in reply.

Ayla heard laughter and saw discreet smiles from other children as they took their seats, and she saw Tamsin's face turn almost as red as her hair. Josh sat down with Ayla next to him and they rode the bus the short distance to the street where she lived. About half way home, the clouds above finally burst. Suddenly everyone was quiet as the rain pummelled the roof of the bus like a billion stones crashing down on a tin roof, and lightning forked through the sky amid deafening blasts of thunder that seemed to shake the very earth beneath them.

Ayla saw bolts of jagged white lightning flare through the dense veils of rain, streetlights and headlamps coming on as the world darkened outside. She could not recall ever seeing such heavy rainfall, and it seemed as though the bus was labouring through the streets as they rapidly filled with streams of water plunging into drains.

'Maybe Fox will get struck again!' Tamsin uttered. 'Here's hoping!'

'It's more likely that you'll get hit,' Ayla called back, feeling more confident with Josh alongside her. 'Bigger target.'

That got a real laugh out of the children on the bus and Josh grinned and nudged her side.

\*\*\*

## Three

Ayla stepped off the bus and into three inches of water, battered by ferocious winds and rain as she turned and hurried along the pavement as the bus waited to pull out into the traffic again.

As she walked alongside the bus she glanced up and saw Josh watching her. He gave her a wave and she waved back, smiling. A moment later she saw Tamsin and her friends rush past his seat and tumble out of the bus in pursuit, violence in their eyes.

'Bigger target?!' Tamsin screeched as she charged at Ayla, her face almost as red as her hair and her fists bunched as she ran.

Ayla whirled and began to run as the bus pulled away. Tamsin and her three friends were almost within arms' reach behind her, all four of them far bigger than Ayla. Their heavy footfalls pounded the wet pavement as Ayla dodged away from them.

'You're going down, Fox!' Tamsin screeched breathlessly from right behind her, one fat hand reaching out for the collar of Ayla's shirt.

The bus was moving with the traffic alongside them, and Ayla could see the children aboard flocking to the side of the bus to watch as Tamsin closed in. Ayla got her rucksack onto her back to free her arms just as Tamsin's hand touched her shoulder, and then she ducked her head down and pumped her arms and legs furiously.

Ayla launched herself away from them as though she had been fired from a cannon, overhauling the bus as it joined the flow of traffic. She sprinted along the pavement and then leaped up onto a wall built into the side of a bridge just ahead. She could hear screeches of delight coming from inside the bus as she ran headlong up the wall as it climbed toward the footbridge. She gauged her pace perfectly as she dashed along the wall above the height of the bus and then leaped the six-foot wide footbridge to land on the descending side of the wall.

Ayla ran down the wet wall as the rain pelted the streets around her and then vaulted off the end, her legs out in front as she landed with cat-like agility and rolled, coming up running again as though it were the most natural thing in the world. She risked a glance sideways and saw the kids on the bus cheering and clapping as she flew along the pavement, the wind in her hair and rain pouring in sheets around her as lightning flared across the sky above.

Ayla glanced over her shoulder and saw that Tamsin and her crew had stopped long ago, hopelessly outpaced and drenched. Ayla grinned to herself and she waved to Josh on the bus, then she turned away from the main street and jogged toward her home.

Ayla loved to run. It seemed to be the one thing that she was good at, her physique naturally lithe and supple. She spent countless hours around the estate, leaping across pathways from wall to wall, scaling stairwells and jumping from heights only to land smoothly and safely, just like her beloved cat, Kitten. Free-running, as it was known, was her only escape from the drudgery of life.

She briefly considered dropping Tamsin's maths book down one of the rapidly flooding drains on her street, but then she thought better of it. Tamsin was as thick as one short plank, her books all filled with untidy errors, and by getting all of the sums correct Ayla guessed that their teacher would figure out that something was wrong. Ayla smiled to herself as she walked along and leaned into the battering winds. She decided to do the maths in a different handwriting style to Tamsin's, making it really obvious that she hadn't done the work herself.

Ayla lived in a modest two up and two down with her mother, Rachel, who worked as a nurse in the local hospital. They had been there for three years, and her mother struggled to pay the bills each month. Life was not cheap and wages were not high, she often said, and it was rare that they had any treats or special days when they could afford to go out together. She often worked fourteen-hour shifts, and as soon as Ayla had been old enough she had been given her own key to allow her mum more freedom to do her job. Tonight though, she was due home at four o'clock, which would mean a rare evening together.

The thought comforted Ayla and made her forget about the pain in her face where Tamsin had hit her. She hurried around a corner and into Marshall Road. The skies were bruised deep grey and she could see the rain pouring in sheets from the sky was bouncing off the road. Another brilliant flare of lightning crashed down nearby and made her jump as she ran the last few paces to her house and dashed through the gate to the front door.

She was inside in a flash and slammed the door behind her. The roaring gale and torrential rain were silenced and she stood for a moment, dripping onto the hall tiles, her hair a lank brown mess in the mirror. She turned to look at herself and saw that one or two of her teeth were stained pink with blood from Tamsin's punch, and her shirt was stained with a dirty footprint.

She cursed and pulled off her coat, dumped her school bag near the stairs and walked through the house. It didn't take long. The kitchen was a small square box that was tidy but had barely enough room for Ayla and her mother to stand together between the counters and the sink. A narrow hall led past the stairs to a living room with a couch and a small television mounted on the wall opposite. A set of French doors led onto a patio and a small lawn, at the end of which was a large tree. Beyond that was a playing field with the back gardens of other houses on the far side of the estate, and rows of ugly high-rise flats beyond.

Ayla dried her hair with a towel and changed out of her wet uniform into jeans and a t-shirt. She was about to put the kettle on to boil some water for her mother before she got home from work when she noticed that the cat wasn't asleep on its mat.

'Kitten?'

Ayla had named their cat when they had rescued it from the shelter some years before, and it being so young and small she had named it with a logic that only a child could understand. Black and white and afraid of its own shadow, Kitten did not like storms.

Ayla looked throughout the house, searching under the beds and behind the sofas but she could not find the cat anywhere. It was only when she looked through the rain soaked windows of the living room that she saw a small black and white patch tucked in among the branches and leaves of the tree.

'Oh no.'

Ayla put her shoes back on and threw a coat over her shoulders. She pulled the hood up and opened the French doors, the rain hammering down on the patio as she stepped outside. Kitten would be soaking wet and freezing even under the huge canopy that the tree offered.

Ayla had been afraid of the tree when she was young, the sound of its branches moving and the shadows it cast across her window frightening her. Now, from its thick branches hung a swing where she had whiled away many summer weekends reading books, the tree a place of peace and solace. *Once you can read you can learn about anything*, her mother had once told her, and she had been right.

Ayla dashed through the rain as flares of lighting forked through the turbulent skies, and hurried beneath the huge canopy. Above her was a thick branch just above head height and sitting on it, tucked against the tree's stout trunk, was Kitten, her head pulled in close to her chest and her legs tucked in beneath her. Ayla heard a pathetic, tiny *meow* from the animal as it saw her.

'Kitten, get down from there and come inside.'

Ayla tried to reach up for the cat but it shied away from her, not fleeing but not willing to jump into her arms either.

Another lightning bolt flickered and then a second later a crash of thunder split the sky with enough force to make Ayla cringe and wince. Kitten whined and seemed to shrink back further against the tree, just out of her reach.

'Come on, Kitten,' Ayla pleaded and tried in vain to reach out for her.

Ayla turned and hurried back out into the rain. A pair of wooden deck chairs were leaned up against the fence. Ayla grabbed one of them and ran back beneath the tree. She unfolded the chair and clambered up onto it. Kitten watched her with fearful yellow eyes, pulled her head away slightly but she still did not get up.

Ayla reached gently across and with both hands and soothing noises she carefully lifted Kitten off the branch and folded her into her arms.

'There now, that was a silly place to hide, wasn't it?'

Kitten whined again and rubbed the side of her face against Ayla's chin.

Ayla was about to move when she froze in place as she felt something strange.

The hairs on her arms rose up and she felt something humming through her as though alive. All at once she remembered the playing field, the bat and the bright light. Graham Holt's voice echoed through her mind. *I read about lightning striking a tree once in a farmer's field. There were fourteen cows hiding beneath that tree, and the lighting fried each and every one of them. Instant barbeque, right there.*

Ayla tried to move but it seemed as though she were stuck in place, her body numb and her limbs frozen. She tried to cry out as the humming around her intensified, and to her horror around the tree she saw a brilliant glowing halo, lights dancing and leaping as though alive from one leaf and branch to the next.

The sky above her flared brilliant white and she saw the lightning bolt as though in slow motion. The entire tree shuddered and a billion water droplets burst as they boiled in an instant, exploding outwards from the tree.

The blast hit Ayla and she felt herself being lifted and hurled backwards through the air, Kitten thrown from her grasp as every one of her senses were cut off one after the other.

She never felt herself hit the ground.

\*\*\*

## Four

It was the voices that she heard first.

They were distant, keening, like the sound of lonely winds soaring through a great wilderness. The voices were indistinct, but she knew that she was hearing living things speaking in a tongue that she could not understand. They shrieked and they howled, like prisoners clawing at the darkness of their cell, and they were coming closer.

Ayla could see nothing, could feel nothing, but somehow the darkness seemed to deepen even further into an abyss that stretched to infinity. From the darkness soared the screams and the wails, the commingled symphony of a thousand souls crying out for mercy. Ayla's heart thundered in her chest as from the darkness she saw eyes appear, countless eyes staring at her and coming closer. Figures reached out for her, implored her to help.

Ayla tried to move but her body would not respond, and then from behind the sea of eyes rushing toward her she heard something new and her skin crawled.

A deep, guttural roar rushed from the darkness to scour the universe of life, something savage and brutal that filled the darkness with a presence so vast and overpowering that Ayla felt her very soul rear up in fear as though trying to back away.

Behind the flowing sea of eyes, two more appeared, and they opened to look it seemed straight into Ayla's soul. Then, she heard a voice so deep it sounded as though it came from the centre of the earth to fill every corner of her mind.

*'She sees.'*

Bright light pierced the darkness and Ayla sucked in a lungful of air as she jolted awake. Cold struck her back and her skin, wet and shivering, her vision blurred and her heart fluttering in her chest as she saw people hovering over her.

'We've got a pulse!'

'She's coming around! Can you hear me, love?'

Ayla's eyes widened as her focus returned and she saw her mum standing over her with two paramedics. Her chest ached as though she had been hit by a car.

'Ayla!'

Her mum burst into tears and one hand flew to her mouth as the paramedics lifted Ayla off the wet ground and onto a gurney that they carried bodily through the house almost at a run. Ayla saw the ceiling of her home flash by and then the turbulent sky roiling above. She saw brilliantly flashing hazard lights reflecting off the damp walls of her home, an ambulance waiting as she was lifted inside while crowds gathered nearby.

Ayla was jostled into position and an oxygen mask fitted over her face as her mother clambered into the ambulance and the doors were shut behind her. A paramedic moved to her side.

'How many fingers can you see?' he asked as he held up his hand before her.

'Three.'

'How old are you?'

'Fourteen,' Ayla replied.

'You're gonna be fine,' the paramedic said. 'Sit tight, we're on our way.'

She felt the ambulance pull away and heard sirens wailing, and she was reminded of the screams she had heard in the darkness. *Had she imagined it all?*

'Mum?'

Ayla's throat was dry and her voice sounded raspy, but her mother was at her side in an instant. Rachel had a kind face and wide brown eyes, long brown hair and slightly coloured skin that never seemed to lose its tan.

'It's going to be okay,' she promised as she took one of Ayla's hands in hers. 'You're gonna be fine.'

'Thanks to your mum,' said the nearest paramedic. 'If she hadn't found you when she did, we wouldn't be having this conversation. She saved your life, young lady.'

Ayla felt tears well up in her eyes as she squeezed her mother's hand. 'Kitten?'

Her mum smiled, but it was not a happy smile now. Sorrow and regret passed like cloud shadows behind her eyes, and Ayla knew that her beloved cat had not survived.

The ambulance raced to the hospital, and Ayla was carried inside and hurried to the Accident and Emergency department. The next two hours passed by in a blur. Doctor after doctor came to visit her, and they ran tests on her muscles and her brain and her eyes and virtually every inch of her.

There was only a single burn from the lightning strike, a jagged mark on her right hand where the skin looked as though it had been scorched. Ayla felt somewhat giddy and tired throughout the entire experience, and she was curious as to why the doctors were so interested in her. It was only when they sat down with her after all the tests that she realised why she had become so important.

'Ayla, we have no idea how it is that you survived,' said Doctor Jared Singh, his dark skin at odds with his silvery moustache. 'The fire service was called to your house, and they found a three–foot wide hole in the ground where the lightning bolt that struck you went into the earth. They estimate that you were hit with over half a million volts.'

Ayla wasn't entirely sure what that meant, but half a million sounded like a big number and she figured that anything that could blow a three–foot wide hole in a patio had some real clout.

The tests that the doctors had run all came back negative, and they assured her mother that there would be no lasting damage from the remarkable incident. They did say that Ayla might experience aches and pains from time to time as the burns healed, but that was all. If anything odd were to occur such as signs of concussion or neurological issues, her mother should bring her right back to the hospital, but they promised that Ayla would make a full recovery in time.

Four hours after she had been rushed into A & E, Ayla walked out of the hospital with her mother and headed for the car park. They could not afford a car of their own, but a colleague of her mother had offered to give them a lift. Ayla hugged her mother closely as they walked, and to her surprise there were television cameras outside with reporters holding microphones and jostling for position with one another as they fired questions at Rachel.

'What's it like to be the mother of the Miracle Child?'

'How do you think that your daughter survived?'

'Do you realise just how *lucky* she is?'

Ayla said nothing as her mother answered the questions as best she could, trying to get to the car and shield Ayla from the reporters. It was then, tucked into her mother's arm, that Ayla saw him for the first time.

He was standing on the opposite side of the road to the hospital, dressed in a long coat that seemed somehow old fashioned and out of place. His features were concealed beneath a hood and his hands were clasped before him. She knew somehow that it was a man, perhaps because of his height, but what she was absolutely certain of was that he was looking right at her. He turned to follow Ayla as her mother guided her across the car park, and he lowered his hooded head in a slow, graceful nod of what could only be recognition.

Ayla tried to point him out to her mother, but Rachel didn't hear her amid the commotion.

A blue car pulled up alongside them and Rachel hastily bundled Ayla inside, and moments later they drove off and left the reporters standing in the drizzle.

'Wow, what's it like to be famous, Ayla?' asked Geraldine, her mother's friend from work.

Ayla managed a weak smile but said nothing as Rachel replied.

'My mother phoned and said there are more of them at the house, and a helicopter doing the rounds overhead.'

'Jeez, she got hit by lightning, she didn't win the lottery. What's the big deal?'

'You haven't seen the tree,' Rachel replied.

Ayla didn't really understand what her mother meant until they pulled up outside their home. Rachel managed to get her past the reporters without too much difficulty, being a bit better prepared for them this time, but it was when they got inside that Ayla realised the enormity of what had happened.

She walked into the living room and looked out of the French doors to see the patio, a wide concave hole furrowed out of the ground by the lightning bolt.

Chunks of shattered patio stone lay all over the place, dislodged soil splattering the fences and the glass doors as though a bomb had gone off in the garden.

But it was the tree that sent shivers down her spine.

The great trunk had been split in two, every branch scorched to the colour of soot, wisps of smoke still coiling from the shattered limbs. The tree had been utterly destroyed, and chunks of timber and branches hurled in every direction across the garden.

Ayla stared at the devastation as her mother moved alongside her and wrapped her in her arms once more.

'You're so lucky to be here,' Rachel whispered. 'What were you thinking?'

'Kitten was hiding in the tree,' Ayla replied, 'she was scared.'

Her mother hugged her tightly once more, and then sat back and wiped a solitary tear from her eye.

'Just promise me that you'll never go under a tree again during a thunderstorm, okay? It's the most dangerous place to be.'

Ayla nodded, just grateful to be back home. Although she looked surreptitiously, she could see no sign of Kitten, and wondered what had happened to the cat after she had been struck by the lightning.

\*\*\*

## Five

Ayla awoke to a bright blue sky shining through her bedroom window, marred only by the blackened branches of the tree in the garden. The headache she had developed before bed the previous night had gone and some of the stiffness in her limbs had eased, but she got a shock when she looked at her bedside clock.

*9.37am.*

Terrified that she was already an hour late for school, she leaped out of bed and promptly fell over as her legs collapsed beneath her. The resulting thump brought her mother racing up the stairs and into her room.

'What happened?'

Rachel helped Ayla back into bed as she replied. 'I'm late for school and…'

Ayla's stomach plunged as she realised that she still had Tamsin's maths book with her. There was no way that Tamsin would get away without doing her homework again, and no amount of excuses would get her out of a detention. Worse, Tamsin would not be able to tell anyone that she had given her book to Ayla, and her retribution would be without mercy.

Her mother saw the distress in her eyes and smiled.

'There's no school for you today, and I've been given the day off to keep an eye on you after what happened.'

Ayla sagged back onto her bed as relief poured over her. She wouldn't have to face Tamsin until after the weekend, as she recalled that today was Friday. It wasn't hard to remember, as it was a Thursday when she had almost been fried alive, not something she would be likely to forget in a hurry.

'Are the reporters still outside?' she asked her mother.

'No, they've already gone on to other things, although you were on the news this morning.'

'I was?'

'You're famous now as the girl who survived one of the most powerful lightning strikes in history,' her mother informed her. 'They had a doctor on the news this morning who said it was a thousand–to–one chance that a human being could walk away from being hit that hard. They think the tree must have taken the worst of it.'

Ayla glanced out of the window and nodded. 'It looks like it's seen better days.'

She turned back to her mother, and with help she got out of bed and got dressed. She wasn't used to feeling so weak, her legs rubbery and her arms sluggish to respond. A sudden fear that she would lose her athletic strength was allayed by her mother, who suggested that they spend the day shopping and eating out in town. Ayla knew that money was tight and that her mother would scarcely be able to afford it, but she also knew instantly that Rachel was relieved that Ayla was okay and wanted to cheer her up.

'What about a picnic in the park instead?' Ayla suggested.

It was always a great feeling, being out and about when everyone else was in school. After the savage storm of the night before the sky was clear and sunny, the air warm. Cars glinted brightly in the sunshine as Ayla and her mother spent a wonderful morning window shopping in town before heading to the park and sunbathing while eating sausage rolls and salad and sandwiches, all washed down with soft drinks. Today was a day when nobody cared about anything other than feeling good, and by the time the late afternoon sun was sinking behind the trees that lined one side of the park, Ayla was feeling very good indeed.

'Movie night?' her mother suggested as they packed to leave the park.

'Done deal,' Ayla replied with a smile as she stood up and hefted her back pack onto her shoulder.

It was then that she saw the horizon. Once again, a line of darkly bruised cloud was building, towering thunderheads brilliant white against the blue like lines of snow castles in the sky. Ayla's legs and arms felt stronger again but she couldn't help but feel a pulse of fear at the sight of the advancing storms.

'Again?' her mother uttered in exasperation. 'That's the second night in a row. Can't we have sunny days any more without a storm afterward?'

She saw the consternation on Ayla's face and wrapped one arm around her shoulders as they walked away.

'Come on, let's get home before the heavens open. We don't want you standing around out here waiting to get fried again, do we?'

But Ayla was not worried about being struck by lightning. What concerned her was the strange feeling she was getting again, the energy that seemed to hum through her. As crazy as it seemed, she felt sure that it was coming from the direction of the advancing storm front.

They walked out of the park, chatting about anything and everything, and Ayla was grateful for the distraction. The way home just happened to put the storm behind them, so she could pretend that it wasn't there and she managed to forget about the strange sensation quivering through her as they hurried along.

People were just leaving work, the streets bustling with cars and commuters hurrying this way and that. Ayla looked up at a giant church as they passed, its ancient walls covered in stone carvings of gargoyles and angels and strange beasts that seemed to look toward the onrushing storms with glee. Above the church spire, white clouds drifted across the blue and a couple of birds wheeled around on the thermals, while higher up a dragon glided between the clouds and…

Ayla stopped dead in her tracks and blinked. She searched the sky, certain that she had seen what had looked like a huge dragon with arced wings soaring across the sky.

'Ayla?'

Her mother had stopped and was looking back at her. Ayla stared at the sky and saw an airliner emerge from behind the clouds, its underside glowing white as it reflected the upper cloud layers.

'What is it?' her mother asked, also looking up.

'Nothing,' Ayla replied, but she glanced over her shoulder again and saw the vast storm closer now, dominating the horizon with a growing darkness that filled her with a foreboding that she simply could not ignore.

They got home just as the upper reaches of the storm began to eclipse the sun and the temperature began to fall. Ayla took off her shoes and hurried up to her room to look at the storm, which by now was shadowing the countryside in the distance with veils of rain pouring from the darkened clouds.

Ayla could hear the news on the television downstairs as her mother switched it on.

'*… more storms tonight and a yellow weather warning for the south east. The storms are being blamed by environmentalists on the result of climate change as western Atlantic weather systems change their behaviour due to the warming oceans. Experts say that things will only get worse, although they also admit that they cannot say for sure what is causing these tremendously powerful storm cells to generate so quickly. In other news today, the government has called for more powers to…*'

Ayla forgot about the newsreader's voice as she watched the storm close in. She saw the first savage flares of lightning crackling across the sky like rivers of jagged white fire that vanished as soon as they had arrived. Thunder rumbled across the heavens like a giant's club being dragged across the ground. She saw the first fat droplets of rain splatter down onto the street outside as pedestrians vanished beneath umbrellas, and a pair of winged gargoyles scurried away through the bushes of a neighbour's garden…

Ayla blinked again. She scanned the bushes near the park opposite her back yard but could see nothing. The memory of the dragon she had seen earlier flared in her mind as brightly as the lightning now flickering like electric swords across the horizon, and she wondered if she was losing her mind.

She looked down at the tree in her back yard, and her heart seemed to stop in her chest as she saw the hooded man again. He leaned against the blackened, shattered trunk of the tree. He was watching her, his face concealed in shadow within the hood, and in one hand he held a thin clay pipe. Slowly, he drew it to his mouth and a few moments later she saw a cloud of blue puff out onto the air and drift away.

She wanted to run downstairs and out into the garden and yell at the man but she could not bring herself to take her eyes off of him, not even for a moment, because somehow she knew that if she did he would vanish once again. For not the first time in her life, she wished that her father were here.

'Mum?' she called.

'Yes?'

'Can you see a man standing against the tree in the back yard?'

There was a momentary pause, and she could visualise her mother thinking for a moment and then going to have a look herself.

'There's nobody there,' her mother replied eventually.

Ayla heard Rachel come up the stairs, but she did not take her eyes off the man even as her mother moved to stand beside her.

'What are you seeing?' she asked.

Ayla kept staring at the man, her eyes going dry as she tried not to blink.

'Am I going mad mum?' she asked. 'He's standing right there in a hood, smoking a pipe and watching us.'

Her mother stared at the tree for a long moment, and then put her arm around Ayla's shoulders.

'Why don't you have a bath and then I'll get the dinner on. After all that's happened, you're probably just a bit stressed and tired.'

Ayla finally blinked, and when she opened her eyes again the man was gone.

\*\*\*

## Six

Although she would never have believed it possible, the second storm was even more powerful than the first. Ayla had got out of the bath as the first lightning strikes ripped the sky apart. The quiet murmur of rain and traffic outside was shattered by deafening cracks of thunder that were loud enough to rattle the windows in their panes.

It was however a relief that there were no power cuts, and Ayla and her mother watched a couple of movies before Ayla finally decided that she wanted to go to bed. The storm had mostly passed by the time they trudged upstairs, and Ayla gratefully got into bed and fell promptly into a deep sleep.

She could not be sure what eventually awoke her.

She was having a dream about an old lady who was beckoning her into a strange, shadowy shop that was full of shimmering walls. Light flared occasionally inside the shop as though the lighting wasn't working properly, and although she was sure she could hear voices from somewhere deeper inside the shop she could not see anybody else.

A very bright flare of light made her squint, and then her eyes opened and she was lying in her bed beneath her duvet. She felt rested, recovered, as though something had changed inside her and the after effects of the lightning strike had finally passed.

Ayla's room flickered with distant lightning that flashed silently, as though the storm were still raging but somewhere far away. She could hear water dripping outside where it must have rained, and there was a strong scent of fresh air coming through her window, the earth cleansed once again.

Ayla rolled over to look out of her window and she saw the storm flickering in the distance, lightning occasionally illuminating vast towers of clouds against the starry night sky. She glanced at her clock and saw that it was almost four in the morning.

Then she blinked as she rubbed her eyes and checked again.

The clock had stopped.

Ayla picked it up and shook it, but the hands were stuck in place. She thought that maybe the batteries were dead. She picked up her digital watch instead and looked at it. To her amazement, the digital figures were frozen in place, even the little dots between the numbers no longer flashing. Ayla frowned and then got out of bed. There must have been some kind of electrical interference that had caused everything to stop, which would mean the old boiler in the hall wouldn't warm the water in the morning for her mother to have a shower.

Alya walked around her bed and past her mirror toward the bedroom door, and glimpsed in the reflection the old woman from her dream who…

Ayla almost screamed as she froze and stared at the reflection before her. The woman's features were elderly but kind, her entire body glowing with a soft hue and partially transparent as she threw her hands to her cheeks in apparent delight. She was smiling at Ayla and to her amazement spoke in a clear and remarkably cheerful Scots voice.

'Ach! It's real, yee can see me and I can see yee!'

Ayla stared dumbfounded at the old woman, and then the woman leaned forward and poked her head through the mirror to look around Ayla's bedroom.

'My my, this is a small chamber for such an important lady. Oooh, make–up!'

Ayla stumbled backwards and toppled onto her bed, her watch clutched in one hand and a scream caught somewhere in her chest. The old lady began trying to pick up items from Ayla's table, but her fingers passed right through them. The hairs went up on the backs of Ayla's arms and neck and she felt her heart suddenly hammer against her chest. She was about to get up and sprint for the door when the woman looked at her again.

'Blasted hands!' she complained with a grimace, but then her face melted in delight and she gazed fondly at Ayla.

'Ach, my own wee little Hybrin! I would never have believed it were I not looking at yee right now.' She fussed a moment as though preparing herself. 'Gosh, it's been so long I can't remember all the things I'm supposed to say. Ah, yes! I know that yee want to run, but you're quite safe my dear. For the now, at least.'

Ayla tried to speak but her throat was dry and her mouth parched. She worked her jaw but nothing came out except for a tiny squeak. The lady in the mirror peered at her.

'Now that's a dialect I nee recognise. This could be difficult as you're not a Highlands lassie now, are yee? Do you speak E–n–g–l–i–s–h? Good heavens, are yee a mowak?'

Ayla got control of her voice. 'What's a mowak?'

'Aha!' the lady replied. 'That's better! For a moment there, I thought a Thundrin had gotten yee tongue. A mowak? Horrible things, they look like us but they're not quite right, y'know, *in the head*.'

She tapped her temple with one finger, which promptly vanished into her skull. She rolled her eyes, part of her finger visible behind them.

'Tsk, I must stop doing that, it's just so un*lady*like. Now, have yee seen the Dragun yet?'

Ayla didn't know what else to do but close her eyes, reach up and pinch herself as hard as she could. She winced at the pain and waited.

'That's an odd thing to do, lassie. It's only a question.'

Ayla opened her eyes. The woman was still there, her arms now leaning casually on the bottom rim of the mirror as she stared at Ayla with what looked like genuine confusion. Ayla stared back for a long moment.

'What's a Dragun, and what are you doing in my mirror?'

'*Your* mirror?' the lady uttered, aghast. 'Young lady, it's yee who are in my mirror. Or, rather, we're both in each other's mirrors. Of course, mirrors belong to people all over the world and I suppose we should let them be, but sometimes things happen and mirrors reveal themselves to be what they truly are.'

The woman peered again at Ayla and saw the confusion there.

'Ach, nee mind,' she chortled, 'yee'll learn quickly enough once Luciffen gets here. They'll be looking for yee by now.'

'Luciffen?'

'The sage, the Great Lightness,' the woman informed her. 'It's always this way when the seal of mirrors is broken, so much to learn and so little time to teach! I must admit I'm a wee bit surprised that a mirror belonging to little old Agnis, which is me by the way, was chosen by forces greater than all of us to herald a new portal but that's just the way the haggis boils. Now, the Dragun, have yee seen it yet?'

Ayla felt as though she was getting dizzy. 'What does it look like?'

Agnis rolled her eyes and flopped her chin onto one supporting hand, her elbow resting on the bottom of the mirror as she waved the other hand in the air.

'Oh, yee know, nothing unusual for your world I suppose. Just a beast of four limbs, two wings and fearsome temperament that flies and breathes fire.'

Ayla's eyes widened. 'A dragon?'

'Dragon, Dragun, are we splitting hairs? Obviously, languages have changed a little since this last happened in 1849! Have yee seen one yet?'

Ayla nodded slowly.

'Yes, yesterday afternoon. I saw one flying around in…'

'Yesterday afternoon?!' Agnis shrieked. 'Good heavens, you're lucky to still be alive!'

'What?'

'The Dragun, it is sent to…' Agnis hesitated as she looked at Ayla. 'It's not *friendly*.'

Ayla thought for a moment.

'I saw gargoyles, and a man in a hood who keeps watching me.'

Now, Agnis was truly concerned and she held out her hand toward Ayla.

'Come, hurry. If yee stay there much longer, yee'll die.'

\*\*\*

## Seven

Ayla stayed right where she was, her gaze affixed to Agnis's hand, which was perfectly translucent and looked like it was made from glowing smoke.

'Hurry along, I don't have all night!' Agnis urged.

Ayla didn't quite know how to respond. She sat in shocked silence as she tried to understand what was happening. She knew that she was not dreaming, but now she was beginning to wonder whether she had lost her mind when that lightning strike had frazzled her brain.

'Oh, here we go,' Agnis mumbled as she rolled her eyes, 'I remember this bit. This is what comes from living in a world of technology, isn't it? You've lost the ability to understand that there is more to your world than yee can see before your eyes. What's your name, lassie?'

'Ayla.'

'Well, Ayla, have yee ever looked at your reflection in a mirror for a very long time and started to feel a bit strange?'

'Er, no.'

'Pfft,' Agnis uttered, 'you button pressers have nee imagination! Have yee ever noticed that cats sometimes stare intently at what seems to be nothing more than thin air?'

Ayla thought of Kitten, of how she used to stare up into the corner of Ayla's room with great interest even though there was nothing there at all.

'Yes, sometimes.'

'Ever felt like yee were being watched and turned to see someone looking at yee,' Agnis went on, 'or thought of someone only for them to turn up moments later?'

'Yes,' Ayla replied, intrigued.

'Good,' Agnis said, 'then you know that there is a reality every bit as present as the one yee can see with your eyes but that yee can feel and sense only occasionally, when the time is just right. Do *I* look like a figment of your imagination to yee?'

'No, but I was…'

'What happened?' Agnis cut across her as she wagged her finger in the air and then thought for a moment. 'Wait, don't tell me. Umm, six black cats crossed your path.'

'No, I…'

'I said don't tell me!' Agnis insisted, her finger now pointed like a weapon at Ayla, and then she studied the ceiling intently as she rubbed her chin with one hand. 'Right, I've got it. One of those fake mediums got lucky and cursed you using crystals and Fort Weed.'

'Er, no.'

'Tsk,' Agnis frowned in concentration. 'Yee encountered a unicorn at midnight, near an elm tree, while dancing a jig to…'

'Will this take long?'

'Oh, so *now* you're in a hurry, are yee?' Agnis uttered. 'Can't let old Agnis have a little fun with…'

Then Agnis saw the shattered hulk of the tree outside the bedroom window against a background of stars, and her eyes widened.

'Lightning strike,' she whispered in awe.

'Yesterday,' Ayla replied.

'Big one?'

'Big enough.'

'Big enough to scorch the tree,' Agnis whispered, apparently stunned. 'So, yee have fire and earth in your soul.'

'I do?'

'You were stuck by fire, while in a tree,' Agnis explained as though it were obvious, but then she leaned further out of the mirror and peered closely at Ayla. 'Were you touching or holding a creature of any kind when it happened?'

Ayla nodded. 'My cat, Kitten.'

Agnis gasped and threw one hand to her mouth, the hand passing straight through her lips and revolving through a complete turn at the wrist to point back at Ayla.

'No wonder the Dragun has hunted yee so quickly!'

'I don't understand.'

'You will,' Agnis replied, but now she seemed concerned and reached out again. 'Please my dear, hurry. Wee old Agnis doesn't want to be the first spectre in the realm to have seen their mirrorsoul die before they even knew what was happening to them.'

'Mirrorsoul?'

Before Agnis could reply, Ayla heard something in the distance. At first, she thought that it was the screech of car tires, as some teenage hoodlum drove his pimped ride at ridiculous speeds through the darkened streets. But it went on for too long and she saw Agnis's features collapse into abstract terror.

'Ayla, please,' she begged, 'listen to old Agnis. I won't last a second against a Dragun and it will be here any moment. Come with me, you'll be safe I promise.'

Ayla made to move toward the translucent hand before her but she hesitated again. The sound of the screeching came closer outside her window, and Ayla was sure that she heard a deep gust after it, as though an immense chest were drawing in more air to breathe.

'Ayla, we won't escape if yee don't come with me now!'

Ayla looked back at Agnis, and then to her shock she saw a black and white cat sitting further back in the reflection, watching her silently. Her heart leaped for joy as she recognised it as her cat, alive and well.

'Kitten?'

Agnis glanced over her shoulder.

'Looks like the lightning bolt changed more than just your perception, Ayla,' she said, and then another horrendous screech split the sky outside the house. Ayla saw the shadow of something huge cross the window and heard a beating of the air that thumped her eardrums like helicopter blades.

'Now, Ayla!'

Ayla leaped off the bed and reached for Agnis's hand, and suddenly she felt a cold, icy grip on her skin. Her feet flew off the ground and she plunged straight through the mirror as she let out a scream.

The mirror passed through her with a flash of light, quivering through her body with a strange sensation a bit like pins and needles. The darkness of her room was replaced by a warm glow of firelight as she crashed down toward the ground. Ayla's free–running instincts took over and she rolled neatly over on her shoulder and came back up with cat–like agility. She felt a brief spell of dizziness after passing through the mirror that faded as she looked around.

She saw that she was in a small cabin of some kind, a bed on one side and a counter on the other with pots and pans stacked neatly upon it. The walls were of thick wood, and the whole was illuminated by a crackling fire opposite a large and heavy door. Kitten was curled up on the bed, watching her with interest.

Before her stood Agnis, a petite woman who was as translucent here as she had been in Ayla's room, her petticoat and legs fading to nothing a few inches above the floor. To Ayla's amazement, Agnis grabbed what looked like a club of hardwood and swung it with all of her might at the mirror on the wall. Ayla could see her own room inside the mirror's reflection, and she could hear a terrific screeching noise and hear the sound of something right outside her house.

'No, mum!'

The club shattered the mirror into shards of glass and a burst of fearsome white light that forced Ayla to turn her head away and shield her eyes. The fragments of the mirror clattered onto the wooden floor all around her, and she opened her eyes to see each shard surrounded by a halo of blue–white light that slowly faded from view. Kitten leaped off the bed and vanished into another part of the cabin.

Agnis dropped the club and her spectral appearance faded as her eyes hooded wearily.

'That'll slow the Dragun down for a wee bit lassie, but not for long.'

Ayla saw how weak Agnis looked and she got up, tried to reach out for her, but her hand passed through Agnis's shoulder and the old lady smiled apologetically.

'Dead for quite some time I'm afraid,' she explained 'I'm not half the woman I used to be, quite literally.'

'But the club?' Ayla said, looking at the weapon now lying on the ground.

'Oh, that,' Agnis replied, 'we spectres all have a little of the poltergeist in us when we want it, but it weakens us greatly for a while. My dear, you must leave. The Dragun will come here and seek you out. I can't protect you in this state.'

Ayla stared at Agnis in shock. She had only met her moments before in the most bizarre of circumstances, but now the thought of leaving her was far more frightening than staying right where she was.

'I don't know where to go,' she said. 'How do I get back home?'

'Luciffen will know how,' Agnis smiled, her apparition fading with every passing second. 'You must find him, quickly. The man with the hood will be waiting for you…'

Agnis kept talking but Ayla could barely see her at all.

'Where, Agnis, where will they be? Can't you stay?'

'Nee the now, lassie,' Agnis's voice replied, 'run, Ayla, run!'

To Ayla's dismay Agnis's spectral form vanished entirely, and then moments later the crackling fire faded from view and the light and warmth went with it. Beside her, the neatly stacked pots and pans became ancient, covered in dust and cobwebs, and the robust walls crumbled to thin, splitting panels through which she could see daylight beyond. Above her head she could see sky through the skeletal remains of the roof, a cold wind blustering through the hollow, abandoned cabin.

'Agnis?' Ayla whispered, suddenly afraid. 'Kitten?'

She thought she heard a distant reply, but then she recognised the screech of something far away but much larger, and she knew that the Dragun had found her already.

\*\*\*

# Eight

Ayla yanked the rickety door of the cabin open and stepped outside, and at once her breath was taken away from her.

The cabin was nestled on the edge of a forest that seemed as deep as eternity and extended into the distance to Ayla's left and right, while behind the forest rose immense mountains that soared high into the sky, their peaks concealed by low scudding clouds that tumbled by overhead. Before her was a valley, and in the distance the silvery thread of a river wound through it with more mountains beyond, the whole vista epic in its scale and yet both beautiful and barren at the same time.

She looked up into the sky and although it was daylight she could see no evidence of a sun behind the clouds, no bright spot that betrayed its location. Instead, through the clouds she could see shafts of light beaming down that changed direction at random and sometimes flickered with rainbow hues, like sunlight reflected off moving mirrors.

The screeching sound got abruptly louder and she dashed away from the cabin and plunged into the forest, dashing this way and that between huge, ancient trunks. She could hear the sounds of the Dragun but she could not yet see it. The thumping of immense wings beating the air vied with the screeches and the rumbling of an immense chest and lungs, along with a strange crackling sound like burning logs.

Ayla ran for another hundred metres through the forest and then she crouched down and waited. She knew that she could not outrun something that possessed the power of flight, but she knew also that a moving target was easier to spot than a stationary one. But that wasn't the only reason she had stopped. She had to *see* it in order to know where it was, or she would not be able to plan her escape.

She remained silent and still, looking up at the dense canopy of trees for any sign of motion against the sky, listening for the sound of beating wings. She could see Agnis's abandoned old hut in the distance through the forest, and then suddenly as she was looking at it she heard a sound like water thundering down a canyon.

From out of the sky streamed a trembling lance of flame that roared into the hut and consumed it amid a seething ball of fire. Ayla saw thick black smoke billow up into the sky as the hut burned furiously and collapsed upon itself amid a billowing cloud of embers that spiralled up into the air around it.

The fearsome stream of flame vanished, and Ayla crouched lower as something appeared over the tree tops and soared out over the clearing. For the first time, she got a good look at the creature that was hunting her.

The Dragun was about as long as two buses, and its wings were even larger than that. As it wheeled upward she could see the light from the sky glowing through the thin skin of them as the Dragun wheeled over in a graceful arc and plunged back down toward the ground. It had a head that looked something like a crocodile and a pair of tails that rippled and twisted for balance as it descended. But what was most shocking was its body, which was entirely coal black but for the seams of what looked like molten metal shimmering between its scales. The skin crackled like burning coals, alive with heat and flame.

The huge Dragun beat its wings and thick, stout arms and legs reached out as it landed in the clearing. Ayla could see the grass smouldering wherever the creature stood as it folded its wings in, and over its back was a shimmering heat haze that rippled the horizon beyond.

The Dragun moved closer to the collapsed cabin, the smoking timbers now collapsed in a pile and burning furiously. The Dragun leaned close and, impervious to the flames, it sniffed deeply. Ayla watched as the beast snuffled the ground next to the hut, little jets of blue and yellow flame spurting from its nostrils as it sought a scent, and then it turned its great head and looked straight toward her.

Ayla saw its glowing eyes, cruel and hot, seem to penetrate the forest and bore directly into hers, and she knew that it had figured out that she was alive and had fled. She also knew that it was too large to move into the forest, and so could not follow her between the trees.

Ayla remained silent and still, waiting to see what the Dragun would do.

With a fearsome blast of air the Dragun beat its wings, the grass in the clearing swaying away from the gusts as it lifted off and turned toward her. The Dragun flew with its nose close to the ground, following the trail she had left as it closed in on her position. She saw the beast open its mouth, its chest swelling as it let out a horrendous screech that rang in her ears as it soared overhead. The Dragun turned out over the clearing and lined up to charge her again.

Ayla remained where she was, gambling that the Dragun was unaware of her precise location.

She could not have been more wrong.

The Dragun thundered in and opened its mouth again to reveal rows of savage teeth glowing like red–hot pokers. A stream of flame burst forth from between its jaws and plunged into the forest in front of her. Ayla saw the flames slice through the trees like a hot knife through butter and saw roiling clouds of embers and smoke race toward her like burning tornadoes.

Ayla leaped up and hurled herself to one side as the flames tore through the forest and scorched the ground where she had crouched moments before. Heat washed over her as she crashed through dense foliage and aimed deeper into the woods, determined to lose the Dragun somewhere where it could no longer detect her scent.

The great, shimmering black beast soared up against the grey sky and wheeled around in a wide arc before it beat its huge wings and rushed back in toward her as she ran.

A flare of violent flame tore through the canopy and she changed direction and hurled herself over the immense bulk of a fallen tree as the forest exploded amid flame and smoke. The Dragun soared overhead again as Ayla rolled through the undergrowth and then came up running again, the scent of scorched wood burning her nostrils and drawing tears from her eyes as she ran.

Thick smoke clogged the air and drifted with the breeze as Ayla sprinted down an animal trail deep in the forest. She saw a rock face ahead blocking her path and she turned left, forced to head downhill through the thick brush. A screech caught her attention and she saw the Dragun at the last moment as it rushed in toward the trees to her left, but this time it did not blast the forest around her with flames.

At the last moment its huge wings flared and seemed to fill the sky above the trees, and then the Dragun folded them back and it smashed through the canopy toward her.

Ayla screamed and ran as hard as she could as she heard tree limbs snap with loud cracks like thunder and heard the Dragun's savage roar as it plunged down onto the forest floor behind her. She felt the ground tremble beneath the impact and she staggered off balance as she tried to get away from the huge beast.

A lance of flame shot by her and a nearby tree crumbled amid clouds of blossoming flame and debris as her escape route was cut off. The Dragun herded her toward the canyon wall to her right, the flames around Ayla now too fierce and hot to pass through. Ayla turned and saw the Dragun on all fours, its wings folded by its sides and cruel, glowering eyes glaring into hers as it advanced toward her.

Ayla backed up until she touched the canyon wall, unable to take her eyes off the hellish beast stalking toward her.

The entire creature looked as though it were forged in the heart of some unspeakable furnace, heat haze shimmering thickly from it and a strong scent of sulphur and ash surrounding it like a choking halo. The Dragun reared up, and a shriek pierced the air and forced Ayla to cover her ears with her hands and grit her teeth against the infernal noise.

Then, the Dragun flung its head toward her and a fierce jet of flame filled her vision.

***

# Nine

The sound of hooves thundered through the forest and Ayla ducked as the Dragun's searing flames rushed in. She flinched a gigantic horse clattered in front of her, the huge bulk of the animal seeming to fill the forest as she looked up and saw a hooded figure upon the stallion's back, a shield in his arms.

The Dragun's fiery blast smashed into the shield and flew in all directions, deflected in some way by a force far larger than the shield itself. As Ayla crouched on the ground, the horseman whirled and flung his shield upon his back as he drew a sword, the blade flashing in the dappled light of the forest as he charged not at the Dragun but at a large tree to its left.

The Dragun turned and lashed out at the horseman, glowing red fangs clashing together, but the horseman was too fast and dodged clear of the strike. The horseman swung the blade as he rode past the tree and the weapon crashed through the trunk, as thick as Ayla's body, shattering it as it passed through and out the other side.

The tree plunged inward and the Dragun shrieked as the trunk rushed down and crashed into the animal, pinning it to the forest floor in a cloud of embers and smoke. The horseman swung back and galloped to Ayla's side, one gloved hand reaching down for her.

Ayla saw the Dragun draw a deep breath to incinerate them both, and she leaped to her feet and grabbed the gloved hand. The horseman lifted her up with immense strength and swung her into his saddle. The huge stallion galloped away from the rock face as a blast of heat and fire crashed into it, billowing embers washing over them as the stallion galloped away.

The horse easily leaped a fallen tree and thundered into the forest, the shrieks of the Dragun fading behind them as they rode at frightening speed between the trees. Ayla hung on to the rider for dear life. She had only ever ridden a pony at walking pace before, not this beast of a horse, jet black and shiny and fearsomely fast as they galloped along.

The rider took them alongside the cliff face for some distance before he was forced to turn as the rocky outcrops spread out before them. He slowed the stallion down to a canter as they followed what looked like an old dried–up riverbed that descended toward the valley and the river she had seen earlier.

The hooded rider said nothing, guiding the horse with casual skill. His back felt hard with muscle, his shoulders broad, and Ayla recognised him as the man who had been watching her. Although she feared to speak, the stranger had just saved her life and she had so many questions that she could not help herself.

'Who are you?'

Her voice sounded small amid the vastness of the forest. She saw the hooded figure's head turn slightly to one side as he heard her.

'My name is Vigoran.'

His voice was rough and raspy and she instinctively sensed the commanding presence in him, that of a leader of men.

'Why have you been watching me?' she asked.

Vigoran rode more easily now, although she could see him checking the sky for any sign of the Dragun.

'To keep you safe,' he replied. 'The Dragun will seek you out again. We're only lucky that a juvenile was sent.'

'That was a *juvenile*?' Ayla echoed.

'Yes, inexperienced and small. Terra clearly thinks that you represent little threat to her at this time.'

Ayla's weary mind tried to figure out what Vigoran meant.

'I'm no threat to anyone,' she replied, 'and I don't know anybody called Terra.'

'I know,' Vigoran replied, 'but there is much that you will have to learn and not long to do so. I was lucky to find you here at all. Were you with someone before the Dragun arrived?'

'Yes, a ghost called Agnis.'

The fact that she was able to casually report chatting to a ghost before being hunted down by a gigantic black dragon spoke volumes to Ayla about her state of mind. Right now, it all seemed bizarrely normal.

'Agnis,' Vigoran echoed as they rode. 'How much did she tell you?'

'She said that I was her mirrorsoul, that people would be looking for me and that I needed to find someone called Luciffen.'

'The sage is on his way.'

Vigoran said nothing more as they rode out of the forest and across a large expanse of swaying grasses toward a broad river that separated the lowland forests from the mountainous heights before them. Ayla was again taken aback by the vastness of the wilderness, of how it felt so wild and untamed, the air so fresh it seemed electrifying.

As they rode down to the water's edge, where she could hear the current whispering above the sound of the wind in the nearby trees, she felt the horse slow down further and Vigoran became alert and cautious.

'What is it?'

Vigoran seemed surprised.

'You are perceptive for one so young,' he observed, 'but there is nothing to fear. We must locate the Riders of Spiris. Agnis was too hasty to bring you into the realm, you're not ready.'

Ayla frowned. 'The Dragun was hunting me, she had no choice but to run.'

Vigoran stopped the horse and looked round at her. To her surprise, she could see only two glittering blue eyes shining like jewels within the darkness of his hood.

'The Dragun was in your world too?'

Ayla nodded. 'And you, and some gargoyles.'

The horse skittered and Vigoran looked to the treeline and then raised his hand, lowered it, then raised it again with three gloved fingers showing.

As if from nowhere Ayla saw a dozen figures emerge from the forest. She could not tell if they had been wearing camouflage that they had suddenly shed or had just been well concealed, but they shimmered into view and walked down to the water's edge.

'Vigoran,' said one of them, a giant of a man with a thick brown beard and a chest as wide as a harbour wall that was covered in matted brown hair. 'You found her.'

His voice was so deep it sounded as though he was speaking underwater and he glanced briefly at Ayla.

'The Hybrin was under attack from a Dragun,' Vigoran replied as he jerked his head, presumably to indicate Ayla. 'It wasn't hard to find them.'

'Where is it now?' asked another, younger man with blond hair and two longbows slung across his shoulders.

'Under a tree Jake, but that won't keep it down for long. We need to keep moving before it burns itself free.'

Ayla could see that there were a number of armed men among what she assumed were Vigoran's Riders of Spiris, but also there were a small number of boys and girls not much older than Ayla.

'We need to lose the Hybrin,' said one of the older men, a stocky swordsman with a shaved head and an arrogant stance. 'She's too young to be of use, and if Terra's looking for her then it puts us all in danger.'

Vigoran glanced over his shoulder at Ayla. 'That will be for Luciffen to decide, Agry.'

The riders regarded her for a moment, and then they turned and the huge man with the beard put his fingers to his mouth and let out a piercing whistle. From the forest galloped a dozen horses, each heading directly for one of Vigoran's companions.

The riders mounted up and Vigoran led them at a gallop down the valley and toward the mountains on the far side. Ayla watched the riders behind them as they travelled. All looked weary and all were heavily armed with various weapons like maces, axes, bows, swords and knives, even the younger ones. Their armour was a mixture of metal and woven leather, much of it studded with brutal stabbing accoutrements so that even defensive material could be used to injure and maim. Ayla had seen nothing like it except in history books at school, where pictures of medieval knights and castles revealed ancient human history as a time of great brutality, of disease and suffering.

They rode for almost an hour until Ayla saw a huge bridge spanning the river beside them. It looked as though it was crafted from timber like any other bridge, but it was only when they got closer that she realised it was built from the bones of some immense creature whose origins she could only guess at. The towering ribcage formed the centre of the bridge, the tips of the ribs almost touching overhead and the spine the base, wherein was a wooden walkway the width of ten horses. Ayla peered at the river and saw the water was as black as night, filled with chunks of ice that were floating down from somewhere high in the frigid mountains.

The horses slowed as they closed in on the bridge, and Vigoran brought his big stallion to a halt and surveyed the wilderness beyond. Ayla could again sense the tension in him, as though he were awaiting something.

Then, quite suddenly, the hairs on Ayla's neck stood up and she felt a terrible dread ripple across the surface of her skin like insects scuttling all over her. Instinctively she looked over her shoulder.

'Dragun, rear!'

The horses whirled as one in time to see the Dragun gliding silently at terrific speed right behind them, its huge fanged mouth open as it blasted them with a tremendous inferno of flame.

\*\*\*

# Ten

The Riders of Spiris scattered as the terrible flames roared between them. The Dragun screeched as it thundered through their midst, flames blazing from its mouth and smoke coiling in vortices over its wings as it soared up into the sky.

Ayla held on grimly as Vigoran galloped toward the bridge, drawing his sword as he did so and yelling at the other riders.

'Agry, Baylien, the vanguard!'

Two of the riders split off and circled back, drawing the Dragun toward them as Vigoran made for the bridge again with the other riders flocking around him. Ayla was confused only for a moment, and then she realised what they were doing.

They were protecting *her*.

The wind howled through her hair as the riders came together, dozens of hooves thundering against the ground and the rumble of clattering armour filling her world with something so terrible and yet so invigorating she almost wanted to cry out in joy.

The Dragun shrieked again, a cruel howl that seemed to echo off the nearby mountains as it dove down toward them.

'Ready!' Vigoran yelled as he looked up at the Dragun. 'Hold!'

The horses thundered toward the bridge as the Dragun dropped down low toward the ground and levelled out, tearing toward them at tremendous speed, its eyes glowing with malice as it opened its mouth.

'Now!'

The riders split in a perfectly coordinated starburst and their horses raced away from each other. Ayla saw the Dragun's head flick this way and that as the sudden multiple targets confused it and it sprayed fire and flame in random directions, trying to hit at least one of the horses.

The riders scattered, but Vigoran had diverted from his course the least and now he turned back toward the bridge as the Dragun raced past in a frenzy of noise, heat and wings. Ayla felt the blast from its wing beats as it flew by, and then Vigoran and several of the other riders clattered onto the bridge and rode hard for the other side.

Ayla looked back and saw the Dragun wheel over and plunge down toward Baylien, who was galloping toward the entrance to the bridge while swinging a huge net over his head and aiming to hurl it at the beast. Her excitement was suddenly shattered as she saw a stream of flame rip across the entrance to the bridge and Baylien vanished into the inferno as the net flew from his hand and landed on the bridge.

The horse plunged from the other side of the inferno streaming flame and smoke, its teeth bared in agony and Baylien consumed in a roiling maelstrom of flame as he toppled from his saddle and crashed onto the ground. The horse galloped onto the bridge amid crackling flames and then leaped off the side and into the river. Ayla saw it vanish amid a blast of white water, but even then it did not cease burning as it sank into the dark and bitter depths.

Vigoran's horse reached the far side of the bridge and galloped clear as he aimed for deep forests lining the mountain slopes just a few miles away. Ayla looked back and saw the other riders racing frantically in pursuit as the Dragun hurled itself into an almost vertical climb and then wheeled over to plunge back toward them.

'We won't make the forest!' Ayla shouted in warning to Vigoran.

Vigoran clearly agreed with her because he suddenly hauled the stallion to a halt and turned it, drawing his shield as he looked back at her.

'Get off.'

There was something in his voice that she knew instinctively not to argue with. Ayla vaulted from the saddle and landed cat–like in the grass. She saw the other riders react instinctively to Vigoran's decision and they wheeled their mounts around to face the onrushing Dragun.

Ayla saw them position their horses in an arc that protected her from the savage beast as it rushed in, saw them draw their weapons and prepare to do battle. Ayla felt the overpowering need to help them in some way but she could think of nothing useful to do as the Dragun sprayed the horses with searing flames.

Vigoran turned his shield and deflected the blast, thick globules of molten material shooting off in all directions and scorching the grass wherever it landed in clouds of fizzing grey smoke.

The riders fired bows and launched spears, the giant hurling a spear twice as long as Ayla that slammed into the Dragun's chest and was promptly consumed by flames as the beast roared overhead. Ayla ducked down as it soared past her and she saw those terrible eyes glaring at her as it did so. The Dragun was moving too fast to strike her so it pulled up into a steep climb, those huge wings beating the air with powerful blasts.

Vigoran's riders thundered by to form another defensive arc, and Ayla looked over her shoulder at the bridge and an idea formed in her mind. She whirled and began running for the bridge. She sprinted as though all the hounds of hell were following her, her heart thundering in her chest and her legs flying in a blur of motion as she hurtled down the hillside and plunged back onto the bridge.

She heard a shriek from behind her and risked a glance over her shoulder.

The riders and Vigoran were engaged in battle with the Dragun, which sprayed them with a ferocious blast of flame that Vigoran only just managed to deflect. She could see flaming spears protruding from the Dragun's body, some falling away as they burned through, and the blond swordsman named Jake had dismounted and was rolling beneath the blasts trying to slash at the beast with his sword.

Ayla ran the length of the bridge, back to the far side where she saw the net dropped by Baylien. He lay nearby, his dead body charred beyond recognition and still smouldering from the heat, and Ayla felt rage build inside her as she grabbed the heavy net. Its edges were lined with small rocks in leather sacks and she understood at once how it was to be used.

Ayla turned and tied one side of the net to a huge rib on the bridge, and then she hurried back to the far end and looked up the hillside at the Dragun. The beast was about to draw breath and blast Vigoran and his riders once again when Ayla raised her hands and outstretched her arms. She drew as big a breath as she could manage and then screamed the loudest scream she had ever managed in her life. It soared across the barren landscape and echoed up into the mountains beyond, loud enough to match even the Dragun's shrieks.

The Dragun looked up sharply and saw her alone on the bridge, and with one great beat of its giant wings the beast lifted up and away from the horses and riders, whorls of dust and grass spiralling beneath from the huge wings. Ayla saw Vigoran whirl in his saddle.

'Ayla, no!'

The Dragun soared down the hillside with the Riders of Spiris galloping in close pursuit, but she could see at once that they would never be able to catch it. The Dragun flew toward her at terrific speed, the wind rippling the thin skin of its wings.

Ayla whirled and sprinted along the bridge, the giant arced ribs flashing by as she ran as fast as she had ever done in her life. She looked over her shoulder and saw the Dragun fly straight down the centre of the bridge, its wingtips brushing the sides as it glared at her and reared its head back, flames spilling from its nostrils and curling from its fangs as it prepared to strike. She heard the roar of air into its throat and saw the web of glowing skin around its chest brighten as oxygen fanned the flames of its scorching heart.

Ayla reached the end of the bridge and hurled herself up and to the left. She grabbed the hidden net and flung it out across the bridge entrance as hard and as high as she could. The rocks flew through the air and the net unfolded in a vast web in front the charging Dragun. The beast turned its head and a jet of scorching flame flared toward Ayla, blasting between the ribs on the bridge like burning fingers reaching out for her.

Ayla dove off the side of the bridge as she felt the hot breath of the flames singe her skin, and she plummeted down into the turbulent black water and plunged beneath the waves.

The Dragun hit the expanding net and the rocks folded back over its wings and trapped them against its body. The huge beast screeched in fury as it tried to pull up, but its wings were useless and with all of their lift taken from them the animal crashed into the ground in a tangle of limbs, the net torn from the bridge by the force of its passing.

Vigoran galloped back through the bridge and the Riders of Spiris fanned out behind him.

'Protect her!' Vigoran screamed as he saw Ayla vanish into the black water.

The giant among them leaped from his saddle and plunged over the side of the bridge and into the churning water.

Vigoran jumped down from his saddle, his sword drawn and his shield up as he sprinted to where the Dragun roiled amid the now burning net in which it was entrapped. Vigoran crouched behind his shield, and as the beast rolled and writhed he picked his moment and suddenly lunged forward and thrust the sword into its body.

The glittering blade punctured its chest and plunged into the heart of the Dragun. The beast screamed in agony, flames spraying from its fearsome jaws as it writhed beneath Vigoran's blade, and then its great head sank back as a cloud of noxious fumes spilled from its lungs in dirty clouds.

Vigoran hauled his sword from within the beast, the blade glowing orange with heat, and as he did so his hood fell from his head. His eyes glowed with their strange blue light, but his face and body were invisible as though he were a ghost. Vigoran yanked his hood back into place as he turned and looked to the river. The waters flowed past them like black oil laced with chunks of ice, the wilderness now eerily silent in the wake of the Dragun's demise.

The Riders of Spiris stood along the shoreline, watching in silence, and then the giant burst from the waves. Water spilled from his great chest and Ayla's body was clutched under one huge arm as he waded out of the river and lowered her onto the grass. Vigoran dashed to his side, and as he reached the side of the river so he heard a cough and a splutter and he saw Ayla spit a mouthful of water out onto the grass, her body shaking.

The giant looked up at Vigoran, his beard thick with droplets of water. The big man's eyes were filled with both wonder and a fiercely protective gleam.

'She took on a Dragun and won,' he said as he looked down at the girl. 'A Dragun, at her age! I've never seen the like of it.'

'Nor I,' Vigoran replied. 'That's what worries me.'

\*\*\*

## Eleven

Ayla travelled the rest of the journey on the saddle of the horse belonging to the big bearded warrior, whose name she had learned was Tygrin. For some reason, he now insisted on keeping her close by. Tygrin's massive arms flanked her and a huge, warm blanket made from the fur of some unknown creature swaddled her against the cold air as they rode into the mountains.

The expressions on the faces of the Riders of Spiris were different now when they looked at her, silent glances that were still guarded but also gleamed with admiration. She had learned that the one called Agry was an aloof, moody man who said little. There was the blond one called Jake, who looked a little older than Ayla, a girl called Siren with dark skin who was always by Agry's side and just as sullen, and a young boy with spectacles called Cyril who was wearing robes and was the only member of the group who appeared to carry no weapons. Quiet and shy, he had said nothing and seemed very much out of place among the hardened warriors who made up the rest of the Riders of Spiris.

Although she had been a terrific runner all her life, Ayla was a lousy swimmer and had nearly drowned the moment she had hit the freezing water. She had been struggling to find her way with her eyes squeezed tightly shut and her arms and legs pumping furiously when she had hit a rock beneath the surface and cried out in shock and pain.

She had barely been conscious when she had felt Tygrin's massive fist close on her collar and haul her from the water, and it had taken some time for the water to fully drain from her lungs afterward. The riders had used the Dragun's smouldering flesh to build a fire to dry her out and warm her, and now Tygrin held her in place on the front of his saddle as they rode through the mountain twilight. In a grim denouement to the battle, Agry had cut out the dead Dragun's scorching heart and now carried it with him in a metal tin strapped to his horse.

Vigoran had guided his men up through a narrow path that climbed between a towering chasm within the mountains, as though a giant had cleaved a path through the ancient rock using blows from a massive axe. The path had taken them high into the mountains, and now the sky was a sea of molten metal laced with streamers of black cloud, while below the deep valleys were masked with the tops of clouds glowing blue in the fading light.

Ayla would have frozen to death up here were it not for the warmth of the giant man guiding his mount along the path. She could scarcely believe what had been happening these past few hours, but she felt both exhausted and exhilarated. The sunset seemed so beautiful as to be alive but once again she noted that there was no actual sun, that the light seemed to have an origin both everywhere and nowhere at once. She looked up to see stars glittering in the darkness and recognised at once constellations like Cassiopea and Orion, the same formations she could see from her bedroom window at home.

They rode for another hour, and it was truly dark by the time they reached their destination. Ayla had never known a darkness like it, so utterly pitch black that she could see nothing of the tremendous mountain heights that were surrounding them. But above, the heavens were alive with a billion stars of all colours that shimmered in the deep cold of space, galaxies swirling in graceful silence and the veil of the Milky Way arcing across the vista.

Ahead in the blackness she saw a tiny fire flickering. The horses rode toward the light, around which were several large troughs full of water. The riders dismounted, Ayla standing beside Tygrin and staring at the troughs.

'Who left those here?' she asked.

The riders said nothing, but Cyril stepped forward. He moved toward an open area where the sheer mountainside rose above them, and within it was a large vertical fissure that to Ayla looked like nothing more than a ragged rockface. In the silence, Cyril began to hum.

Instantly Ayla felt something in the air, an aura around her that was similar to the fear that she had felt when seeing the storms back home, but this time it was warm and inviting. She stared at Cyril, and the notes he hummed seemed to strike her core and make the hairs on the back of her neck rise up. It sounded like the coolest, most moving tune she had ever heard, and it seemed to carry far further than Cyril should have been able to project it. The air around her became alive with a hundred more unseen voices keeping perfect harmony with Cyril, souls whose presence she sensed but could not see.

To her surprise, the rocky fissure suddenly glowed with a warm orange light as Cyril lifted his hands, his eyes closed, and then he bowed at the waste and drew his hands to one side as though opening a set of invisible curtains. Before them, the rocky fissure sparkled and from its darkened depths Ayla saw what looked like a temple carved into the living rock of the mountain side. The temple rose up with spires that blended into the mountain, its magical veil drawn aside by Cyril's sorcery. She realised that even now it would have been invisible from further down the path or up in the sky. Cunningly placed in the natural fissure and visible only from the path when approaching from directly in front of it, now its windows glowed with light and warmth before them as the humming faded away into silence.

Cyril approached the doors, which were made from heavy timbers, and he held out one hand to them. The doors creaked and opened, letting a shaft of bright warm light out into the cold night. Ayla realised why Cyril was the only member of the group not to carry a weapon – he must have been some kind of wizard or something, his weapons magical and not physical. Vigoran rested one hand on her shoulder and gestured for her to join him as they followed Cyril into the temple.

The interior was far larger than the exterior, and to her surprise Ayla saw carvings on the walls much like those she had seen in churches back home.

Gargoyles, serpents and what looked like angels and other heavenly beings shimmered in the light, all with their eyes raised to the heavens. In between the carvings were immense shelves filled with ancient books, and the entire building smelling of dust and age, of an ancient history completely different to the one she knew from home.

'What is this place?' she asked in a whisper, feeling as though she were in something like a cross between a church and a library. Rose would have loved it in here.

'The Well of Memories,' Cyril replied, speaking for the first time and his voice reverential. 'This is where all history resides, where all magic that can be earned through work is found. This is the place that Terra most wants to find and destroy, and she has sought it for centuries.'

From out of thin air a wisp of smoke appeared and took shape, and Ayla's eyes widened as she recognised its form.

'Agnis!'

'Ach, there yee are my child!' Agnis rushed across and threw her arms around Ayla's neck, passing right through her and out the other side. Ayla turned and saw Agnis spin in mid–air, her hands clasped to her cheeks in adoration. 'I knew yee'd find this place safely, you're special Ayla!'

'I had help,' Ayla said as she gestured to Vigoran.

To Ayla's surprise, Agnis curtsied in mid–air. 'Your Majesty,' she intoned.

Ayla looked curiously at Vigoran, who ushered her along before she could ask any questions.

'Come, the great sage is waiting.'

Agnis hovered alongside Ayla as they walked, her hands still clasped before her in delight.

'I met my great grandmother here once,' she enthused, 'grumpy old thing she was though, yee'd not have liked her. She now spends most of her time haunting stately homes in your world, such a waste of her talents.'

'This is where ghosts come from?' Ayla asked.

'Ach, nee, not so much! Ghosts in your world are shadowy images of your past that sometimes flicker into view, brief reflections of times gone by. Here in the Mirrorealm the dead thrive alongside the living, although not so much since Terra came to power.'

Candles that were not really candles but balls of incandescent light hovered in the air and illuminated the hall, the lights drifting toward them and helpfully guiding them as they walked. Ayla was in awe of everything around her and realised they were walking toward a great crackling fire, in front of which were several ageing leather seats.

Vigoran and Cyril led her to the seats, and there she saw that one of them was occupied by an old man with a thick beard. He leaned on a thick staff by his side, watching her in silence as she approached. Behind him, leaning against the wall beside the fire, was something tall and flat that was hidden behind large, thick blankets.

Vigoran immediately lowered himself onto one knee before the old man, but the old man shook his head and waved the warrior's humility aside.

'You of all men have no need to bow down before me, Vigoran,' he said.

Vigoran stood, and with one hand gently eased Ayla forward. 'This is…'

'Ayla Fox,' the old man said before Vigoran could finish.

Ayla stared at the old man for a long time. He was grey, tired and dressed in old rags that made him look like a homeless beggar or perhaps a fortune teller. His limbs were thin and pale, like the twigs of a silver birch tree, but his eyes reflected the firelight with a mischievous twinkle that danced with light and life.

'How did you know my name?' Ayla asked.

'Come, sit,' the old man said, 'there is much that you need to know. My name is Luciffen.'

Ayla glanced at Vigoran, but all she could see were those twin points of blue light inside his hood watching her. Ayla moved forward and sat down on a seat on the opposite side of the fire to Luciffen. The old man regarded her for a moment before he spoke.

'I understand that you have many questions, Ayla, but right now we have little time and so I must ask you that you merely listen and try to understand.'

Ayla nodded and said nothing, waiting for Luciffen to go on.

'The Mirrorealm in which you now sit is a universe that in many ways is the opposite of your own, and through a series of unfortunate events you are now a part of it. Whereas in your world it is technology that has come to reign supreme, here it is sorcery and what you might refer to as magic that holds sway.'

Luciffen wafted his hand near the fire and the glowing logs and coals brightened, embers spiralling up from the flames. To Ayla's amazement they formed the shape of the Dragun that had pursued them earlier in the day.

'There is much here that will surprise you, much that will frighten you and much that is dangerous to you. You are what is known here as a Hybrin, Ayla, a person from another frame of reality who has crossed over through the mirror and is now as much a part of this world as you are your own.'

Luciffen let his hand drift again through the spiralling embers and they reformed into the shape of what looked like an immense fortress of some kind, set against towering mountains.

'We are a shadowy reflection of your own world. There is duality in all things; the Yin and the Yang, the large and the small…,' Luciffen leaned closer to her, '…the light, and the darkness. For every action, there is an equal and opposite reaction. For every technological advance in your own world, so magic becomes more powerful in ours. With every act of violence in your world, the darkness grows greater in our own, and there is much darkness here Ayla.'

Ayla couldn't help herself. 'Why am I here?'

Luciffen twirled his finger in the air and the fortress of embers dissolved into something else, something cruel and evil that surged out of the flames. Ayla recoiled slightly as the image of a stunningly beautiful woman's face appeared in the embers, but that beauty was much like the ferocious beauty of a force of nature, captivating and yet lethal at the same time.

'Terra,' Luciffen whispered the name, as though to say it might conjure up the woman in the very temple in which they sat. 'Be not fooled by her great beauty, for it is only her powerful dark magic that retains her once human features.' As Ayla watched, the gorgeous face dissolved into a disfigured, twisted visage of pure evil that caused Ayla's stomach to feel as though it were twisting upon itself with disgust.

'Terra is the most powerful wytch in Mirrorealm, an ancient evil as old as mankind itself. She has reigned in one half of this world for millennia, but every now and again the forces that are always in flux are altered and she gains in power. The darkness closes in upon Stormshadow Citadel even as we speak, and our forces are greatly depleted. But nature always finds a balance, a way to even the score, and from time to time Hybrins appear in our world who are uniquely gifted.'

Ayla figured that he was talking about her. 'What happens to them?'

A familiar voice, that of Vigoran, spoke from behind her. 'They fight the forces of darkness alongside us, and give us the chance to restore the light that once shone across the Mirrorealm and dispel the evil that now surrounds us.'

Ayla was about to ask another question when a familiar voice interrupted them.

'Did yee also tell Ayla that the poor wee things normally die horribly in the process?'

Agnis popped into view and floated out over the flames of the fire to confront Luciffen.

'Agnis,' Luciffen smiled, 'you've recovered from your exertions I see?'

'Nee thanks to the Dragun and my mirror being shattered!' Agnis snapped but then she became apologetic. 'I did my best, but the Dragun had already been in Ayla's world and it came for her right away and we had to run so there was so little time to…'

Luciffen waved Agnis down. 'I understand, Agnis, you did a fine job.'

'Aye, I did that,' Agnis agreed, and then looked at Ayla and clasped her hands to her cheeks as she went all doey–eyed again. 'My own wee little Hybrin.'

'Agnis is right,' Vigoran agreed.

'I am?' Agnis replied, apparently surprised.

'Terra is growing more powerful by the day so we must move quickly. I've never heard of a Dragun making it out of the realm before, not like that.'

'Nor I,' Luciffen agreed. 'Terra is preparing to strike and will be raising her armies as we speak, but I don't know how she became powerful enough to send Draguns into Ayla's world.'

'What does this Terra want with me?' Ayla asked. 'Why would she send a Dragun after me? I'd never even heard of her until I came here.'

Luciffen looked at her, and it seemed that his rheumy old eyes bored deep into hers, the flames reflecting the gruesome apparition of Terra in the flames.

'Because by having arrived here, you are the only force in the Mirrorealm that can destroy her.'

\*\*\*

## Twelve

'Me?' Ayla asked.

Luciffen adjusted the long, thick robes about himself as he spoke.

'Yes, Ayla, you. There have been eleven Hybrins in the Mirrorealm in the past thousand or so years, all of whom have come here and fought alongside us in the never–ending war to maintain balance between the forces of darkness and light. You are the latest, and by far the most capable if what Vigoran is about to tell me is true.'

'Ayla outwitted and defeated a Dragun in battle,' the warrior explained, apparently unperturbed by the fact that Luciffen appeared to already know what he was about to say. 'It was a young one, but none the less an impressive feat.'

Agnis gasped adoringly and patted Ayla's head. Her hand sank through Ayla's skull with a tingling sensation and wafted in front of her eyes.

'Impressive indeed,' Luciffen agreed.

'Now don't go getting none of yee's big ideas,' Agnis said protectively as she hovered alongside Ayla and folded her arms over her chest. 'Tell her about what happened to Percival Longbottom in 1743.'

Luciffen shifted in his seat and Vigoran remained silent and still.

'What happened to him?' Ayla asked.

'The poor wee lad had his arm and leg bitten off by a horde of Vampyres,' Agnis announced. 'Then there was Mary McDonnell in 1296, who lost her head, literally. And don't get me started on Lewis of Argylle in 824 who…'

'Yes, Agnis, we all know about Lewis of Argy…'

'I don't,' Ayla said.

Luciffen sighed. 'Lewis was a young Hybrin who was captured by Terra. The great wytch took him back to her lair in the Towers of Vipera, and cast poor Lewis into the Mirror of Souls.'

There was something about the way that Luciffen spoke that sent a chill through Ayla.

'What's the Mirror of Souls?' she asked.

Vigoran moved to the fire and sat down in one of the seats, and to Ayla's surprise she realised that all of the Riders of Spiris were now variously standing or sitting around the fireplace as Luciffen spoke, their approach having been absolutely silent.

'There is one Great Mirror in the realm, Ayla,' he explained, 'although we suspect that there are others out there as yet undiscovered. They are not of this world. They were forged in the heart of a star, like your sun, that once burned in our own heavens along with a second smaller star. But the stars were much older than yours, just as our world is, and when they grew old they also grew larger and eventually collided. The smaller of the two was shattered by the unimaginable forces while the other was flung out into space.'

Luciffen got to his feet and trudged around the fireplace to the towering object leaning against the wall, covered in blankets. He reached up and pulled the blankets aside, and Ayla stared in wonder as she saw the most perfect mirror she had ever seen.

It was a deep black in colour and yet it seemed to radiate an energy that she sensed but could not see. Utterly perfect in its reflection, so that the reflection actually seemed more intense than reality itself, she saw the flames of the fire and the temple around them but strangely neither she, Agnis nor the riders were reflected.

'The shattered star's remnants were also cast into the cosmos, but several large fragments landed here on this world and changed it forever,' Luciffen explained. 'Exotic materials, these mirrors are made of. As hard as diamond and yet as light as a feather. One fragment like this should have the weight of billions of mountains, but we feel its mass and gravity not physically but as the magical properties that brought life back to Mirrorealm long after it should have been destroyed in the wake of the loss of its suns.'

Vigoran gestured to the mirror as he chewed on a piece of what looked like dried meat.

'The largest of the mirrors were found and mounted in Stormshadow Citadel, and has radiated light across the realm for thousands of years, along with the sorcery and alchemy of which Luciffen speaks. But then a powerful sorceress betrayed the Council of Stormshadow and tried to take the mirror for herself.'

'Terra,' Agnis said in a disgraced tone as she patrolled up and down in front of the fireplace. 'She has much to answer for.'

'Terra was a white wytch who became consumed by hatred and a lust for power,' Luciffen said, 'and turned to the dark arts. She used the mirror to conjure a small force of demons and other unnatural beings, giving them life in this realm in return for their servitude. The Army of Stormshadow was sent in to oppose her, and she used the Great Mirror to entrap all ten thousand of them. She also captured the White Wytch, Gallentia, the head of the Council of Stormshadow, and had the rest of the council slain. With her remaining power she conjured an immensely powerful Dragun to guard the Mirror of Souls, so that we would be unable to liberate our army, and then fled. The Great Mirror became known as the Mirror of Souls.'

Luciffen sat back down by the fire, one hand resting again on his staff.

'Have you ever stared into your own reflection in a mirror for a long time and started to feel strange, Ayla?'

Ayla had denied doing so to Agnis, but she had been confused and shocked at the time. In fact, she had occasionally stared into a mirror in such a way. She knew that others had done it too, and like them she had looked at herself for long enough to feel a strange sensation coming over her. She remembered that the longer she stared at herself, the stranger it felt and that there was a powerful need to look away, that something was terribly wrong.

Luciffen saw the response in her eyes and he nodded.

'Then you began to sense your own presence in another realm,' Luciffen explained, 'your mirrorsoul. Had you not stopped looking you would have seen things that cannot be explained, things that are often frightening and confusing or magical and wonderful, depending on how lucky or unlucky you are. The reflection in a mirror only travels so far, however, and it is not possible to cross physically into another realm unless there is some other force at work, usually one of either nature or sorcery.'

Ayla remembered the lightning strike, but Agnis spoke first.

'Ooh, silly old Agnis, I almost forgot! Ayla was struck by lightning while standing next to a tree and holding a cat. Which now lives with me, by the way.'

Luciffen nodded slowly as he smiled at Ayla. 'The forces of nature, and with them earth, fire and soul. You are a "*seer*", Ayla, one who can now see the evil both in your world and here in Mirrorealm.'

Ayla wasn't sure what to say about that, and knew even less what to do about it. Luciffen spoke before she was able to conjure up a question or two.

'Terra will seek your death, because a Hybrin is a form of life that she has no direct ability to control. All Hybrins are immune to the sorcery that dominates our realm, Ayla. Terra cannot lure or deceive you with magic as she deceives others, and she will always appear to you to be the evil that she truly is.'

'So Terra has control over the Mirror of Souls?' Ayla said.

Tygrin spoke from one side of the cave, his solemn, deep voice echoing back and forth in the flickering light.

'Not yet, for the Mirror of Souls remains beyond her reach but also beyond ours. Terra's sorcery puts her on an equal footing to us, but she has an army at her side while ours dwells in misery within the Mirror of Souls. It's an advantage that has allowed her to grow truly powerful. Soon she will be strong enough to launch a direct attack on Stormshadow Citadel and capture it, and we have no way of stopping her.'

Vigoran nodded slowly as he carried on the story.

'Our simple weapons are no use against the power of Terra's occult. The entire army was consumed by the Mirror of Souls and most of us were lucky to escape with our lives. The citadel was abandoned as we could not summon enough men to defeat the Dragun, and so we hid here in the Well of Memories, afraid that Terra would try to take that too. Our forces were broken up, scattered into the wilderness where we now hide in small bands, like this.'

Ayla looked at the Riders of Spiris around her, young men and women not much older than her.

'When did this happen?' Ayla asked.

Luciffen replied, his face half in shadow from the firelight.

'Terra's betrayal was long ago, but the capture of the Army of Stormshadow occurred here in the year 1939 in your world, the outbreak of what you call World War Two.'

'The Second World War caused this? How?'

'Because what happens in your world affects ours, and all others,' Luciffen replied. 'The growth of evil in one world will give strength to the evil in another. Your world is suffering, Ayla. The Second World War caused a rise to power of Terra in ours, and although the forces of darkness were defeated in your world we did not prevail. Now, the forces of darkness in your world are growing again and we are weakened already. There is little to stop Terra from conquering the entire realm and gaining control, and if that happens then the balance of forces will be lost forever and Terra will be able to advance in *all* realms.'

'Ach, that's not the half of it!' Agnis said as she floated around, gesturing as she spoke. 'The worlds we inhabit often collide, and darkness is the result. When evil takes hold in your world you see it in the acts of men, of wars and disease. In our world, we see it in the form of Urks and Draguns, Vampyres and demons rising to harm us. But if Terra controls all the mirrors and is able to project herself and her minions into other worlds, then yee'll see them as they truly are. The Black Death, the Inquisitions and the Crusades were all driven by the rise of darkness here in the Mirrorealm, evil leaking into your world. The legendary monsters of your ancient legends such as the Titans, the Minotaur, the Kraken and others that yee'll have heard of, all were demons that slipped from our world into yours lassie, when the darkness grew very powerful.'

'The Minotaur was real?' Ayla gasped. 'And the Kraken?'

'Seamen in your world reported the Kraken for many centuries,' Luciffen confirmed, 'and the Greeks built a great maze that can be visited today to try to keep the Minotaur from escaping its underworld lair. These beasts were not the figments of the imaginations of men, but demons from the Mirrorealm embodied physically into your world. Werewolves, sea serpents, vampyres and demons, all have stalked your world from time to time and caused great distress wherever they were seen.'

Ayla began to sense how the war that Vigoran and Luciffen spoke of was affecting her home. She thought of everything happening there; of climate change, the Gulf Wars, the lies of politicians and the spectre of poverty, the rise of hate and fascism and terrorism and suddenly she understood. Luciffen's next words rang through her mind and echoed into an eternity that seemed larger now than it had ever done.

'Terra is rising again, stronger now than ever before, and if she is not stopped here then she will eventually become powerful enough to cross the boundary between realms. If that should happen, untold chaos will enshroud your world once again.'

'What will she do?' Ayla asked.

'We don't know, lassie,' Agnis said, 'but whatever it is, it's coming already and it'll nee be good for yee or your kind. Wars, pestilence, even an extinction canny be ruled out. If Terra takes control, then your world and ours will be changed forever.'

Luciffen watched Ayla as he spoke, as though assessing her.

'Like it or not, Ayla, you're the next Hybrin and the key to defeating Terra and restoring balance not just to our realm, but also to your own.'

\*\*\*

## Thirteen

A silence filled the hall for a long moment, and Ayla shook her head.

'I think that someone picked the wrong mirror,' she said finally.

'We don't choose the mirror,' Luciffen smiled at her. 'The mirror chooses us.'

Ayla felt mildly dizzy. So much had happened in such an incredibly short space of time that she didn't know where to begin. She felt overwhelmed by the enormity of this new world and what she apparently meant to it, and the thought of such great change filled her with fear. Would she survive this? Would she ever be able to return home?

*Home.*

She thought of her mother, Rachel, and wondered how on earth she was going to be able to explain all of this to her.

'I can't do this,' she whispered.

To her surprise Luciffen smiled in what seemed like relief as the flames crackled alongside them.

'I would not have expected you to say anything else,' he murmured, 'and I am glad of your honesty. Had you rushed to help, I would have feared that you had underestimated the enormity of what lies ahead. There will be great danger and many obstacles to overcome, and we haven't even started to work out how we will rescue Gallentia, or regain Stormshadow Citadel and defeat the Dragun that Terra has placed there to…'

Ayla, suddenly overwhelmed, stood up and strode out of the temple.

The air was cold outside, the night sky glittering with a million stars. Ayla's mind was so full of concepts and names and fears that she had to clear it, to try to think straight. She was standing there staring up at the stars when one of the Riders of Spiris approached.

She saw the blond swordsman, Jake, behind her with a thick blanket in his hands that he draped over her shoulders. She smiled her thanks as she wrapped the warm blanket about her and looked back to the stars.

'It's a lot to take in,' he said.

Ayla sighed. She still couldn't believe where she was standing, and the thought that she had left her room in the middle of the night suddenly struck her. Her mother would be going insane with worry.

'I have to get back,' she said.

The tall warrior looked at her for a moment, and then he shook his head. 'Time moves differently here. If you go back you'll be right where you left, same time, same place.'

Ayla frowned. 'How?'

'I don't know,' he shrugged. 'Time ebbs and flows but it always equalises eventually, just like water always finds a level.'

Ayla looked back to the stars, somewhat soothed that her mother would not be on the verge of cardiac arrest with panic but still concerned for her.

'This isn't my world,' she said. 'I can't stay here.'

'It's not my world either,' Jake replied.

Ayla turned to look at him. 'You're a Hybrin?'

He threw her a lop–sided salute and crossed his eyes in a comical way. 'At your service.'

'But I thought that Hybrins were rare?'

'They are,' said Jake, 'but there have been three in the past sixty years, more than anyone can remember, which is not good news. The forces of nature are trying harder to restore the balance and it's not working.'

Ayla looked at Jake for a long moment. He was handsome in a quirky kind of way, with a warm smile and blond hair that hung in strands either side of his face. His jaw was wide, and there were shadows of pain behind a pair of grey eyes.

'Where are you from?'

'Arkansas,' he replied and stuck out a rough, calloused hand. 'Jake.'

'Ayla.'

She shook his hand, and found herself hanging on for just a tiny but too long. Jake's smile broadened.

'Yeah, I know.'

'How come you're not the one they're relying on to save the realm from Terra?' Ayla asked him.

'Because I shouldn't be here at all,' Jake replied with a shrug. 'My father had a crystal meth habit and my mother died when I was four. I was on the streets by eight years old. Got caught out in a snowstorm one night a year or so back, lost my bearings and collapsed on a farmer's electrified fence while trying to get into a barn for shelter. Thirty thousand volts later I woke up here. Vigoran thinks the windows in the barn acted like mirrors, reflecting the light when I was electrocuted. One in a million chance.'

'I'm sorry.'

'Don't be,' Jake assured her, 'life's been kinder to me here than it ever was in Arkansas. I wouldn't go back for all the money in the world.'

Ayla smiled, understanding why Jake would now so willingly ride into battle with Vigoran, and also why he was standing here.

'They sent you to talk to me.'

'I came here of my own free will,' Jake countered. 'I saw what you did on the bridge, Ayla. I've never seen anyone move that fast.'

'I was being chased by a fire–breathing dragon the size of a bus. It's quite motivational.'

'Still,' Jake shrugged with a smile, 'you bagged it just the same. You may not think that you're up to this but believe me, this place, it has the ability to bring things out in you that you never even knew you had.'

Ayla smiled faintly. 'Both the good and the bad?'

Jake nodded, his pep–talk slightly derailed. 'They're fighting a war here and they're losing. These are good people and for whatever reason, you've been sent here to help them. Don't waste it before you know the value of what's here, Ayla.'

Jake turned and walked back into the temple.

Ayla stood for a while and looked at the stars, the same ones she saw on every clear night at home, and she made her decision. She turned and walked back inside, and all the Riders of Spiris and Luciffen stood to face her. Agnis hovered up into the air, her hands clasped before her.

Ayla spoke as clearly as she could, even though she felt strangely nervous, ashamed even.

'I want to go home. I can't just leave my mother alone, for this. She was left alone once before, and…' Ayla felt it hard to speak of what had happened, and her throat felt suddenly tight as tears welled in her eyes. 'She has never gotten over it. We're all we've got, together, the two of us. I can't leave her.'

She saw the faces of the riders pale slightly, and then fall. One by one, they turned from the fireplace and filed out of the hall. Vigoran paused alongside her, placed one hand on her shoulder and squeezed before he vanished into the night.

Agnis drifted across and threw her arms around, and through, Ayla's neck.

'I understand, my love. You look so much better with your wee head still attached to your neck.'

Ayla smiled, and in a sprinkle of light Agnis was gone.

Ayla felt somehow bereft as she saw Luciffen turn toward the mirror he had recently unveiled. There were no recriminations, no begging for her to reconsider. Ayla thought that the forces of nature might send another in her place perhaps, but regardless she knew that she could not leave her mother alone to face life without her. Jake's promise of the ebb and flow of time did not quite match up to her fears of her mother's suffering should she vanish as her father had once done, so long ago.

'Look into the mirror,' Luciffen said. 'You must keep looking until you see yourself. It will feel strange, but you must not turn away.'

Ayla took a breath to relax, and then she looked at the mirror. At first, she could see nothing but the reflection of the temple and the flames. Then, slowly she saw the temple become blurry and indistinct, and then she saw the flames smear into a hazy glow of light that pulsed as though alive.

The temple vanished from the mirror's reflection and she saw the faint outline of something rectangular and patterned, and she realised that it was her bed.

'That's right,' Luciffen whispered, his voice filling her mind, 'keep watching.'

Slowly she saw the rest of her room materialise before her, as though she was standing on the inside of her bedroom mirror looking out, and then she saw herself lying in her bed, fast asleep. The room felt warm, the air stuffy, the covers brushing her skin.

Ayla realised that her eyes were closed. She opened them and saw her bedroom wall beside her and her watch, the digital display flashing normally.

*4.07am.*

Ayla sat up in the bed and looked at her mirror, but there was no sign of Agnis and there were no signs of a Dragun having blasted her bedroom with flames. The sky outside was clear and filled with stars, and Ayla breathed a sigh of relief. That had been the most amazing, incredible dream that she had *ever* had, and she couldn't believe how long and realistic it had been.

Ayla turned over, closed her eyes and pulled her duvet closer about her shoulders.

She opened her eyes again as she felt something strange against her neck, like fur.

The duvet was not a duvet, it was a blanket. With a start, she realised that it was the same blanket that Jake had put over her shoulders outside the temple, and which she had still been wearing when she had stared into Luciffen's mirror.

\*\*\*

## Fourteen

'What's wrong?'

Ayla's mother watched her curiously as she ate a slice of toast without any real interest, staring into space and her mind lost amid the lonely mountains of Mirrorealm. Ayla didn't even hear the question until Rachel repeated it a second time.

'Nothing,' Ayla managed to reply, barely looking at her mother.

As usual Rachel was in a rush to get to work on time, and worried about the fact that she would be leaving Ayla at home, alone, while she slogged through another fourteen–hour shift.

'I'm okay mum, honest.'

'You seem preoccupied with something.'

'I'm just tired mum, that's all.'

'Are you sleeping badly, are you ill or is it because you..?'

'Mum,' Ayla interrupted, 'it's been a tough couple of days, okay?'

Her mother grabbed her coat and hugged Ayla, then looked deep into her eyes. 'You haven't seen more strange men wandering about in the garden, have you?'

'No,' Ayla replied.

'Okay,' came the reluctant reply, 'but if you have any more hallucinations you call me right away and come to the hospital, understood?'

Her mother pecked her on the cheek and a moment later she was away and out of the front door. Ayla sat for a few moments in silence and then she hurried upstairs to her room and reached under her bed. She pulled the blanket that Jake had given her and smelled the soft odour of it, the blanket woven from some kind of super–soft wool that seemed warmer and more comforting than it had any right to be.

She had found herself thinking about Jake a lot more than she had expected, and now she realised that he had been telling the truth and that there had been almost no change in the time of night from when she had entered Mirrorealm to when she had returned. She thought about that for a moment, and then she hurried back downstairs and opened up her mother's laptop computer.

They had only enough money for the one ancient computer, and she had to wait impatiently for the computer's drive to start up and open Windows 1876 BC or whatever version it used. As soon as the Internet was available she typed in several words into the search engine.

*JAKE ARKANSAS ELECTRIFIED FENCE ACCIDENT*

To her surprise she saw a news article appear from a publication in Arkansas detailing the hospitalisation of a young man by the name of Jake Shaw, 15, whose unconscious body had been found near an electrified fence during a freezing January night. As Ayla read, she discovered that Jake was now on life–support in a hospital in Pine Bluff, Arkansas, with doctors uncertain of whether he would make it through the next forty–eight hours.

What really leaped out at her was a picture of Jake, presumably taken when in police custody at some point or other. While he looked several years younger in the image, there was absolutely no doubt that it was the same Jake who now lived in the Mirrorealm.

Ayla sat back in her chair and stared at the screen. She had not imagined the night's adventures, and the confirmation of Jake's story and the blanket still under her bed were all the evidence she needed. What bothered her now was that everything Luciffen had said might also be true. Had she made a terrible mistake?

On impulse, she moved to the television and switched it on. She selected a news channel and watched as report after report came in, detailing a seemingly endless series of disasters both natural and man–made around the world. Tremendous storms were battering countries on both sides of the Atlantic, with the most powerful hurricanes ever recorded leaving terrible destruction in their wake, while the United States was on the verge of conflict with a number of rogue nations and states harbouring terrorists of one kind or another. Hate crimes were rising, intolerance of religion and of those with no religion were commonplace, violence toward minorities of all kinds and mistrust of politicians of all nations seemed endemic as did polarised and confrontational politics. Some countries were even testing nuclear missile technology again, threatening their neighbours with all–out war. Then, the broadcaster's tone changed and the image turned to one of presenters Helena and Mike.

*'…and in the bizarre news section, strange reports flooded in yesterday from passengers aboard a British Airways flight waiting to land at Heathrow.'*

*'That's right Helena,'* said Mike, *'the airplane was preparing to land when over sixty passengers erupted into panic having seen what they insisted was a real–life dragon flying in the opposite direction.'*

Ayla froze in place as she watched the television.

*'The crew of the airliner refused to comment this morning,'* added Helena, *'but what's stranger is that a source inside the airline reported on condition of anonymity that both pilots reluctantly filed a near–miss report with an unidentified flying object that same afternoon. Although neither of the pilots described the object as a dragon, both agreed in their reports that the object was alive and not a machine.'*

*'As if our skies weren't busy enough already, eh Helena?'* Mike chortled. *'Do you think they'll be using low–flying dragons as a reason for delays at airports now?'*

*'You're such a card, Mike.'*

Ayla switched off the television. She needed to clear her head, and she could think of no better place than in the warren of alleys and housing estates. She had her trainers on within moments and was out of the door, locking it behind her as she set off at a jog.

The sun was shining and there was a breeze gusting her along as she ran to the housing estate and vaulted up onto a low wall. She ran along it at an easy pace, cutting left and jumping the gap as she ran directly up a forty–five–degree incline in the wall beside a flight of concrete steps. A young mother was trying to coax a screaming toddler down the steps while holding two bulging bags of shopping, but both she and the toddler fell silent as they watched Ayla race up the steep incline and vault from the top. She heard the mother gasp as Ayla plummeted down to land smoothly as she continued on her way at a run.

Ayla made her way into the estates, running and leaping across stairwells and pathways, always moving from wall to wall, never letting her feet touch the ground. Her mind cleared, her only focus her movement, and as she reached a building with a concrete–encased stairwell on the side, separated from the main building by a narrow gap, she vaulted up between the two walls and pinned herself in place, feet on one wall, back and shoulders on the other.

Ayla shimmied her way up the wall and then pulled one leg in and pushed off over the twenty–foot drop, grabbing the opposite ledge and flipping herself through a windowless cavity into the stairwell. She ran hard, pushing herself up the steps to the twelfth floor where the steps ended. There, at the top, was a staggering view over the city through a window whose glass had long ago been vandalised and removed.

Ayla leaped up into the open cavity and swung out over the drop, reaching up for the ledge above that she knew was there. She hauled herself up, the wind whistling past her at this height as she clambered up onto the roof of the building and turned to look out across the city.

She could see everything from up here, and as nobody ever visited the rooftop she often sat for long hours in peaceful solitude. Now, the view over the city was marred by a long line of dark clouds moving briskly in from the west. Ayla could see the marching thunderheads once again and the hard–won tranquillity in her mind was broken by the sight of the turbulent clouds.

Ayla thought that she saw something in their patterns, the image of a face towering over the city as the thunderstorms approached. She squinted, saw vivid flashes as lightning flickered this way and that, and then she felt her skin crawl as she sensed the evil within the storm. It grew upon her, like an awareness of being watched, creeping up her back and tingling in her shoulders and neck. Whatever she had gained in the Mirrorealm had not left her yet.

*You're a seer, Ayla.*

A vast thunderhead towered up into the sky, and within its depths she thought she saw the face of a beautiful yet cruel woman glaring down at her. Lightning illuminated the cloud and she heard the first threatening rumbles of thunder echoing back and forth across the land.

'Terra,' she whispered.

She searched the sky for any sign of a Dragun but she saw nothing, only the presence of great evil before her. It felt as though it had always been there, but only now was she able to truly see it. She sucked in a breath of fresh air and closed her eyes as she tried to clear her mind again. Terra had no interest in her, right? She had returned home and presented no threat to the realm.

Ayla opened her eyes and it seemed as though the thunderhead had doubled in size, Terra's huge visage towering over her as lightning raged beneath the rain shadow cast by the storm front. The wind turned cold and Ayla saw the sun being eclipsed by the highest clouds once again.

Ayla's cell phone rang in her pocket, and she pulled it out to see Geraldine's name on the screen. She answered it.

*'Ayla, it's Geraldine. Can you come to the hospital?'*

'Why? I feel fine, honestly.'

There was a pause.

*'It's not you, Ayla. It's your mum.'*

Ayla's heart felt as though it had stopped in her chest and she looked up at the fearsome face of Terra in the clouds. Ayla was leaping back down into the stairwell an instant later, running faster than she ever had.

\*\*\*

## Fifteen

Ayla had never liked hospitals. There was something about the clinical smell of the halls that made her want to run outside for fresh air every five minutes. Now, breathless from tearing straight across town, she hurried through the bustling Accident and Emergency department and saw Geraldine coming the other way.

'What's wrong? What happened?' Ayla asked.

Geraldine waved her down.

'It's okay, your mum's fine. They're just keeping her in observation for now.'

'Why? What's wrong with her?'

Ayla allowed herself be led into one of the wards, where the same doctor who had treated Ayla just a day before was now deep in discussion with another doctor, his brow furrowed and one hand stroking his chin.

Doctor Singh saw her coming and he smiled as he made his way toward her.

'How's my favourite miracle girl?' he asked.

Ayla managed a brief smile in response but she was in no mood for small talk. 'Where's my mum?'

'She's in the ward,' Doctor Singh replied. 'I'm afraid that she collapsed earlier today while at work.'

'Collapsed?' Ayla uttered in horror as she felt tears well up in her eyes.

'She's fine,' Doctor Singh promised her as he squeezed one of her shoulders. 'We think that it's stress, probably due to her high workload and your near miss with death of the other day. She's just over tired and she needs some time out.'

Ayla wasn't sure what to make of that but she followed Doctor Singh to a hospital bed and saw Rachel at once, lying in the bed with a saline drip in her arm and a tired look on her face. She brightened as soon as she saw Ayla, who raced to her side and flung her arms around her mother.

'It's okay Ayla, I'm alright.'

Ayla squeezed her mother tight as Doctor Singh read from a recent report on her mother's condition.

'Hyper tension,' he said as he looked at her. 'Have you been experiencing any chest pains, headaches, that sort of thing?'

Rachel nodded wearily. 'Some.'

'She's been having a headache almost every day,' Ayla said helpfully.

Doctor Singh nodded and put the report back in place.

'You need rest.'

'I need to get back to work,' Rachel replied. 'I can't afford to take time off.'

Doctor Singh smiled in understanding. 'I know you feel that way Rachel, but you're no good to Ayla if you're in here suffering from hypertension. You're a nurse, you know well enough where that leads if left untreated.'

Rachel sighed but Ayla could sense the frustration in her and she held her hand.

'I could maybe get a Saturday job to help,' she offered.

Rachel smiled, but her eyes were filled with tears now.

'And I've got your back too,' Geraldine said from nearby. 'I can't stay at your home but I can check in every day.'

'I can handle the chores,' Ayla reminded her mother. 'You need to stay here for a while, get some rest and then you'll feel better.'

'Since when did you become so grown up?' Rachel asked, resting one hand on Ayla's cheek.

Doctor Singh grinned as he gestured to Ayla and Geraldine.

'It would appear that your personal support network is in full swing,' he announced, 'and as you're here in the hospital then, technically, you're still working. I will leave you to supervise the operation of this saline drip for the foreseeable future, Nurse Fox.'

Doctor Singh turned away with a mischievous smile as Ayla held onto her mother's hand. She looked so tired, drained, as though she were carrying the world upon her shoulders. Ayla was struck for the very first time by just how much her mother was doing and of the strain that it was placing on her, and suddenly Ayla felt ashamed as she realised how much she had come to rely on her. Without a father figure in her life, her mother had become her entire world, but Rachel too had lost someone close to her.

Ayla could not remember her father. Although she rarely mentioned it to her mother, she knew that he had walked out when Ayla was only a year old and had never been seen again. She did not know why he had gone or where, only that she had been too young to even remember his face. Rachel kept no photographs of him in the house, so that there was nothing to remember him by, not even a name.

'We'll sort this out,' Ayla said to Rachel, her tone serious. 'We're not going to have to live like this forever mum, okay?'

Rachel seemed more upset than ever, crying openly now. She hugged Ayla tightly, and Geraldine stepped in and took Ayla's hand.

'I'll get this one home,' she informed Rachel. 'You, get some sleep and don't worry about a thing, *got it?*'

Rachel managed a reluctant nod in response, and then Ayla left with Geraldine. They walked out of the hospital together for the second time in two days, and outside the quiet and sterile interior of the building she saw the deep grey skies and the torrential rain pouring in sheets at an angle across the car park.

'Jeez, again? What the hell is this country coming to?' Geraldine complained.

Geraldine hurried off to her car and returned a few minutes later to collect Ayla and take her home. They drove through the rush hour traffic, headlights flaring through the rain–drenched windscreen until Geraldine pulled in outside Ayla's home.

'Are you sure you're going to be okay?' Geraldine asked her. 'You can stay at our place if you want?'

Ayla shook her head. 'I'll be fine, really, and I can do some chores for mum ready for when she comes out.'

Geraldine nodded. 'Okay, you've got our number. If you need anything, at any time, just call.'

'I will.'

Ayla got out of the car and ran through the rain to her doorstep, unlocked the door and hurried in. She shut the door behind her and locked it both with the key and the latch to ensure that nobody could get inside. She thought for a moment, and then she hurried to the phone and dialled a number from memory.

*'Ayla?'* Rose answered her mobile phone on the first ring. *'My God what happened to you? You've been on the news and I thought you were dead when you didn't call and…'*

'Rose, forget all that. I need your help. Can you meet me at the library in one hour?'

*'The library? But you just got hit by lightning and…'*

'It's important, Rose. Can you be there?'

*'Yes, of course I will. One hour.'*

Ayla put the phone down. She didn't really know whether this was the right thing to do, only that sitting around doing nothing was no longer a possibility. Her mum was ill and the entire planet seemed to be going insane, and Ayla had the sense that the events in the Mirrorealm were to blame.

She *had* to do something.

\*\*\*

## Sixteen

The funny thing about the library was that it had once been a church. Ayla walked up to the ancient, imposing building with its towering ornate spires and ugly gargoyles and figured that nobody in their right mind would want to walk inside the place anyway – it wasn't exactly inviting.

She had read on her phone on the way to the church that it had been built in the year 1412, a time when most people were living in abstract poverty in the medieval Dark Ages. The churches had been powerful back then, and thought nothing of enlisting the people into building their great monuments while those ordinary people struggled to find enough food to eat. Failure to worship was harshly punished, and denial of a god resulted in people being tortured or even burned alive at the stake. The church towered over the rest of the street even today, so back them it must have seemed impossibly powerful and overbearing. Fortunately, society had moved on from those dark days, and Ayla had shuddered as she imagined what it must have been like to have suffered through them.

Ayla walked inside and into the deep hush that pervaded all such buildings, as though some omnipotent god really were watching them from the lofty heights of the rafters. Rose saw her coming and at once rushed over and threw her arms around Ayla's neck.

'Wow, I'm so glad you're not dead!'

Ayla chuckled. 'Yeah, good to see you too.'

'So, what's so important that you're out of bed and down here at the library? What do you need help with? Boy trouble? Girl trouble? How to avoid thunderstorms?'

Ayla ushered Rose down one of the long book aisles and spoke in a whisper. 'I need to know everything that you know about the underworld and the occult.'

Rose blinked. 'Seriously?'

Ayla knew that there was no way she could tell Rose what had happened. First, Rose would think that she'd gone insane. Second, if word got back to Ayla's mother it would only increase her anxiety.

'Yeah, seriously. Look, the world's getting pretty odd out there and I wondered if all of this had happened before, y'know, back in the past.'

Rose narrowed her eyes. 'Okay, but I still don't get why you'd want to know all of that.'

'Just help me out here, okay?' Ayla asked.

Rose led Ayla to a set of shelves in the Ancient History section of the library, the books there as old it seemed as the church, and she hauled a particularly large one off the shelves. They hurried to a table in an alcove nearby in a secluded part of the library, and Rose opened the huge book up and found what she was looking for.

'The underworld,' she announced, 'otherwise known as Hell or Hades in our part of the world. It is the legendary and mythical realm of the dead, a place where all souls reside in the afterlife.'

'Sounds great,' Ayla said.

'Every single religion and mythology in the world speaks of the underworld, in religious texts or through oral traditions, but they're all pretty much the same.'

'Okay,' Ayla said, 'so even cultures that are far apart speak of the same or similar things?'

'Identical things,' Rose said. 'The names are different, but all describe beasts that are chimeras, one species mixed with another, ghosts, vampires, dragons and so on. Most also have a head figure, a great evil of some kind. Here, we'd call that dude Satan or Lucifer.'

Ayla frowned as she thought of Luciffen. 'Lucifer is the bad guy?'

'Not really,' Rose said. 'The name actually means "bright star" or the "coming of dawn light" and was given to the star Venus in ancient times. The early Christians took the name and gave it to the devil, as they liked to demonise older pagan religions on their heads to confuse people into thinking that something once seen as good was in fact evil.'

'So, the name originally meant the light, not the darkness?'

'Pretty much,' Rose agreed. 'Most of what religious people believe in now is false, all twisted up with time and history. Easter, Christmas and things like that all had different meanings back then and were nothing to do with religions. It's only in fairly recent times, historically speaking, that they came to be associated with a person at all.'

Ayla looked at the pages of the book, which were filled with images of folklore creatures, dragons and sprites and angels.

'Do you think that these people actually saw these things?'

'They certainly believed that they did,' Rose replied. 'Fear of the creatures of the underworld is as old as humanity, and comes from the Middle East in what's called the Fertile Crescent, where civilisation first took hold. What's odd about that is that most of the legends of the underworld also say that's where civilisation will end too.'

'Why is that odd?'

'Because all of the world's creation myths say the same thing, that our world sprung into light and life after a great darkness, and will end when the forces of darkness return to fight the last great battle with the forces of light. You'd know it as Armageddon.'

Ayla thought of the darkness that must have consumed the Mirrorealm after the loss of its suns, as Rose turned the pages of the book to an image of what looked like the most apocalyptic storm that Ayla had ever seen. The painting showed demons and angels warring in a turbulent sky filled with fire and lightning.

'That's the end of the world?' Ayla asked.

'The End of Days,' Rose said as they looked at the painting.

Ayla felt something stir inside of her as she looked at the image, and somehow she knew that she was on the right track.

'A war,' she echoed, thinking of how Luciffen had said that life in the realm was a reflection of life here on earth. 'How does the war happen?'

'Well, nobody knows as it hasn't happened yet,' Rose admitted, 'but usually it's said that there will be an increase in war and pestilence around the world, rising unrest, suffering and general bad–vibes all around. Eventually, people turn against each other and amid the chaos and confusion the evil becomes strong enough that the underworld opens up and the dead and the living go to war. There have been all kinds of supposed *seers* in the past who have described the event, like Nostradamus.'

*Seers*. Ayla stared at the image as she thought about the state of the world around them, the increasingly violent weather, the wars and suffering, the famines and the increased sightings of strange beasts she had heard about on the news. She looked at the depictions of the warring angels and lightning bolts and wondered if the supposed seers had merely painted what they *thought* they were seeing; angels and demons, when they could have seen flying machines fighting as cities burned in nuclear fires below.

'The underworld opens,' she whispered to herself.

If the Mirrorealm was anything to do with the current global woes, then Ayla was sure that the great evil that would rise to conquer the earth was Terra and her army. Luciffen had been right. The last time this had happened had been World War Two, and the forces of light in Ayla's world had barely avoided utter defeat at the hands of Hitler's Third Reich before rallying and winning the conflict. Now, the evil was rising again. This was no longer about a war in some other realm that would never affect Ayla and her mother if they just stayed away. This was something that was affecting them all, *already*, and there was nothing that anybody could do about it as there was nobody on earth who had any idea of what was really happening. Except Ayla.

'Is there anywhere in the world any evidence that the underworld is opening, I mean, right now?'

Rose nodded. 'Sure, if you believe in that sort of thing. They're opening up all over the planet right now in the far north.'

'You're kidding me?'

Rose tapped some search terms into her phone and the Internet returned a series of sites.

'They're calling them megaslumps,' Rose said, 'but the local people are referring to them as the Gateways to Hell.'

Ayla looked at the images on the phone's screen and her skin crawled. The open wilderness of a vast forest filled the screen, and within it an immense chasm that seemed to plunge into the very depths of the earth. It looked literally as though the planet were turning itself inside out.

'Batagaika Crater, in Siberia,' Rose said, 'the largest of them all at half a mile long. The local people won't go near it as they say they hear strange creatures crying out in the night and fear that the underworld is coming out to get them.'

Ayla saw other images of similar chasms, gigantic seismic scars torn into the earth, their depths lost in shadows and darkness. One of them was a pit of fire, the earth literally burning within.

'Sinkholes are opening up all over the earth,' Rose added, 'and this pit of flames is Darvaza Crater in Turkmenistan that's been burning for decades. Scientists say that it's caused by burning gas but nobody believes them. The locals call it the Gates of Hell and…' Rose looked at Ayla. 'Are you okay, you look like you've seen a ghost! Are you sure that lightning bolt didn't, y'know, do anything to you?'

Ayla stood up and hugged Rose. 'I'm fine, honest, thanks for helping me.'

Ayla turned and hurried away, leaving Rose in the library and looking a bit confused.

*\*\**

## Seventeen

Ayla hurried home and locked all of the doors as soon as she was there. She shut all the windows and made sure that the answerphone was on and that the television and cooker and everything else was switched off. Happy that the house was secure, from normal human beings at least, she then walked into the kitchen and opened the fridge.

There wasn't much inside, but she grabbed a few sausage rolls and sandwiches left over from the picnic with her mother and packed them into a belt bag that she had bought on holiday in Cornwall the year before. She hadn't realised how hungry she was, and she ate half of it while packing.

She walked into the living room and turned on the television. Mike and Helena were still there, chatting away to the camera with their bright perma–smiles.

*'… and more incredible reports are coming in of unusual phenomena, this time from farms where cattle mutilations are on the rise.'*

*'That's right Dave,'* Helena agreed. *'Vets in the area have been baffled by farmers reporting livestock found dead in the mornings with puncture wounds in their necks, their bodies entirely drained of blood! The phenomena have existed for decades, but this time there have been witness reports of pale figures feasting on the remains. Dale Angus reports.'*

Ayla watched as a windswept reporter appeared with a microphone in his hand. He was standing on the edge of a boggy field, and behind him were several white tents, rigid cow's legs poking from beneath them.

*'This single farmer has lost over twelve head of cattle in two days, all of them drained of blood. What's worse is that local people have signed sworn statements saying that they have seen what they describe as "pale, winged creatures of a human form" eating or drinking from the remains before apparently flying away into the night when disturbed. While local police have not ruled out some kind of occult worship, they say that local veterinarians cannot see any evidence of tampering with the remains and that the cows appear to have been attacked by some kind of local predators.'*

The screen snapped back to Mike and Helena.

*'Better stock up on garlic then, folks,'* Mike quipped as Helena rolled her eyes.

Ayla switched off the television. She stood for a long moment, staring into space as she thought again about what Luciffen and Vigoran had told her. Ayla turned and walked through the house, checked that the French doors were locked, and looked again at the blackened bulk of the gnarled tree in the garden before she hurried up the stairs and into her room.

The storm outside had cast the room into near darkness, but she did not turn on the lights. Instead Ayla moved to the window and looked outside at the storm raging in the heavens. Lightning forked angrily across the bruised clouds, and she felt her skin tingling with the knowledge that something out there was watching her. She sensed it in the darkness, in the shadows, something cold and cruel slithering from one place of hiding to the next. It was as tangible as the air that she breathed, and she knew that it wasn't going away.

Her mother was ill, stressed by the struggles that they faced in the same way that Ayla was stressed by her problems at school. But now, there was something else hunting them and Ayla could not shake off the feeling that her mother's sudden illness was due to more than just bills and Ayla's brush with death in the garden.

She looked up into the sky and she could almost feel Terra watching her, smiling with malice as the storms raged and the rain lashed down around the house. She could hear Luciffen's voice in her mind, whispering with the rain. *Now, the forces of darkness in your world are growing again and we are weakened here already. There is little to stop Terra from conquering the entire realm and gaining control, and if that happens then the balance of forces will be lost forever, and Terra will be able to advance in all realms.*

Ayla took a breath, and then she turned to her bedroom mirror. She sat down before it and checked that the bag was securely tucked around her waist, and then from beneath her bed she pulled the blanket that Jake had given her. She placed it around her shoulders and breathed deeply upon it for a moment, savouring the scent and letting it fill her mind with thoughts of the Mirrorealm.

If Terra was going to try to come to Ayla's world and hunt her down, perhaps even her family, then she wasn't going to just sit back and let it happen. Her mother needed help and Ayla was going to make sure she got it, one way or the other.

She looked into the mirror, composed herself, and then silently stared at her own reflection.

The room flickered with lightning from outside, and thunder raged across the heavens. Ayla flinched at the powerful blasts that seemed to rip the sky open right above the house, as though Terra were enraged at what she was attempting to do.

The darkness around her seemed to deepen, and gradually her reflection seemed to lose definition before her. Her eyes blurred and her face became little more than a blob of unfocussed light hovering amid the darkness. She kept her eyes open, fought the growing need to look away as she sought some sign of the Mirrorealm in the faint light beyond the blurry reflection of her room.

The sound of the crashing thunder and the angry flares of lightning faded from her awareness as she stared into oblivion, and quite suddenly she realised that she was not staring at anything at all. Her mind had gone completely blank and she was not conscious of her surroundings.

Ayla blinked and her vision returned.

She was sitting before her mirror, in her room, and nothing had happened.

Ayla cursed herself and thumped her thigh with one fist. She had abandoned the one place where she could have made a difference, and now she could not return. She thought of Agnis and Vigoran and Jake, the giant Tygrin and the strangely exhilarating atmosphere of the realm and she knew that she had made a terrible mistake.

'Damn it, Jake,' she uttered, 'where *are* you?'

Ayla stood up, frustrated and turned away from the mirror.

It was then that she felt the hairs on her neck stand on end and what seemed like the air rushing from the room into the mirror behind her. She tried to turn but it was already too late.

Ayla felt herself lifted off her feet. She screamed as she hurtled backwards through the mirror, the sensation of pins and needles racing through her body as she plunged into the Mirrorealm.

\*\*\*

## Eighteen

Ayla flew backwards through the air and saw a grubby, stained mirror flash into view as she tumbled out of it. She landed hard on her back but managed to roll over to minimise some of the impact, and saw the walls of a gloomy subterranean cave around her and flaming torches casting flickering light and shadows. She got onto her feet and stood up, and saw a big brute of a figure with a thick chain around its neck and huge, round yellow eyes snarl as it swung an enormous club at her head.

Ayla shrieked and ducked as the huge club flashed past inches above her scalp and crashed into the mirror. The impact shattered the mirror into a thousand pieces as Ayla scrambled beneath the giant's thick, hairy legs and leaped to her feet.

The huge figure turned toward her, its back hunched and its head hung low on a thick neck that sank into broad, rounded shoulders. Its back was matted with a thick forest of hair, its skin pale and flecked with large bunions that shone in the light. Ayla could see that it was something between a man and a beast, its legs ending in cloven hooves and its arms as thick as her torso and bulging with muscle. The troll–like creature turned its bulbous head and glared at her, drool streaming from its thick lips as it dragged the club around. Then, it grimaced and the heavy club swung again as it lumbered toward her.

Ayla ducked and backed away from the troll, and she saw over its shoulder what appeared to be a tunnel that led away from the cave. The problem was that the way to the tunnel was barred by an iron gate that was sealed with a padlock the size of her head.

The troll's features twisted in fury as he heaved his great shoulders and swung the giant club at her head. Ayla ducked and rolled beneath the blow, heard a swish of air as it flashed past and smacked into the wall of the cave. She scrambled to her feet again and leaped back two paces as the club swung back and missed her chest by an inch, the troll handling the enormous club with surprising agility.

The troll turned smoothly as his attack missed, swinging the club up and over behind his head to bring it crashing down toward Ayla. Ayla dodged left and the club smacked down into the stony floor of the cave, spraying her with sharp stone chips.

Ayla got to her feet and backed up further as the troll hauled the club up again and scowled at her, thick, yellowing teeth bared behind its fat drooping lips. He moved toward her, one hoofed leg extended for balance as he swung the club again.

Ayla ducked beneath it and dashed for the cell gate. The troll reached out for her with one hand and she darted left and ran up the wall of the cell as the troll's dirty, fat fingers brushed past her shoulder. Ayla hit the ground running and dashed to the cell doors, grabbed them and pulled hard.

'Somebody get me out of here!'

Her voice echoed down the tunnel and she heard moans in response as shadowy figures appeared before other cell gates, the bulky bodies and dim–witted eyes of other trolls glowing in the darkness. Ayla turned and saw the troll rush in, the club raised above his head as rage radiated from his eyes. Ayla backed up and felt the gates behind her, and the padlock dug into her back as she saw the club come crashing down.

She twisted aside at the last instant and the thick club smashed down across the huge padlock with a metallic clang. Ayla saw the padlock smashed apart and the huge gate swung open. She leaped past the ogre's club and out into the tunnel, then sprinted away as fast as she could toward the light of flaming torches lining the walls.

The tunnel filled with a roar of countless trolls, all of them reaching out of their gates for her with thick fingers stained with soil and grime. Ayla glanced over her shoulder and was surprised to realise that the troll was not pursuing her down the tunnel. She slowed down, looked left and right at the gruesome faces staring at her, and she saw not anger in their eyes but suffering. Ayla stopped in the tunnel for a moment, but the troll did not appear. Slowly, she turned back and walked to where the gates of the cell hung open, the shattered hulk of the padlock in the tunnel where it had fallen.

Ayla crept along until she could see inside the cell again, and there she saw the troll kneeling on the ground, his back turned to her. She could see that he was trying to pick up the shattered fragments of his mirror, but his thick fingers and clumsy hands were no good for such work. The shards of glass cut into his skin but he seemed impervious to the pain, engrossed in his work and he had tossed his club to the far side of the cell.

Ayla could not help herself, for she sensed something unusual in this hulking creature, something familiar.

'Hello?'

The troll glared over his shoulder at her and for a moment she thought that he might stand and pursue her, but instead the troll turned back to his work. Afraid and yet curious, Ayla crept back into the cell. She knew that she should be fleeing and beginning her search for Luciffen and the Riders of Spiris, but she could not shake the feeling that something was very wrong down here in these strange catacombs.

She walked to a spot near where the troll was kneeling, close enough for him to see her, not close enough that he could reach out and grab her. He was still trying to pick up the pieces of his mirror and failing miserably.

Ayla carefully knelt down and picked up two matching shards of the mirror. The edges were glowing with a pale white light. She pushed them together, and to her amazement they fused perfectly in a flash of light.

She looked up and saw the troll watching her, its eyes wide.

Ayla, mastering her fear and revulsion, reached her hand out with the repaired mirror section for the troll to take. The huge creature frowned in confusion, but then it reached out and gently took the piece from her. It was large enough for the troll to handle, and it gently began matching the piece to other smaller shards. As Ayla watched she saw piece after piece of the mirror fuse again, and the dexterity the troll showed was anything but simple–minded.

'Why are you locked in a cell?' Ayla asked, curious as to whether the troll could speak at all.

The creature glanced at her, as cautious as she was, but then it spoke in a gruff voice that sounded like boulders rolling down a hill.

'Leave, or you too will become one of us.'

The mirror was becoming larger now, the troll moving about on its knees to collect more pieces and let them fuse back together again. Ayla picked up more of the smaller shards and joined them together as she replied.

'I will. I have to leave, but I want to know why I ended up here?'

The troll scowled as he worked, not looking at her.

'This is the Catacomb of the Cursed,' he rumbled. 'Those who have been cursed are sent here, and you must be a Hybrin, the most dangerous of all accused souls. Leave, before I take my club to you again.'

'I'm not cursed,' Ayla said. 'I only just got here.'

The troll *humphed* but said nothing as he got to his hooves and hefted the mirror upright. Ayla lifted her own section and then hesitated. The ogre looked at her, cradling the mirror protectively in his arms, and Ayla offered him the other piece she had reconstructed.

The troll's eyes narrowed, but he finally relinquished half of the side of the mirror and allowed Ayla to push her own piece back into place. The mirror's edge shone and joined with the rest, and as she watched so thousands of tiny filaments of the mirror lifted up off the floor of the cell and flew back into position in a sparkling display. Ayla watched in fascination as the mirror seemed to come together in the reverse motion of the way in which it was shattered, and she saw little pieces fly from her hair and clothing where they had lodged and re–join the main mirror.

The troll waited until the display had ended, and then he leaned the mirror up against the wall. Ayla could see that there was no reflection of herself in the mirror, but the troll's solemn face stared into his own eyes and his shoulders sank as though in despair

'Where are we?' Ayla asked.

The troll sighed miserably as he replied.

'The Mines of Poisor. Terra captured and cursed us all, then imprisoned us down here in this catacomb to search for fragments like these.'

It took a moment for Ayla to register what the troll had said as he gestured to his mirror.

'Terra is searching for pieces of mirror?' she asked.
'Of course,' the troll rumbled. 'She's building another one to conquer the realm.'

\*\*\*

## Nineteen

Ayla stood bolt upright and scanned the tunnel outside the cell, suddenly fearful that she would see the much–feared wytch charge into the cell with the hounds of hell at her heels. But there was nothing but the sullen gazes of the ogres in other cells.

Luciffen had not mentioned the fact that Terra might be building another great mirror, and there was no reason to suspect that he or Vigoran knew anything about it, but if it was true then they could find themselves hopelessly overpowered when Terra launched her attack. Luciffen had mentioned that there was the suspicion that more mirrors could exist in the realm, fragments of the star that had exploded so long ago. Ayla realised that another mirror of darkness, perhaps even a small one, could explain why Terra had grown in power so quickly.

She had not heard of the Mines of Poisor before now, and she had no understanding of why she would have emerged through the mirror of an enslaved troll right under the nose of Terra herself.

'I need to get out of here,' Ayla said as she turned for the cell gate.

The troll moved and blocked her path. 'And I need you to stay.'

'A moment ago, you were telling me to leave.'

'That was before I thought about it. You destroyed my mirror and now it will never be the same again.'

'The mirror is fixed,' Ayla pointed, 'and I didn't smash it, you did.'

'After you came flying through it and nearly hit me in the face!' the troll roared, spittle flying from his thick lips and one fat finger pointing at her. 'I should crush you like a worm where you stand.'

The troll turned and grabbed his club, but Ayla stood her ground as he raised the weapon.

'If Terra finds out my cell is broken she'll think I've attempted escape, and that will mean certain death for both of us!'

'Then leave with me,' Ayla replied.

The troll stared at her as though she were insane. 'I'm not able to leave, and even if I was I would be alone out there in the realm! You don't understand!'

'That's right, I *don't* understand,' Ayla shot back. 'You could walk out of here with me this very moment and yet you're standing there threatening me with your lump of tree! I don't have time for this.'

Ayla marched past the troll, batting the end of the club out of her way as she walked out of the cave and turned left, heading for the light. She heard the troll hurry out of his cell in pursuit, his hooves clicking on the stony ground. She turned and saw his bulky form tip–toeing on his hooves with a dainty gait, a nervous look on his face.

'You can't go up there!' the troll whispered. 'It's not *safe*.'

'It's not safe down here either,' Ayla replied tartly, 'as there are trolls here who apparently will crush me like a worm.'

The troll reared up and frowned at her. 'You think that I'm a troll?'

'Well you're not a bloody unicorn.'

There was a long silence and she saw a sadness overwhelm the troll as he stared down at himself. Ayla felt suddenly ashamed and she softened her tone.

'Do you have a name?'

'Ellegen,' the troll replied in a soft voice, his gaze not meeting hers.

It seemed a strange name for a troll, but then Ayla had to admit to herself that she had never met one before, and therefore had no real right to know what they should be called.

'Well, Ellegen, my name is Ayla and I'm leaving this place right this moment. You can come with me or, you can stay.'

Ayla turned and continued marching toward the lights, while behind her she heard Ellegen tip–toeing along again to hide the clicking of his hooves.

'We can't just *leave* the Mines of Poisor,' he insisted, drool spilling from his lips that he wiped away with one chubby hand. 'Terra would notice and that would be that.'

'She'd kill us?'

'In an instant,' Ellegen replied. 'You haven't seen what happens to those of us who try to escape the catacombs.'

'I can't stay down here forever,' Ayla insisted. 'I have to find Luciffen again.'

Ellegen froze in motion, and she noticed every other troll in the cells that had been able to overhear her stare at her with eyes wide.

'You know Luciffen?' Ellegen asked, awestruck. 'You've actually met him?'

'Sure,' Ayla shrugged. 'Just yesterday.'

The trolls all watched her in utter silence for a long moment, and then as one they all collapsed into fits of laughter, their great bellies shaking and their hands over their mouths as they tried to keep their voices down.

'What?' Ayla asked, both annoyed and confused by their mirth.

'You were with Luciffen yesterday, and today you're here in the Mines of Poisor,' Ellegen gasped, tears streaming down his face to mix with the drool on his lips. 'That's a new one!'

'It's true,' Ayla snapped and stamped her foot in fury. 'I was being chased by a Dragun, and Vigoran and the Riders of Spiris defeated it with me at a bridge and…'

'Vigoran!' roared one of the trolls between showers of spittle. 'She knows the King too!'

The other trolls sunk to their knees and rolled about in laughter in their cells, and Ayla gave up. She turned and continued walking, the sound of laughter fading away behind her. She had gone some considerable distance when she noticed that the tunnel was climbing steadily uphill and the air was cooling.

Ayla slowed down as she sensed something. Despite the increased light coming from the torches, their flames flickering and snapping, she could see a darkness ahead. It was hard to define; she could not actually see it with her eyes and yet as she looked ahead she could tell that the light from the torches was dimming steadily. Her skin tingled as though insects were swarming across her arms and neck and she was overcome with the powerful need to escape, to withdraw from the coming darkness in the same way that she had felt compelled to flee the storms back home.

Then she heard something that sent a chill down her spine, a growl so low and so deep that it stirred a primal fear within. She began to step backwards through the tunnel, retreating away from whatever was coming toward her.

Ayla turned to flee back down the tunnel but a pair of huge arms wrapped around her from nowhere and lifted her up and away from the ground. She was about to scream when she saw Ellegen's face close to hers.

'Cerberus,' he whispered, his face ashen, 'Hell Hounds. They're coming.'

Ellegen hurried back to his cell with Ayla in his arms. He set her down and then he closed the cell gate behind him and managed to balance the padlock in place as though it were still sealed. He turned to her and ushered her to the back of the cell, before he slumped down in front of the mirror and pretended to be asleep, his bulk blocking her view of the cell gates.

The grumbling and muttering of the other imprisoned trolls fell silent and was replaced by the low growling she had heard moments before. Ayla sat in silence and listened, unable to see but knowing that whatever was outside the cell was coming into view. She closed her eyes and heard the heavy padding of feet on the cool stone, heard the rasp of air moving in and out of massive chests and smelled something rank and thin, like the smell of old rags and fear. Her legs turned to jelly where she sat and she felt her breath trembling in her chest.

The Hell Hounds sniffed at the cell gate, and then she heard them move on and away from the cell. Ellegen waited until they were gone, and then he turned his great head and looked at her.

'You were right, you must go, now!' he whispered. 'Terra might know that you are close by. You're putting us all in danger!'

'What about you?'

'I'll be fine.'

'Come with me,' Ayla insisted. 'We can get out of here together!'

Ellegen's head bowed in sorrow. 'None of us can ever leave, Ayla.'

'But when they find the padlock is broken…'

'Nothing, compared to what will happen should they find you in my cell. Now go, before the hounds come back! If they get in front of you, you'll never make it out of the mines. Go, keep moving upward and don't look back!'

Ayla turned to the cell gate, and then something crossed her mind.

'I don't know where to go,' she admitted.

'Keep going *up*,' Ellegen insisted. 'Follow the light.'

Ayla took a breath and then peered out into the tunnel. She could still smell and sense the Hell Hounds but they were out of sight. She eased the cell gate open and crept out into the tunnel, then turned and as silently as she could she sprinted away toward the light.

\*\*\*

## Twenty

Ayla reduced her speed to a jog to conserve energy in case she needed it later. She had no idea how big the Mines of Poisor might be, but she figured that the most powerful wytch in the realm would probably have acquired herself some serious real estate.

The sound of metal on metal caught her attention, and to one side of the tunnel she saw a narrow fissure that glowed with an orange light. She crept up to it and looked inside, and saw an immense vertical shaft on the other side of the rock face. The shaft had been physically dug into the earth and was illuminated by flaming torches and ringed with gantries and unstable looking ladders. Across the faces of the shaft, trolls wielded pick axes as they laboured in the heat, digging into the walls in search of fragments of the ancient star. Ayla saw them picking fragments out and placing them together, each troll working on their own section. Ayla thought about Ellegen's mirror, likely forged from fragments inside this shaft, and of the hundreds of trolls all slaving away at the rockface, and she realised that the finished mirror would dwarf anything that had gone before in the realm.

The tunnels climbed out of the catacombs where she had seen the imprisoned trolls, and she could feel the cold creeping through her bones as she jogged along. There were flaming torches on the walls but they were spaced further apart and Ayla found herself surrounded by shadows and darkness. Strangely though she realised that she was not afraid because she could not sense anything hiding around her.

Since the lightning strike, she had begun to realise that she could feel when evil was close by, and she recalled Luciffen referring to her as a "*seer*". If Terra and her hordes of darkness relied on stealth to creep up on their enemies, or deception to lure them to their fates, then Ayla's ability to detect the evil around her would be a valuable weapon to Luciffen and his allies, not to mention a great threat to Terra.

Even as she thought about her strange new ability, her skin crawled and the hairs went up on the nape of her neck.

The tunnel levelled out and Ayla slowed as she saw a set of huge gates before her, massive wrought iron as tall as a house and guarded by two huge figures with their backs to her. Ayla ducked to her left and hid in the shadows. The figures were massive, cloven hooved and bulky just like Ellegen and the other prisoners, and both were armed with heavy clubs as long as Ayla's entire body, but that was where the similarities ended. These ogres had twisted horns poking from their skulls and cruel faces that were alive with malice, and they stood almost twenty feet tall.

The massive iron gates were designed to stop Ellegen and his companions from escaping, but the bars were spaced widely enough apart that Ayla knew she could slip between them, her body half the size of any of the prisoners.

Ayla checked behind her, and then she began to edge closer to the guards. She could hear their great chests breathing, the rush of air in and out of their lungs, and their huge hooves clicked every now and again on the stone floor as they shifted position. Ayla crept closer until she could smell their hair and hides, which reminded her of a horse's stable that had not been cleaned for some time. They wore nothing over their legs and hooves but thick fur, and their immense upper bodies were draped with loose tunics of cloth and old leather stained with years of neglect.

Ayla slipped up close to the gates and watched the ogres, waiting for a chance to slip through a gap in the gates and hurry away. She could see that beyond the gates was a hall enshrouded in semi–darkness, polished stone flags on the ground and ornate walls filled with grotesque carvings of gargoyles and Dragun heads that glared out at her from the shadows.

Ayla was almost touching the thick gates when she felt the darkness come upon her again, a cold chill and a feeling of impending doom. She looked over her shoulder and she sensed rather than saw the presence of the Hell Hounds, heard their growls as they came closer. They would be tracking her scent now, moving faster as they hurried to catch her. Ayla felt panic rise inside her as she realised that she could not go back and she could not go forward, the massive guards blocking her way.

She looked up, seeking a way to escape from the hounds when she heard a noise that chilled her to her core. A wailing, mournful cry echoed up through the tunnels from behind her as though a thousand wolves were howling at once, and then she saw the beasts emerge from the darkness.

She saw their eyes first, glowing like those of a Dragun as the Hell Hounds moved into view. At first she thought that there were six of them, twelve eyes glaring at her, but then they moved closer to the flickering torches and she saw that they were a pair of animals, each with three snarling heads and sets of drooling jaws. Their bodies were bulky and muscular, covered in thick black hair that rippled with the muscles beneath their skin, and she could see what looked like smoke spilling from their nostrils as they advanced.

The Hell Hounds growled and all at once they broke into a run and charged straight at Ayla with their glowing fangs bared and their claws clicking loudly against the stone floor of the tunnel.

Ayla looked up and saw the two ogres slowly turn toward the sound of the howling, Ayla almost at their feet and below their line of sight. She whirled and saw the hounds right upon her, their grim jaws smiling with malice it seemed as they converged on her position and launched themselves at her.

Ayla leaped out from the shadows, turned sideways and shoved herself into the largest of the gaps between the iron bars. She got halfway through and then realised that she was stuck. The hell hounds rushed in and she smelled their rank skin and fur and the sulphur smell of their breath, and with a supreme effort she blew all the air out of her lungs, pinned one foot firmly on the ground and shoved hard.

The gate's bars squeezed by and she popped out the other side as the nearest Cerberus slammed into the gates with a loud clang of muscle on metal, its drooling, snarling fangs just inches from where Ayla stood. She staggered away from the gates as the ogres turned and looked down at the Cerberus.

Ayla sprinted away from the prison gates. The huge guards roared in unison as they noticed her for the first time and they turned and lumbered in pursuit, their thick clubs swinging and their footfalls shaking the ground. Ayla ran as fast as she could and changed direction this way and that as the huge clubs crashed down behind her.

The ogres' blows shattered the stone flags and smashed into the ornate carvings either side of the corridor, Ayla ducking aside as clouds of stone chips sprayed around her. Ayla dashed clear of their attack and began to pull away from them. Despite their huge size the ogres' pace was not quick enough to catch her and she immediately began looking for an escape route small enough that they would not be able to follow.

Ayla reached a corner at the far end of the corridor. She risked a glance behind her as she heard another of the Hell Hounds' terrible howls echoing through the hall. One of the ogres had turned back, and she saw that he was fumbling with a set of giant keys hanging from his belt. She knew that if those Cerberus got out she would not be able to outrun them, four legs always far faster than two.

Ayla dashed out of sight and sought a doorway or exit of some kind as the ogre still pursuing her lumbered around the corner and hurled the giant club in his hand directly at her, hoping to smash her to the ground.

Ayla ducked and rolled as the club flew over her head and clattered into the stone flags as she came back up onto her feet and kept running. Another howl echoed in pursuit, this time twisted with fury and elation, and she knew that the hounds were free of the gates.

The corridor she was in was still immense, with a high roof and massive windows to her right that overlooked a mountainous valley filled with darkness. She could see no moon or stars, no evidence of anything other than thick, low clouds and flickering lightning that forked angrily across the sullen skies.

Ayla ran on and into a vast hall, the ceiling a hundred feet above her as though she were inside some kind of cavernous church that had been abandoned for centuries. There were few torches flickering around the hall, the entire area feeling cold and desolate, filled with shadows and dust. Vast windows to her right looked out upon the lonely landscape outside, and she could see frost upon the glass.

A sensation of dread crept upon Ayla and she ran across the hall as she sensed the hounds closing in upon her from behind. She dashed toward a long table in the centre of the hall, empty chairs arranged around it before a towering statue of what appeared to be a woman draped in robes, one hand holding aloft a torch while the other held a book tucked against her side. Her face was exquisite, her hair falling in stone locks across her bare shoulders, her face stern but fair. The statue looked remarkably like the image of Terra that she had seen in the flames of Luciffen's fire.

Ayla realised that there were other shadowy statues around the hall of men, women and several species that she could not be sure of but all of which shared human characteristics.

A growling from behind Ayla made her turn, and she saw the two Hell Hounds bound into the hall, their jaws drooling and their fangs bared.

\*\*\*

## Twenty–one

Ayla dashed to the table, then vaulted up onto it as the two Cerberus bounded toward her.

The table was laid with cutlery and glasses that were thick with dust as though the hall had been awaiting overdue guests for decades. The glasses and cutlery clattered to the floor as Ayla dashed along the table's length with the hounds close behind.

Rows of huge chandeliers dangled over the table from the dizzy heights above and she knew that her only choice was to go up. She heard plates shattering behind her and turned to see one of the Cerberus leap up onto the table and bound toward her. Its heads were snarling and snapping at her as it closed in, and the other animal was accelerating to intercept her from one side.

Ayla sprinted as hard as she could and then jumped up and caught hold of a chandelier as the Cerberus beside her leaped onto the table, the fangs of its nearest head gnashing as it reached out for her legs. The chandelier swung out as Ayla pulled her legs up and the hound passed by just beneath her. She hauled herself up onto the chandelier and scrambled up the supporting cables as the chandelier reached the zenith of its swing and arced back toward the table.

The Cerberus leaped up, their savage fangs fastening on the chandelier and slowing it down. Ayla climbed up out of their reach, but she could see that there was nowhere left to go. The Hell Hounds hauled down on the chandelier and she heard the mountings in the ceiling grind and creak as the weight of the two animals bore down upon it.

Ayla was praying that it would hold when she saw the two ogres lumber into the hall, their clubs swinging as they saw her clinging to the chandelier and the two hounds hauling down upon it.

One of the ogres snarled in delight and swung his club at the chandelier's support cables. The massive club slammed into the chandelier and it was torn from the roof in a shower of masonry. Ayla shrieked and held on for dear life as the chandelier flew across the hall toward the towering windows and crashed down onto the stone floor.

Ayla was thrown clear and tumbled along the ground. She managed to find her feet and staggered upright as she saw the Cerberus stalk towards her, their heads hanging low and their eyes cruel as they circled either side of the shattered chandelier.

Ayla scrambled back and away from them and bumped against the cold glass of the windows. She glanced over her shoulder and saw a dizzying drop down the sheer face of a vast cliff of black rock that plunged toward a deep and turbulent maelstrom of freezing black water. There was nowhere left for her to run and now the hounds were close enough to smell, the ogres right behind them.

Ayla felt dread coursing through her bones, her blood running like ice through her veins as the nearest of the hounds reared its heads. Their jaws opened and she saw the rows of fangs glowing with an unnatural light as the huge animal lunged at her.

Suddenly the huge hound was yanked away and its teeth and fangs clashed together. The Cerebrus turned and a huge fist appeared from nowhere and socked into one of the hound's skulls with a crack like a gunshot. The punched head slammed into its neighbour with a dull crack, and the centre head smacked into the other as the hound howled in pain. Ayla stared in astonishment as two thick arms hauled the beast up into the air and threw it at the other hound. Ayla saw the two animals collide and tumble across the ground as Ellegen leaped to her aid, his muscles bulging and his toad–like features twisted with anger.

She felt a joy like nothing she had ever experienced as the troll moved protectively in front of her, but she knew that there was no way he could fight off the two massive ogres before them. Ellegen turned and she saw a volatile mixture of regret and anger in his expression, and then he lifted her with both arms as he threw her onto his back.

'Get down!' he yelled.

Ayla ducked her head down behind Ellegen's massive neck as he suddenly ran straight at the huge windows. Ayla heard her own scream as his immense bulk smashed through the glass and it shattered as surely as if someone had fired a cannonball through it.

Ayla saw the precipitous drop open up beneath them, plunging away into the abyss below as they fell. Ellegen threw his arms out and dove willingly toward the rocks and freezing water.

The wind howled in Ayla's ears, competing with the rapidly fading wails of the Hell Hounds far above as they lamented their lost victim, and then she realised that she and Ellegen were surrounded by a blossoming halo of golden embers as though they were on fire. Ayla stared in disbelief as Ellegen's immense bulk seemed to shine with the colour of molten metal, a bright meteor plummeting to earth from the darkened heights and leaving a trail of glowing embers behind him. Then his form changed, spreading out around her as they plummeted to their deaths.

Quite suddenly the spreading embers became great wings and Ellegen's bulky, muscular body transformed beneath her and pulled up out of the deadly dive as the wings beat the air with powerful strokes. Ayla was dumbstruck as the powerful beats pulled them up into the turbulent skies, the glowing embers fading away behind them like an old skin as the troll's hideous face vanished to reveal that of a handsome man, his chest broad and his hair thick and black and hanging down his neck like a mane. Ayla looked down and saw galloping hooves moving in time to the huge wings.

'What happened?' she yelled above the wind whistling past them.

The reply came in a voice every bit as deep as Ellegen's voice had been, but more human now.

'Thanks to you, I just betrayed my entire species to get you out of there.'

'Thanks to me? You told me to run!'

Ellegen nodded, not looking back at her as he replied. 'And I should have left you to it! Who knows what Terra will do to my family when she learns that I have escaped and you are with me!'

Ayla looked down at Ellegen's body, that of a horse with wings and a man's torso and head where ordinarily a horse's neck would have been.

'What are you?' she asked.

'I am a Centaur,' Ellegen replied, his voice filled with pride. 'No time to explain, I must get you to Luciffen as fast as I can. There will be no stopping Terra's fury now, and her reach already extends across much of the realm. If someone doesn't attempt to stop her soon, I fear that our suffering will be nothing compared to what will come afterward. Hang on!'

Ayla felt the Centaur accelerate, the huge wings thrusting them through veils of cloud and rain over the blackened, shadowy land below, and ahead in the distance Ayla could see a line of brightness across the sky. She could sense the warmth and the light emanating from it, could almost feel the invigorating fresh air beyond these cold and cruel mountains, and she began to understand what it was that Luciffen and his friends had been trying to explain to her. This region was what was becoming of the realm under the rule of Terra; a barren, cold, dark wasteland devoid of life, devoid of the light of its magical suns.

Ayla's ears turned slightly of their own accord, a strange and primal response to fear as she felt evil close behind them. She whirled to look behind her and straight into a pair of eyes glowing like red suns.

'Dragun, right behind us!'

\*\*\*

## Twenty-Two

Ellegen pulled up into a steep climbing turn as a blast of flame roared past on their left. The dramatic manoeuvre caught the pursuing Dragun off-guard and it overshot, racing past in a blur of huge wings and glowing scales.

Ellegen turned in mid-air and began to follow the Dragun, preventing it from bringing its fiery breath to bear on them. The Dragun pulled up and wheeled back toward the Mines of Poisor, and Ayla knew that they could not risk getting too close to the place they had just escaped from.

'The clouds!' she yelled, wondering if they could escape by not being seen.

Ellegen responded instantly and they climbed hard, the Centaur's huge wings beating the air with muscular thrusts as the Dragun circled out wide in order to come back in at speed and catch them. The Dragun raced in as Ayla looked back, and then suddenly it was lost in the clouds as Ellegen climbed out of sight.

Ayla felt moisture cling to her clothes and hair, the interior of the cloud cold and damp. She could see nothing but a murky grey in all directions, and the lack of a horizon made it hard to tell which way up they were. She heard a distant screech from somewhere below and she guessed that the Dragun was waiting for them below the clouds.

'It won't follow us up here,' Ellegen called to her above the wind as they travelled. 'The moisture is no good for its lungs.'

Ayla had not thought of that, hoping only that the clouds would conceal them from the Dragun's view. Either way, she didn't care just as long as they were out of danger from being fried alive by the awful creature. She heard its fierce but lonely calls for several minutes as they flew along, Ayla tucking in behind Ellegen's broad and muscular back for warmth as they flew through the clouds.

Around her, the sky became gradually brighter as they flew further away from the Mines of Poisor, and she could feel some semblance of warmth returning to the air. The clouds around them began to break up and she saw shafts of light beaming this way and that, the clouds a disorientating vista of moving light and shadow that shimmered around them in a kaleidoscopic display.

Ellegen risked a descent out of the clouds and the wilderness emerged beneath them. Ayla saw immense forests and tracts of wild grasses, saw mountains to her left and open plains to her right. Veils of falling rain nearby were shot through with rainbow hues as a beam of light travelled through them, and rivers flashed silver as they reflected the light.

'Where is Luciffen right now?' Ellegen asked her.

Ayla was surprised. 'He could be anywhere, I don't know.'

'You know where the darkness is, do you not? You can find the light too, if you try.'

Ayla sat for a moment between Ellegen's beating wings, and then she closed her eyes and tried not to think about anything other than where she felt was the warmest and the most inviting direction to fly. To her surprise, the answer came to her instantly.

'That way,' she pointed to her right. 'Toward the forests!'

Ellegen turned right in a sweeping circle as they descended lower over the pristine wilderness. Ayla looked down and saw wild horses with slender horns protruding from their heads running in an open clearing, looking up at them as they flew overhead. She saw hawks and owls in flight, geese and ducks, all manner of wildlife just like at home, but she also saw strange beasts among them that she could not identify.

Ellegen revelled it seemed just as much as she did in the light and the life around them, and they flew on for almost an hour before Ayla felt something tugging at her awareness, a need to slow down.

'I think they're somewhere down here,' she said to Ellegen.

The Centaur slowed, looking down at dense forest beneath them. It was tough to see anything beneath the tree canopy and Ellegen shook his head.

'I can't see anything down there. Can you get us any closer?'

Ayla had the sense that Luciffen was somewhere close by but she could not seem to focus any closer in than she already had.

'Sorry, no, can we land somewhere?'

Ellegen headed toward a small clearing and descended gracefully in a tight turn before he settled down on his hooves. Ayla saw him fold his huge wings neatly in alongside his flanks and she suddenly understood why the name had fitted his troll personification so poorly. Ellegen was a perfect name for a Centaur of his grace and power.

Ayla dismounted and landed smoothly alongside him, and she got her first look at his face. Ellegen's jaw was wide and strong, his eyes a fierce blue like Vigoran's, his hair shiny, curly and black and his skin tanned and smooth. He looked like some kind of Greek God and Ayla found herself staring openly at him.

Evidently, Ellegen was used to the response.

'Beauty is only on the surface,' he said to her. 'Yours is that you befriended me when I was cursed to look like a troll, even after I tried to kill you with that club.'

'You're a lot less grumpy like this,' she observed. 'Why did you look like a troll before?'

The answer came not from Ellegen but from behind her.

'Because Terra's sorcery is only powerful enough to hold sway within her own territory.'

She turned to see Luciffen walking across the clearing toward them, Vigoran and the Riders of Spiris behind him. Ayla could not conceal her joy at seeing them, and she wondered how it was that she could feel this way about people she barely knew. Vigoran nodded at her from within the shadows his hood, those strange blue eyes shining brightly, and she saw Tygrin and Jake beaming at her. She smiled back brightly as they approached, and Luciffen moved to stand alongside her and looked up at Ellegen.

'A Centaur,' he said appraisingly. 'It's been far too long since we have seen your kind in the realm. By what name do you go?'

'Ellegen,' Ayla answered proudly for the Centaur. 'He saved my life.'

'And Ayla mine,' Ellegen replied. 'She appeared in a mirror in the Mines of Poisor. She said then that she knew you and the King, although I could scarce believe it.'

Luciffen bowed his head graciously. 'Terra's magic is not yet done with us, and we are greatly reduced in number.'

Luciffen turned to Ayla and he slowly shook his head.

'In the passing of just one day you have defeated a Dragun, escaped from the Mines of Poisor and liberated a Centaur, revealing where Terra has imprisoned them all of this time. We have never known the like of you, Ayla. Why did you come back?'

Ayla glanced briefly at Jake as she replied.

'Some things are worth fighting for,' she said.

Jake smiled but said nothing as Luciffen rested his hand on her shoulder. 'Terra will know by now that you've returned, and she will endeavour to hunt you more than ever. Come, we must travel quickly as there is much to do.'

'That's why we're here,' Ayla replied. 'Terra is trying to build another Great Mirror to dominate the realm.'

\*\*\*

## Twenty–Three

The Riders of Spiris set up a camp in a deep forest that seemed as ancient as the universe itself. The trees were twice as large as anything that Ayla had ever seen before, and because of the shifting light from the darkening sky their branches leaned and swayed slowly in a graceful dance to follow the light.

The camp was built around a fire that was coal black and long cold, the horses tied up to trees and nuzzling their feed bags as Ayla walked with Luciffen into the centre of the camp and sat down. She gratefully drank from one of the water bottles and chewed on cured meat as Luciffen sat down with her and rested on his cane. Then, he waved one hand in the general direction of the fire.

The coals glowed and hummed with energy and Ayla felt warmth wash over her as the fire was rekindled and flames crackled into life. Ayla watched in fascination as the fire took hold and burned with an unearthly energy and glow, comforting and yet alien at the same time.

'I see that you have kept Jake's cloak,' Luciffen observed, the warm cloak wrapped around Ayla's shoulders.

'It's colder here,' she replied, perhaps a little too defensively. She saw Jake look at her and smile.

Luciffen did not pursue the matter.

'Ayla, by now I suspect that you have seen how powerful Terra has become. Did you see her at the Mines of Poisor?'

Ayla shook her head as she chewed on the food.

'She has grown powerful enough that the realm is now drawing toward her,' Luciffen explained. 'Any more Hybrins that come through may end up in her clutches before we can find them.'

'You think that there will be others?'

Luciffen shrugged. 'Now that you are back, perhaps not, but it is hard to say how nature and the realm will react. Theirs are powers beyond our own understanding. But it is true to say that never in history have we ever had two Hybrins in the realm at the same time.'

Ellegen moved to stand with them, his powerful body glowing in the light from the fire and his long tail swishing idly from side to side.

'Terra was nearby,' he said with a knowing gleam in his eye. 'We encountered only Hell Hounds, ogres and a single Dragun.'

'*Only?*' Jake uttered as he sharpened the blade of a sword on the opposite side of the fire.

'Terra could have sent more,' Ellegen pointed out, and Luciffen nodded in agreement.

'She may not have been aware that Ayla had emerged from a mirror so close by, but by now she will be prepared. You cannot travel back to your own world and then return here again, Ayla. It is almost certain that you would arrive right in front of Terra.'

Ayla nodded as she finished her meal.

'I don't think going back is going to help anything,' she pointed out. 'There were more storms and I sensed that she was there.'

'She is gaining power,' Vigoran said in his husky voice. 'Much longer and she will draw enough power to launch a final assault on us and root our people out from wherever they're hiding. More ogres, more Draguns, more everything. If she takes Stormshadow Citadel and the Mirror of Souls, it's all over.'

Luciffen nodded, absorbing it all before he spoke.

'Terra will begin the march of her army soon, and we have little to oppose them. How soon can we rally the tribes?'

Ayla listened as Vigoran listed a series of tribal names that sounded both alien and familiar; the McHollians, the Fyters, the Bannisters and the Dwarves of Dellhanny. Ayla imagined tribes of ferocious warriors armed with swords and axes and spears all gathering on some barren plain to stand up to Terra's massive army. Vigoran spoke of the long ride and the need for messengers to carry the warning that Terra's final assault on the rest of the realm was imminent.

Ellegen replied: 'I can travel faster and more freely than any of you, and can rally the tribes who are willing to fight.'

Luciffen nodded his gratitude but then his eyes saddened. 'The rest of your kind?'

Ellegen's noble head sank.

'They remain imprisoned and will suffer dearly for my escape. Terra needs them to work the mines in search of fragments of the dead star to build her new mirror, but she also cannot control her impulses for revenge and retribution. I fear for them greatly.'

'If Feeher gets two mirrors under her control, she truly will be unstoppable. Without Gallentia, we're defenceless.'

'Who is Gallentia?' Ayla asked, recalling the name that Luciffen had spoken of before but knowing little about the person.

'Gallentia is a white wytch,' Luciffen explained, 'and the head of the Council of Stormshadow. She was captured by Terra, who is using Gallentia's power to further her own aims.'

'How?' Ayla asked, curious.

'Have you ever heard of the concept of *chi*, a life force energy generated by all living things?'

Ayla's eyes narrowed. 'I don't think so.'

'In your world, it goes by many names,' Luciffen explained. 'In Japan it is known as *Ki*, from which Reiki is named. In China it is *chi*, in India, *Prana*, in the Middle East *Baraka* and *Ruach* in Hebrew. All describe the same phenomena, an energy generated by all living things from which other living things can draw strength. It is believed that any world with life upon it becomes as one under the influence of this force.'

Ayla got the impression that Luciffen had travelled extensively in other worlds, or had at least read widely about them.

Ellegen sighed.

'The realm is a place where anything is possible, where life can grow in many different forms that would seem out of place to a Hybrin like yourself. Centaurs, Griffons, Unicorns, Draguns and all manner of beasts roamed this world, but each was an independent spirit and slave to no master. When Terra rose to power she began to entrap as many species as she could, to use their life force energy for her own ends. She has captured many of the most magnificent animals and imprisoned them over the centuries, and in doing so drawn sufficient strength from them to build her army.'

Luciffen spoke softly, his eyes lost in the dancing flames.

'Life is like gravity; it seeks itself out, draws species together like gravity draws matter together to build stars and planets and galaxies. Within them, life thrives, but beyond are the great expanses of darkness and cold, the places where Terra and her like gain their strength.'

Ayla thought for a moment. 'So, what are we all going to do about it?'

Luciffen looked at her and smiled. 'What we have always done, fight back. But for that we need an army, and we need Stormshadow Citadel.'

'Does Terra control the citadel?' Ayla asked.

'Not yet,' Vigoran replied. 'The Mirror of Souls is within and its power is what keeps the darkness at bay in this part of the realm. Before she fled, Terra was powerful enough to put in place a single, very powerful Dragun that now lairs at the citadel. No man has been able to come close to it since.'

Lucifffen stirred the flames with circular motions of his hands as he spoke.

'Our purpose is to regain Stormshadow Citadel, but first we must liberate Gallentia. Without her we will not have the strength to oppose Terra's sorcery. Only united can we stand against her. If we should fail, then the war will be over and there will be nothing to stop Terra from conquering this realm and many others after it, including your own world.'

Luciffen was looking at Ayla as he said this, and she ordered her thoughts before speaking.

'How many are there in Terra's army?'

'The hordes of darkness,' Ellegen replied, 'forged by black sorcery from the very rocks and soils of the realm, number in the tens of thousands. She recruits any and all comers; Vampyres, Werewolves, demons and sprites and Draguns, any of the forces of chaos that will rally to her banner.'

'Okay,' Ayla replied. 'And how many can we muster to face them?'

At that, Vigoran lowered his head.

'With *all* of the tribes, we could field perhaps two thousand.'

Ayla realised that the odds they were facing were almost overwhelming and for a moment she wished that she could just go back home and pretend that none of this was happening. Then she saw in her minds' eye her mother in the hospital bed, and her resolve strengthened.

'What about the other prisoners in the Mines of Poisor? Ellegen, how many Centaurs are there?'

Ellegen thought for a moment. 'Perhaps two or three thousand, although many have perished in captivity.'

'And the Mirror of Souls?' she asked Luciffen.

The old man raised an eyebrow as he considered the question.

'Over the decades Terra had entrapped tens of thousands of souls, not all of them warriors mind, but doubtless an entire army's worth. But the Mirror of Souls is too powerful and dangerous for us to pursue alone, and Terra's Dragun will guard it with its life. It is beyond our reach for now.'

'Desperate times,' Ayla replied. 'You've all said it yourselves: you can't win an open battle with Terra, her forces are already too powerful. So, you need subterfuge. You need the Centaurs freed, the Mirror of Souls opened, Gallentia liberated and the tribes on your side before Terra can get her army to Stormshadow Citadel.'

From behind her, she heard Agry's voice.

'Oh, that's all right then. We'll just pop off and pick them up for you. What do you want us to do *after* breakfast?'

'Cut it out,' Jake snapped.

'Gallentia will be hidden somewhere in the Towers of Vipera,' Vigoran said, 'a labyrinth so vast that it could take years to find her. The tribes are fearful and in retreat, and the Centaurs are likewise imprisoned in the mines, a place no man dares to tread. We couldn't get in there and even if we did, we wouldn't get out alive.'

'We did,' Ayla replied with a gentle smile as she glanced at Ellegen

She got to her feet and looked at them one after the other as she spoke.

'Ellegen, you escaped and your fellow Centaurs remain, afraid to leave for fear of what will happen to those they leave behind. So, why don't you convince them to *all* leave at once? Dictators use fear to control populations, just as Terra is doing – they pitch us against ourselves in the hope that we won't rise against them. Unity is the only thing that they fear. Vigoran, Gallentia is someone that I can find. I can sense the darkness of evil, but I can also sense the light, something that Ellegen taught me. As for the tribes…'

Ayla walked to Jake and took hold of the sword that he had been sharpening. She tested its weight in her hands, and for some reason that she could not understand it felt right at home in her grasp, as though she had been holding such a weapon all her life and never known it.

'You ask them whether they want to die on their knees, or fighting on their feet.'

The flames of the fire crackled and spat, and in the flickering light Ayla saw smiles spreading on the faces of the Riders of Spiris. Tygrin stood, his immense bulk towering over the others.

'I'm with Ayla,' he growled.

The other riders looked at him, and then Vigoran stood. 'Aye.'

Jake got up. 'Aye.'

Ellegen stood forward. 'Aye.'

Siren and Cyril exchanged a glance, the warrior girl and the apprentice wizard like chalk and cheese but somehow inseparable, and then they stood and spoke in unison.

'Aye.'

One by one they all stood but for Agry, who shook his head and cursed for a moment before he slowly got to his feet. 'Aye,' he spat.

'We can't reach the Towers of Vipera on foot in time to reach Gallentia, it's too far and the terrain is far too harsh so we'll need a ride,' Luciffen pointed out. 'Fortunately, I know just the person for the job.'

'Not *him*,' Jake uttered, appalled.

'In war, one cannot be too choosy about one's allies,' Luciffen replied. 'We shall leave in the morning.'

'But he's a *pirate*,' Jake snapped. 'He'd sell his own mother for the right price.'

'Who are you talking about?' Ayla asked.

'You'll see,' Jake replied with a scowl, 'but don't expect a hero.'

\*\*\*

## Twenty–Four

They awoke early the next morning. Ayla crawled out from beneath her blanket to see Luciffen rekindling the fire. The forest around them was obscured by thick fog that deadened all sound, although she could hear countless thousands of water droplets splattering down amid the trees as moisture fell from their leaves.

There was time for a short breakfast of whatever could be found among their meagre belongings, and then Ellegen moved to her side and looked down at her.

'I leave to rally the tribes,' he announced. 'Luciffen wants the army to rendezvous to the south of Stormshadow Citadel, so I will meet you there. I have no doubt that you're in safe hands, Ayla.'

Ayla glanced around her at Vigoran, Jake, Luciffen, Tygrin and the others as they worked to clear the camp and prepare the horses. Siren was solemnly polishing a sword and Cyril was practising sorcery, making fluttering birds from the embers of the fire spiralling up into the foggy dawn sky.

'I think so to,' she agreed. 'Fly safe and watch out for Draguns.'

'They won't be about in this fog,' Ellegen replied with a smile, 'but there are plenty of other forces of darkness now haunting the wilderness. Make sure you stay alert, for all of them will be hunting you.'

'Good to know.'

Ellegen turned to Vigoran. 'The valley of Maryn Tiell?'

'The valley,' Vigoran nodded, 'if the tribes come we will occupy the high ground on the river, opposite the citadel, and pray for fog like this.'

Ellegen nodded and then walked clear of the fire. Ayla watched as he spread those enormous white wings, and then with powerful beats he galloped away and lifted off. She saw him vanish up into the fog within moments, and the beating of his wings faded to silence.

'You have done great things, Ayla,' Luciffen said as they mounted their horses, Ayla climbing up into Tygrin's saddle with him. 'It has been a long time since any Centaur roamed these lands. His presence will give the tribes confidence that they can stand against Terra.'

'I didn't do anything,' Ayla said as they began to ride through the misty forest. 'Ellegen came after me.'

'At great risk to himself,' Vigoran said. 'He must have felt it was worth it.'

'He must've lost his mind,' Agry muttered from behind them. 'Even if the tribes do gather, and don't start fighting each other in the meantime, we won't have enough warriors to win any battle and I don't trust our chances in the Towers of Vipera.'

'Then stay behind and keep yourself safe,' Jake snapped back. 'Wouldn't want that delicate little hide of yours to become endangered, would we?'

'You watch your mouth, Shaw, or I'll…'

'Be quiet,' Luciffen uttered. 'Division is precisely the tool that Terra wields most deftly, more so even than her dark sorcery. We *must* remain united in all our endeavours, or this will be for nothing regardless of the size of our army.'

They rode on in silence for the next two hours, leaving the cover of the forest and riding out over vast tracts of wilderness. The fog lifted as the morning wore on to reveal an immense valley that stretched almost as far as the eye could see. As they reached the upper heights of the hills flanking the valley, Ayla could see a distant line of dark cloud much like those she had seen preceding the storms back home. The other riders moved their horses alongside Tygrin's as they stared out into the distance.

'Chaoria,' Luciffen identified the region, 'the underworld, the land of the dead. The Towers of Vipera are within, although for many centuries few have trodden that road and lived to tell the tale.'

'This is dangerous,' Jake said, 'we're walking right into the enemy's backyard.'

Ayla thought about the Mirror of Souls for a moment.

'What does it take to get the souls out of the mirror?' she asked curiously. 'And can the Dragun that guards Stormshadow Citadel be defeated in any way other than brute force?'

Luciffen dismounted, as the other riders followed suit and allowed their horses to graze on the hillside.

'The Dragun can be slain in the normal way with a sword or other edged weapon through its heart,' Luciffen replied as he sat down on the grass and rested his weary back and legs. 'Which will be no easy feat, given that it is likely a very large and very fierce beast. The wound allows the heart to cool and returns the Dragun to the rock and stone from which it was forged by Terra's dark sorcery. The only other way a Dragun can be slain is with a blast of its own flame, reflected back at it using a mirror forged in the fiery breath of another Dragun. The chances of that happening are limited, to say the least.'

'And Terra?' Ayla pressed. 'She cannot be immortal or invulnerable, right?'

The other riders looked at her in surprise.

'Sure,' Agry muttered, 'she can be killed, with a sword that has been dipped in the fiery blood of a Dragun that she has forged through her heart. Probably not the easiest job in the world, don't you think, as a Dragun's heart remains flesh for only a limited time after its death.'

Agry opened the box in which he had placed the fiery heart of the Dragun that they had slain by the bridge, and he poured out nothing but grey ash from within.

'The Mirror of Souls is another matter,' Luciffen said.

'In what way?' Ayla asked.

'The Mirror of Souls is immensely powerful but it only entraps the souls within, it cannot control them. Another mirror placed before it would allow the imprisoned souls to see themselves and cross over. But we only possess the one fragment, and bringing it with us to Terra's lair would be foolhardy in the extreme.'

'Not to mention awkward,' Jake added. 'Given the size of the thing.'

Ayla nodded, recalling the mirror that stood twice as tall as a man.

'How big is the mirror of souls?'

'Huge,' Jake replied. 'Twenty times the height of a man. Only magic can move it, which is why Terra couldn't take it back to Vipera with her.'

Ayla thought for a moment.

'Ellegen had a mirror through which I passed, and he broke it with his club but then was able to put it back together again.'

'The magic that allows a mirror to become a portal lingers long after the mirror is shattered,' Luciffen explained. 'Bring the pieces back together in time and rejoin them and the mirror will become powerful again. Such is the way of the magic of the realm, but for now magic is the least of your concerns. Vigoran?'

Ayla turned as the warrior stood, and from his pack he lifted a bow and quiver. Ayla was commanded to stand, which she did, and Vigoran handed her the bow.

It was crafted from some kind of burnished wood that was both light and yet extremely strong. When her hands touched it she sensed an energy within the bow, as though it were alive, humming and vibrating through her body like a live current.

'One of only four Bows of Archadian remaining in the realm,' Vigoran said to her. 'It will protect you when your speed and agility is not enough, but it draws its energy like all things from the life force around us. Use it only when you most need it.'

'Where are the arrows?' Ayla asked.

Luciffen gestured to the quiver, the line taut as steel and yet as thin as a hair from her head.

'Taken from the mane of a Griffon,' he explained, 'the only beast in the realm that hunts Draguns, although there are scant few of them left. The arrows will come when you need them.'

'From where?' Ayla asked again.

'From within,' Luciffen replied, as though it were obvious. 'There is no need to worry about it for now, for when the time comes you will know what to do.'

Vigoran stood aside, and Tygrin came forward. From his pack he produced a shield, not much larger than a dining plate, but Ayla had already seen what such shields could do when wielded by Vigoran against a Dragun.

'Forged from iron and the bones of a Firedrake,' Tygrin explained. 'It will deflect all but the most powerful of blows, but weakens quickly and takes time to regenerate. Again, use it wisely.'

Ayla took the shield from Tygrin, who ruffled her hair with one giant hand and winked at her as he stood aside. Jake came forward and from his pocket he produced something that he handed to her but she could not see. It too felt alive with energy and she could sense its proportions as it touched her skin, those of a small knife.

'Slim, beautiful and dangerous,' he said to her, his blue eyes seeming to bore into hers, and then he smiled. 'So is the knife, and it'll cut through anything.'

Ayla felt her skin flush red and she struggled to control the broad smile that spread across her features as Jake stepped away. Now, Agry moved forward and tossed her something with an irritated flourish that she caught in her free hand.

'Dragun's tooth,' he uttered. 'Like you it starts fires in an instant, which we then have to put out.'

Ayla saw the tooth in her hand. It was black and shiny, felt warm to the touch and was also vibrating with unseen energy that was less comforting than that of the other gifts. She tucked the tooth into her pocket and looked at the riders around her.

'I don't know what to say,' she uttered. 'Thank you, all of you.'

Luciffen stood and gripped her shoulders in his hands.

'Thank you for coming back to us,' he said simply. 'Now, we must head into Terra's lair and find Gallentia.'

\*\*\*

## Twenty–Five

They travelled throughout the rest of the day, stopping only to rest the horses and gather supplies. Ayla spent most of her time with Tygrin, the towering warrior showing her which berries and fruits were safe to eat and which ones were poisonous. Some of the plants in the realm were flesh–eating and permanently ravenous, capturing their victims by spreading addictive odours that dulled the mind and lulled the unwary to their fate. Others grew upside down in the earth and only came out at night, while others still appeared entirely sentient and would chat away happily as their petals or berries were plucked. Tygrin pointed out to Ayla that as they moved closer to Chaoria, the life would become less abundant and that there were more poisonous plants than edible ones.

Ayla noticed Jake loosely following their every move, chopping wood here or gathering fruits there, always within earshot.

'I think that Jake has a candle burning for you,' Tygrin said as he eyed the young warrior. 'He'll have to come through me to get to you though, don't worry.'

Ayla was only mildly surprised at Tygrin's protective tone, but she felt that it would be something of an insult if she were to say that she rather enjoyed the attention she was getting from the American. It made a great difference to the general apathy that most of the boys at her school displayed.

'He's on *our* side, remember?' she admonished Tygrin. 'It won't do us any good if you thump him over the head.'

'It might do *him* some good,' Tygrin rumbled back. 'He's too enthusiastic and charges into situations without thinking. He'll get himself killed if he's not careful.'

'We're not exactly taking the safe and secure route ourselves, Tygrin.'

Ayla gestured to the darkened skies to the east, closer now and easily visible through the trees of the glade where they were camped. Tygrin looked up at those skies, where it seemed the light could not penetrate, just like the fading images in two mirrors facing each other.

'Terra's minions will be about, goblins and gargoyles, demons and spirits. It's only a matter of time before we're spotted.'

Ayla reflected on that for a moment, and she realised that he was right. How could they get close enough to the Towers of Vipera without being spotted and overwhelmed by Terra's army? She put the question to Luciffen, who seemed unconcerned.

'Terra is not the only wielder of powerful sorcery in this realm,' he replied. 'Getting in will be fine.'

Ayla did not ask what he meant, but Agry looked up from where he was polishing his sword and mace.

'And getting out…?' he murmured.

Luciffen's smile slipped a little. 'Once close to the Towers, my magic will weaken considerably just as Terra's weakens when outside of her own lair.'

'Thought so,' Agry replied, shaking his head as he continued to polish the sword.

The light began to fade as they worked, and Ayla became so engrossed in helping Tygrin while learning how to survive in this strange new world that she was mildly surprised to find that the sky had darkened considerably as they returned to the camp and the air had begun to cool, a mist forming as in the distance drifting columns of light cast rainbow hues over the hills and valleys.

Ayla slowed as she entered the camp and found herself transfixed by the darkening skies above. The fire was crackling gamely in the camp and casting its warmth across them all, but somehow she still felt cold.

'You sense it,' Luciffen observed as he looked at her.

'The cold,' she replied. 'Like death.'

'Terra's power grows by the day, perhaps the hour,' Luciffen replied as he looked up at the low, sullen clouds billowing over them. 'Her reach is extending further out into the realm.'

'Then you'll need warmth,' Tygrin said as with one hand and a folding shovel he scooped up a long line of earth and tossed it to one side.

Ayla watched as Tygrin excavated a long, narrow cavity in the earth that was as long as she was. Then, the big warrior gestured to the fire and to Luciffen. The old sage turned and looked into the flames, and as Ayla watched several glowing coals levitated out of the fire and drifted across to the cavity that Tygrin had created. The coals dropped and scattered across the ground, and Tygrin quickly shovelled the earth back over them and stamped it down with his boots.

'There,' he said triumphantly, 'that'll keep you warm through the coldest of nights.'

Ayla settled down after a meagre meal with the rest of the riders, and she found herself thinking of home as she lay down on the ground and wrapped the blanket around her. To her amazement, the ground was warm and within minutes she was as cosy as she had ever been in her bed. Her mind was on her mother when she realised that Jake had placed his bedroll close to hers and was watching her silently.

'Thinking of home, right?' he said.

'My mum,' Ayla replied. 'She's in hospital recovering from stress.'

Jake watched her for a moment and then glanced up into the darkness around them. 'And that's why you're back.'

Ayla nodded but said nothing more, turning over so that she was facing the fire. She looked into the flames and could see there whatever she wanted. She was still staring at them when the warmth and the light lulled her into a deep sleep.

Jake lay in silence and watched Ayla sleeping. He was motionless for long enough that everyone assumed that he also had fallen asleep. He saw Vigoran move across the camp, as silent as errant thoughts. Jake closed his eyes almost completely, but kept them open just enough to see. Vigoran knelt down alongside Ayla and gently tucked the edges of her blanket closer about her neck, and then rested one hand protectively upon her shoulder. Ayla stirred and smiled gently, then fell asleep once more.

Vigoran remained with her for several minutes, staring at her much as Jake had done, and then he slipped away to his own bedroll.

Jake watched him in silence and then he fell to sleep, wondering.

*

Ayla wasn't sure what woke her, but she opened her eyes hours later to see the fire now a pile of glowing coals shimmering in the darkness like a small, slumbering Dragun. Tygrin was snoring loudly, his breath condensing on the cold air in great glowing gusts, and the other riders were all sleeping soundly. Ayla was about to go back to sleep when she spotted movement on the edge of the camp.

She squinted to see someone creeping away into the night. She remained silent and still, and she saw the person glance over their shoulder. Agry seemed to check that everyone else was still asleep and then he vanished into the forest.

Ayla gently threw off her blanket and grabbed the invisible knife that Jake had given her. She slipped around the edge of the fire, wide awake now as she snuck to the spot where Agry had disappeared, willing her eyes to adjust to the cold darkness.

The forest was inky black, but she could just make out Agry's form hurrying off through the trees. She watched where he went and was considering what to do next when a hand suddenly slipped over her mouth to silence her. Cyril pressed the tip of his finger to his lips as he released her.

'I saw him go too,' Cyril said.

Ayla's heart was racing in her chest as she scowled at him. 'Stay quiet and behind me.'

Ayla crept in pursuit of Agry, one hand gripping the knife as she slipped through the forest with Cyril behind her.

She could feel a chill in the air, more than just ice or mist, that seemed to creep into her bones as she eased her way between the trees. Her eyes began to adjust to the darkness and she found that she could see Agry more clearly than before. He was moving in absolute silence and if she hadn't noticed him leave the camp she realised that she would never have been able to find him again.

Ayla moved steadily along behind Agry, never getting too close. Above them she could see the vague outlines of the massive trees silhouetted against a dark sky, the branches and limbs still now in the absence of any light and the trees thinner and less robust than those they had encountered earlier the previous day. It was as though the closer they got to the Towers of Vipera, the more life struggled to survive.

She slowed as Agry reached the edge of the treeline, at a clearing filled with the ancient stumps of dead trees. Ayla could feel a cold breeze drifting into the forest from the clearing, and with it a stale odour of decay. Agry crouched down on one knee as though awaiting someone important. Ayla crouched down also with Cyril alongside her, watching and waiting, and then from the night sky something sinewy and grey fluttered down like a dark thought and landed opposite Agry.

Ayla was startled at how she recognised the creature at once, its appearance almost the same as the stone gargoyles carved into the big church near where she lived. Its wings were ragged like the sails of a ghost ship, its head horned and with a beak like that of a parrot. Its eyes glowed as it moved forward. On the ground its gait was awkward as it approached Agry and emitted a short, harsh bark.

Agry glanced around him to ensure that nobody was looking, and then spoke several words that she could not hear before he slipped something into the gargoyle's open beak. The creature appeared to swallow whatever it was that Agry had handed to it, then it turned and fluttered off into the darkness.

Ayla turned and with Cyril they hurried back to the camp, slipping into their bedrolls and feigning sleep. She did not relax until she saw Agry return and slip silently into his bedroll, careful to avoid waking any other of the riders.

\*\*\*

## Twenty–Six

They broke camp the next morning. Ayla and Cyril watched Agry closely but said nothing to Luciffen or the others. She had wanted to, but Cyril had insisted that they keep their silence, at least for now. Agry had no idea that he had been spotted, and as such they had an advantage over him. Ayla was less certain of delaying. Was Agry a traitor? What if he was planning to betray them all to Terra for some reason? He seemed a grumpy and combative sort, but Vigoran and the others accepted his presence none the less. What if there was some other reason for his secret meeting that she could not fathom? She knew that Cyril knew the riders better than she did, and felt compelled to accept his judgement, at least for now.

The worst of it was that Cyril could not share their knowledge with Siren, who walked always with Agry and seemed allied to him in ways that Ayla did not yet understand. Siren could not be trusted to keep the information to herself and Cyril felt that she might even become angry if they shared what they knew with her. Ayla got the impression that Cyril would be upset if the friendship he shared with Siren were compromised in any way.

They set off into a gloomy, foggy morning that had enshrouded the realm as they rode alongside a forest that began to thin out around them. Ayla noticed quickly that the trees were losing their leaves, a brown slush covering the ground as immense numbers of them fell and rapidly decayed. It felt as though they were travelling through different seasons, heading from a summer into a deep autumn, and as they moved so the trees became bare and black.

Then, ahead of them in the gloom, Ayla saw a river moving sluggishly beneath the mists and the lights of buildings and houses. Beyond them she saw the masts of sailing ships anchored out on the water and some nearer the jetties. The entire town was perched on the edge of the great river, and at once she sensed that all was not well.

Tygrin brought his horse to a standstill on the edge of a bluff and they overlooked the ragged, rundown settlement before them, flaming torches flickering in the gloomy light.

'Port Ranken,' Luciffen uttered as though he had something unpleasant in his mouth. 'Nowhere else in the realm will you find such a den of thugs and thieves.'

'Why can't we just go and liberate the Centaurs and ride them to get to the towers?' Ayla asked. 'Why bother with this place?'

'The Centaurs themselves will not willingly join us if they fear for their brethren and their families,' Vigoran pointed out. 'At least here we can get the help that we need, at a price.'

They rode down into the town, passing drunken sailors who staggered this way and that, many with an equally drunk woman on their arms. The air was laden with heady scents of rotting wood, damp, horse droppings and wine that seemed to seethe in the misty air. Tygrin guided his horse to a large building in the centre of the town and they dismounted. A big sign above their heads was flanked by two flickering torches.

### *The Dragun's Head Inn*
*Abandon hope, all ye who enter here*

'Inviting,' Ayla said as she glanced at Luciffen.

'Stay with me,' he replied, 'these places can get very rough.'

'Rubbish,' Tygrin said as he dismounted, one giant hand resting on Ayla's shoulder as they approached the drinking house. 'It's not so bad in here really, once you get to know people. They wouldn't say boo to a goondock.'

The door to the inn flew open and a man tumbled out backwards and crashed to the ground, one of his eyes blackened by a punch as a dwarf appeared in the doorway and growled.

'And *stay out!*'

The dwarf was half his victim's height and adorned with the longest red moustache Ayla had ever seen, drooping down to his knees. Fierce, cold blue eyes glared out into the gloom as though challenging the world itself.

'They're just a bit misunderstood,' Tygrin added with a shrug.

The dwarf's glare settled on Tygrin.

'Well I'll be a mowak'sh backshide, if it ishn't Tygrin Fletcher!'

The dwarf swaggered down the steps of the inn and wiped the back of his hand on his mouth as he looked up at Ayla's towering bodyguard.

'Fyter,' Tygrin nodded at the dwarf. 'Still picking on the natives?'

Fyter glanced at the unconscious man snoring on his back nearby. 'Pah, they're nothing but dogs, shtealing anythin' they can shee and touch, including my girlsh.'

Fyter seemed to notice Ayla and he bowed unsteadily. 'And t'whom do I pleashure the have?'

Fyter almost toppled over as he bowed. Tygrin steadied the dwarf with one hand and pushed him gently back upright.

'We need a ride,' Tygrin said, 'someone reliable and honest.'

The dwarf stared at Tygrin for a moment and then burst out laughing.

'Reliable and honesht, here, he saysh! And where would you honesht folksh be shailing to thish fine ev'ning?'

'The Towers of Vipera.'

Vigoran stepped forward and the dwarf stared at him in awe and bowed, more convincingly this time.

'Your majeshty,' he intoned. 'You won't find many who will shail to the towersh, or even into Chaoria at all, but I know of one who might be crazshy – I mean, courageoush enough. Come with me.'

Ayla followed with Tygrin and the others as Fyter waddled up into the hall and inside. The air was thick with smoke that rolled and spiralled near the ceiling in a yellow cloud. The bar was filled with men, women, creatures that Ayla could not recognise and a couple of ghosts who chased each other around with broken bottles of beer, zipping through doorways and walls as though they were not even there.

Several people were asleep at wooden tables surrounded by tankards and bottles, while others quietly played cards or dice and watched with suspicious gazes as Ayla walked by with her motley crew of friends. Fyter led them to a booth near the back of the bar where the light was lower. Ayla got the impression that they were entering the most dangerous part of the inn, where trouble lurked in every shadow.

'Herric,' Fyter called, 'I've got trade for you.'

Ayla saw a young man look up at them from beneath the tip of a beaked hat. He was lounging in a corner booth, a tankard before him, his boots up on the table and a disinterested look in his eye. Ayla reckoned he was fifteen, maybe sixteen but he was younger than most in the bar and had a cavalier air about him that she instantly both liked and detested.

'Vigoran,' Herric said in a lazy drawl as he spotted the warrior king. 'I didn't know this was a fashionable bar now.'

One hand wafted in the direction of chairs opposite, of which Vigoran took one. Ayla sat alongside him with Luciffen, the other riders standing behind. If Herric was at all intimidated by the armed warriors confronting him he betrayed no indication of it.

'We need passage,' Vigoran announced without preamble, 'as soon as you're ready.'

Ayla noticed a huge, muscular man as large as Tygrin move to a position near the booth. His skin was as dark as obsidian, and his face was laced with bizarre tattoos that glowed with a bioluminescent light.

'Who says I'm going to be ready to go anywhere?'

'It's important,' Luciffen urged. 'We must travel east, as fast as we can.'

Herric raised an eyebrow and smirked. 'East from here is into Chaoria, and nobody's going in there right now and coming back alive.'

'Two thousand gold pieces,' Vigoran said.

Herric's cool blue eyes fixed on Vigoran's and he leaned forward slowly. 'Four thousand.'

'Three,' Vigoran responded. 'You know we're good for it, but we're in a hurry.'

'Looking for something?'

'Nothing that would interest you,' Jake hissed from nearby.

Herric didn't respond to Jake, his eyes fixed on Vigoran. 'Four, or I won't be movin' from this seat.'

Tygrin shoved his way forward and pulled the great axe from his back as though he was about to haul it over his head and split Herric's table in two. Before he could lift the weapon a gang of tattooed, muscular men leaped from their seats in the surrounding booths and a bristling array of swords were pointed directly at the big warrior. The glittering blades rasped against Tygrin's beard as he stood rooted to the spot, the huge dark–skinned man grinning at him with shockingly white teeth. Herric smiled quietly up at Tygrin, not having moved even an inch.

'Somethin' you need?'

Luciffen leaned forward. 'Can you take us, Herric? We would need to leave within the hour.'

Herric glanced at the old man and then his gaze settled on Ayla. For a moment Ayla felt herself blush as the piratical captain watched her for a long moment, and then without taking his eyes off her Herric wafted one of his hands in the air. As if by magic, the armed men moved away from Tygrin and slid their swords and knifes into sheaths.

'Case you hadn't noticed the whole world's heading west, away from Chaoria,' he said. 'I'll be doing the same in the morning.'

'That's called running away,' Jake pointed out.

'It's called good sense. You should try it some time.'

'You watch your mouth,' Siren snarled at the pirate captain.

Herric appeared amused as he looked at the Riders of Spiris.

'Look at you all, charging around the wilderness for your fortune and glory. How does it feel, Vigoran, to no longer be on a throne and down here with the rest of us?'

Vigoran leaned on the table. 'I was never anywhere else. If you ever earn anything honestly, let me know how it feels so that I don't have to lock you in irons again.'

Herric's hand idly caressed the handle of a sword at his side.

'Those days are long gone,' Herric replied with that casual smile. 'I'm the one who decides who gets what these days, and a passage east isn't high on my list.'

'You'd let the realm burn for spite?' Ayla asked, stunned.

Herric looked at her again but he seemed not to have an answer. For a moment she thought she saw something that might have been shame flicker behind his eyes, but then the mask fell again and he shrugged.

'This war of yours isn't anything to do with me,' he murmured to Vigoran. 'You want your little castle back, go get it yourself.'

'We don't want your help,' Siren snapped, 'just the ride east. Then you can run away and hide with the rest of the scu…'

The seamen around them growled and Ayla heard the sound of metal against sheaths again as they began drawing their weapons. Vigoran stood up and Tygrin clenched his fists as he glared at Herric's crew.

'This is what Terra wants,' Ayla said, eager to avoid any violence in the confines of the bar. 'Us all fighting each other, instead of fighting her.'

The seamen seemed to consider this. Vigoran slowly sat down and removed his hand from his sword. Tygrin forced himself to relax and even Herric seemed to become more reasonable.

'This isn't our fight.'

'Not now, it isn't,' Vigoran agreed. 'But one day, like it or not, if a stand is not made then it'll become your fight.'

'Nobody can run forever,' Luciffen agreed, 'but if they should keep running, then one day there will be nowhere left to run and they will ask themselves – why didn't we fight back when we had the chance?'

Herric watched the old sage for a long moment. Then he glanced at his crew, who were watching him expectantly.

'Four thousand, all in advance.'

'Four thousand,' Vigoran agreed.

'I have berths for eight,' Herric said finally. 'The rest of your little clan will have to stay here.'

Luciffen nodded. 'That will be enough.'

Herric sighed as though reluctant to stand, but he slid his boots off the table and got to his feet. For someone so young he was well built and seemed to have an aura of command about him that rivalled Vigoran's. Herric leaned against the edge of the booth, his hands on his hips as he surveyed them.

'Meet me at the docks in two hours. Where are you all going?

'The Towers of Vipera,' Vigoran said, 'as close as you dare to take us.'

\*\*\*

## Twenty–Seven

'Make way!'

Herric's First Mate, the giant dark–skinned man whom he referred to as Jenson, led a gaggle of burly seamen who split the busy crowd on the wharf like whales crashing through a turbulent sea. Ayla could see Herric striding along just behind Jenson, his gait casual and his long black greatcoat trailing behind him as he swaggered toward a battered but sleek schooner moored nearby. The ship's masts were elegantly raked, her bow narrow and her hull low in the water, suggesting a vessel built for speed, and beneath her bowsprit was carved her name in graceful letters.

*Phoenix.*

Around them the port was a flurry of activity, ships loading and queues of people all struggling to get aboard vessels that were illuminated by hundreds of glowing lanterns that shone like constellations of stars in their rigging. To Ayla, it looked very much like everyone was leaving town.

'Where are they all going?' she asked Luciffen as they walked.

'They're fleeing the darkness,' the sage replied. 'Terra's army must march this way and cross the river at the Bridge of Caya D'on, and people don't want to be here when the Urks come rampaging through and destroy the town.'

They followed Herric to the schooner, his crew hurrying aboard to prepare the ship for sail. Vigoran led the way up the boarding ramp, with Tygrin and Jake behind, Cyril and Siren alongside Ayla and Luciffen at the rear. Agry snorted and huffed as he followed them miserably up onto the ship's deck.

The captain was about to haul up the boarding ramp when a gruff voice called out.

'Herric!'

Ayla saw the captain turn to look at a cruel looking man with a scarred, shaved head, pot belly and big fists standing with a gang of rough–looking thugs. He was dressed in black leather and had thick gold earrings in his ears and another through his nose that gave him the appearance of an unshaven pig.

Jenson moved to Herric's side, one hand on his cutlass. 'You wish me to remove them?' he asked in a deep, sombre voice.

'Nah,' Herric said. 'I've got this. Get the Phoenix ready to sail.'

Herric sauntered back down the boarding ramp, and Ayla moved to the ship's bulwarks so that she could overhear the conversation.

'Dunfig,' Herric drawled, 'I see you've bought your boyfriends with you.'

'You're overdue,' Dunfig growled.

'You're overweight, but I'm not here to judge.'

The men behind Dunfig sniggered, then fell silent at a savage glare from their leader.

'Forty eggs,' Dunfig snarled, 'that was the price. You said you'd have them a month ago and my boss isn't happy.'

'Yeah, sorry about that,' Herric replied with a shrug, 'bad weather, apocalyptic takeovers of the realm, you know how it is.'

Dunfig took a pace closer to Herric and Ayla saw that there was a knife in his hand.

'I'll gut you right here and now if you don't pay up.'

'You gut me right here and now, you definitely won't get anything,' Herric replied without concern. 'You can tell your boss the money's coming, I'm guessing she'll be here soon anyway. Wonder what she'd do if she found out you'd iced the only chance she has of protecting her Draguns from attack?'

Dunfig sneered at Herric. 'You're too clever for your own good.'

'You're not.'

Dunfig turned and stalked away with his thugs, while Herric casually strode back onto the deck of his ship as though nothing had happened. Ayla found herself watching the captain with interest as he swaggered around and directed his crew with an authority far greater than his years.

'Reed, look ye to those top gallants, they're not drawing as they should!'

'Voight, lash down the 'tween deck hatches and report to the bosun!'

'Marrin, secure that bulwark or I'll take the lash to your spine!'

The seamen hurried to carry out his orders under Jenson's watchful eye, scurrying up the ratlines and onto the yards as hatches were closed and boarding ramps lashed down.

'Don't be fooled,' Jake said as he moved to stand alongside Ayla, 'he comes from a long line of buccaneers and he's every bit as untrustworthy as they were.'

'You really don't like him, do you?' she said as the schooner drifted away from the dock and out into the river. Above them, her sails unfurled with booms like cannon fire.

'He sails under no flag, is allied to nobody but himself,' Jake replied. 'He's as likely to sell us out to Terra as he is to help us, and I suspect that he's involved in illegal trade of one kind or another.'

'What makes you say that?'

'The scent,' Jake replied, 'haven't you noticed it yet?'

Ayla sniffed the air, but it was so laden with unfamiliar odours that she could not tell one from another.

'It's coming from the lower decks,' Jake whispered. 'There's something in the holds that Herric's keeping out of sight.'

From the dock there echoed a mournful wail across the foggy isle as a signal was blared from a tower, and Ayla saw everyone grab hold of something to steady themselves.

'What's happening?' she asked Jake.

'We're leaving,' Jake replied as he gripped the bulwarks.

Ayla saw the schooner's sails bulge in the meagre breeze, and she saw other ships departing *en masse* from the docks, all heading across the water and away from them.

And then the unthinkable happened.

The deck of the Phoenix heaved beneath them and the ship surged forwards through the water as though it were powered not by the wind but by engines concealed somewhere beneath the surface. Before Ayla could react to the movement she slumped against the mainmast, watching as the sails filled with a wind whose breath she could not feel. The water rushed by the hull as the ship cast ripples in the glassy surface of the river, and then the bow rose up and the hum of water crashing by below faded to silence. Ayla felt her stomach tingle as the Phoenix glided up into the air, and then she looked behind her and saw the flotilla of vessels lift off out of the water of Port Ranken and fly into the gloom.

Like starlit sailing ships of old they soared up into the air, their sails rumbling in the fluking winds as they climbed up into the fog and the lights of the port vanished below them. Through the misty skies she heard the sombre toll of ship's bells, informing others of where they were in the gloom to avoid collisions.

The Phoenix climbed upward, the moisture of the fog clinging to Ayla's clothes and hair as the ship heeled gently over and turned, her roguish captain balancing easily against the movement as he stood behind the wheel and directed the helmsman.

'Make your height eight hundred leagues and keep a sharp eye open for Draguns.'

'Aye, cap'n.'

Ayla watched in fascination as the fleet of corsairs, privateers and pirates floated away from the port below and then they were gone in the mist, heading west toward safety as the Phoenix climbed away toward the east.

Luciffen made his way to Herric's side.

'The forces of darkness will be amassing by now, and Draguns will guard the Towers of Vipera.'

Herric did not look at Luciffen as he replied. 'I can take you within fifty leagues of the towers, but any closer and we risk being toasted alive by whatever the Wild Wytch is cooking up out there. You sure you want to go through with this, old man?'

'There is nobody else.'

From where they stood, Jake and Ayla could overhear the conversation and she could see that Jake didn't like it one little bit.

'He's got no reason to take us, and every other pirate has sailed west. Why would he bother with this flight?'

'There's got to be something in it for him,' Siren said. 'He's up to something. The Phoenix is one of the fastest pirate ships in the realm, he could be smuggling or running weapons, anything.'

'Supplying Terra,' Cyril suggested, surprising them all. 'I'm just sayin', people like Herric work for anyone and everyone, the highest bidder wins. If Terra's minions have already been out here, you can bet your life the pirates would have struck a deal with her to protect their ships and port.'

Ayla thought about Herric's confrontation with the thugs at the dock, and wondered whether there was more to the captain's presence in Port Ranken than just waiting to pick up passengers.

'Why don't we take a look around?' she suggested.

'The lower decks are sealed,' Jake replied, 'I already checked.'

Ayla reached into her pocket and felt the handle of her invisible blade, the one that Jake had given her. 'Then we should use a key, shouldn't we?'

Jake looked at her and grinned. Cyril and Siren moved to her side, and they walked together toward their berths while Herric was engaged in conversation with Luciffen and Vigoran.

The hatches to the 'tween decks were all lashed closed save for one, and Ayla walked down a steep set of steps into the deck below. The area was lit with glowing lanterns, giving it a shadowy appearance, and it smelled of wood and oil and dust. To either side of the ship were a row of cannons that gleamed a cruel glossy black in the light. Concealed behind closed gunports, Ayla would never have imagined the weapons were there at all when she boarded.

'Herric's ready for a fight,' Siren said as she admired the arsenal with a gleam in her eye, 'and he knows how to look after his weapons.'

'And he's dabbling in things that he shouldn't,' Cyril added as he too looked at the cannons. 'These are some of the Guns of Solelle, an old fortress that fell centuries ago. Each contains the heart of a young Dragun, sustained by magic alone. Herric's no sorcerer, so how did he come by these and how does he control them?'

Jake shot Ayla an inquiring look, but she shrugged.

'I don't know, but we can't judge him on that alone.'

'Doesn't exactly make me want to trust him either,' Jake replied.

Ayla eased forward through the schooner's gundeck and saw a hatch in the centre of the deck that was secured with metal padlocks. She crept alongside the hatch and crouched down as she felt for the knife in her pocket. The others kept watch as she cut through each of the padlocks, the invisible blade passing through each as though it were made from nothing more substantial than air. Carefully, she reached down and lifted the hatch, and almost at once she smelled something that was a cross between straw and skin. The scent reminded her of horse stables, and Jake spoke quickly.

'There's something alive down there.'

Before Ayla could react there came from the darkened depths of the ship's hold a terrifying screech and two angry eyes flared in the darkness and shot toward her.

\*\*\*

## Twenty–Eight

Ayla hurled herself back from the hatch as a huge, feathered head jerked up and smashed the hatch aside. She landed on her backside on the hard deck as she stared in amazement at a creature that she did not recognise.

It had the head of an eagle, its beak as thick as her thigh, but behind its head was a long mane that would have looked more at home on a lion. The mane glittered like gold dust in the light from the lanterns, shimmering as though alive as the fearsome creature turned to look at her with those cruel, hunter's eyes.

'Get the hatch down!' Jake yelled. 'It's a Griffon!'

Siren swung her sword at the Griffon and the ferocious looking beast snapped its head toward her. Its beak clamped down around the sword and snapped it as though it were a twig, the two pieces of the weapon clattering down onto the deck. Siren leaped backwards out of the way as the Griffon clambered up out of the hatch, and Ayla felt true fear run like poison through her veins as she realised how big the creature was.

It stood as tall as a horse, with the thick and muscular body of a lion and twin tails that swirled and writhed. Tucked in along its flanks were folded wings that shimmered with iridescent light and colour like rainbows through falling rain. The whole creature was so spellbindingly beautiful and yet so large and powerful that Ayla froze on the spot, unable to move.

'Get back!' Jake snapped as he moved to stand protectively in front of Ayla.

The Griffon roared and one heavy forelimb wafted Jake aside as though he wasn't even there. Jake hit the deck hard and his sword spun from his grasp as Cyril leaped forward and waved his hand.

'Protector meus, lumen est!'

A wave of sparkling light glistened from Cyril's hand and washed across the Griffon, but the huge animal merely shook it off like dust and stalked forwards. Cyril yelped and jumped behind Ayla as she scrambled to her feet.

'My sorcery doesn't work on it!' he squeaked. 'It's too strong!'

Ayla began backing up as the huge Griffon prowled toward them, and Siren whirled for the exit. She was stopped right there as men tumbled down the steps into the gundeck, Herric's crew with their swords drawn and murder on their faces.

Ayla saw Herric jump down onto the gundeck. His eyes took in the scene as the Griffon closed in on Ayla and her friends, and an infuriating grin spread on his face.

'Don't smile at it! Shoot it!' Jake yelled.

Herric glanced at the Griffon, and then he raised one hand and clicked his fingers. *'Sit!'*

The huge Griffon stopped moving, its beak inches from where Ayla cowered, and then the big beast ruffled its feathers and sat down, its yellow eyes fixed upon hers as though it were an eagle glaring down at a dormouse.

Jake stared at Herric. '*Sit?* That's all?'

Tirga and Vigoran stepped down into the hold as Herric strolled casually across to the Griffon and ruffled its thick mane. Ayla stared in wonder as the captain folded his arms across his chest and leaned against the animal's neck, the huge Griffon nuzzling him.

'And what were the four of you doing down here?'

Jake stood up. 'You're smuggling Griffons,' he countered. 'Their eggs are worth a fortune on the black market, there are hardly any left in the realm.'

Luciffen joined Vigoran on the gundeck as Tygrin growled at Herric. 'I knew it, nothing but a common thief. Terra would pay handsomely for the last Griffon eggs in existence, they're the only native species in the realm that willingly hunt Draguns.'

Ayla slowly got to her feet as the Griffon made soft purring noises at Herric. The captain ignored the animal as he looked at Ayla, measuring her up.

'You're trouble,' he said finally, the first words he had spoken directly to her since they had met. 'You've got an adventuring spirit you don't know how to control. I should lock you up in the brig.'

Ayla fought to build a wall of dignity around her embarrassment.

'Like you lock this beautiful animal up in your holds?'

Far from being admonished, Herric merely smiled at her as though he was enjoying the banter.

'Hybrin,' he guessed, as though he could see right through her, 'you knew that something was down here, didn't you?'

Ayla raised her chin in defiance but she said nothing. Herric's smile did not slip as he turned to the Griffon and made a couple of strange clicking noises in the back of his throat. The Griffon turned, lumbered back to the hatch and descended into the darkness once more.

'Secure the hatch,' Herric ordered his men as he turned to look at Jake, 'and place a watch on our guests. We don't want them becoming lunch for the Griffon, do we?'

Herric strolled from the gundeck without another word, leaving Ayla and the others apparently unpunished and yet admonished all the same. Luciffen moved across to her and frowned as he watched the Phoenix's crew securing the hatch.

'Griffons,' he murmured. 'Just one egg can be worth thousands, enough to buy ten ships this size.'

'He can't be trusted,' Tygrin whispered as they left the gundeck. 'We're walking into something we can't control and Herric holds our lives in his hands. We need to get off this ship.'

'We need to get close to the towers,' Luciffen reminded him, 'or all of this will be for nothing no matter what happens to us. We cannot be choosy about with whom we travel, for few others would have taken us this far.'

The Phoenix sailed on, rising up into a brilliant blue sky and skimming the surface of the clouds as though she were sailing on a rolling, pure white sea. Ayla stood for much of the time on the stern deck, watching the huge clouds glide silently by as the ship's sails rumbled and boomed and the deck creaked beneath their feet.

Despite the uncertainty of her friends she found herself watching Herric far more than she knew that she should. The captain's roguish nature and cavalier disregard for authority was the most compelling thing she'd ever witnessed. This was nothing like the handsome cruelty of Schwarz or the noble friendship of Jake – Herric was like a force of nature that had thundered into her world as forcefully as had the Mirrorealm, and now it seemed as though everything was in orbit around the captain.

'How come he's the captain of a ship when he's so young?' she finally asked Vigoran, whom she found sitting quietly near the bow of the ship smoking his clay pipe.

'His father was a buccaneer named Jack Rackam,' Vigoran replied. 'They called him Calico Jack because of his vibrantly coloured clothes. Calico Jack sailed further and faster than any before him and amassed a fortune in stolen goods, exotic beasts and minerals, jewels, everything. He grew powerful enough that he had his own island, but when Terra grew to power his land was consumed into Chaoria and so was Calico Jack.'

'Terra killed him?'

'Nobody knows,' Vigoran said, 'but Herric fled with one of his father's schooners and a loyal crew and has continued the family business ever since. He may be one of the youngest of the buccaneers out there, but he's as ruthless as his father ever was. He grew up rough, Ayla, with brethren among whom only the strong and the heartless survive. You'd do well to stay away from him.'

Ayla heard Vigoran, but she wasn't sure that she agreed with him. Unlike others she had met here in the realm, she felt nothing of the darkness around Herric. But she had only been here a short while and in truth she knew nothing of the man who now was sailing them into what could be their last days. Luciffen was right – they had to remain with Herric, or how else would they get out of here again?

The captain turned on the deck, and in his hand he held a strange device that he held up to the four corners of the compass. He seemed to take some readings and then he called out to Luciffen.

'Get your stuff ready,' he said with far more enjoyment than Ayla felt was truly necessary. 'We're coming up on Chaoria! Helm, down with the bow! Brace the main yard and unshackle the guns!'

Herric turned to Ayla and flashed a bright renegade smile.

'If you came here looking for adventure sister, you're about to get it. Wanna go for a ride?!'

Before she could answer, the Phoenix dove for the clouds and plunged into the darkness of the storms raging below.

\*\*\*

## Twenty–Nine

The Phoenix descended into the storm clouds like a submarine diving beneath the waves and instantly the serene silence was replaced with a deep darkness and flashes of distant lightning that crackled around them.

The crew fell quiet as the ship sailed through the towering cloud formations, rocking this way and that on the winds that now gusted across the deck. The Phoenix heeled into the gales as Herric stared ahead into the storm.

'What do you see?'

Luciffen's voice burst into Ayla's awareness and she took her eyes off Herric as she realised the sage was speaking to her. She focussed on the realm around them.

'I can feel cold, darkness and it's not just the storms,' she replied.

Herric spoke from nearby, never taking his eyes off the clouds around them, and she realised that he was gauging the conditions like a sailor might assess the sea.

'Terra can conjure her storms but they're still weather,' he said. 'Thunderheads there, up draughts and downdraughts over there, storm cells all around us.'

'Can you navigate through them?' Vigoran asked.

Herric offered him a hurt look and pressed both hands to his own chest. Vigoran ignored the captain's bravado and turned to Luciffen.

'We are close. Terra might sense that you're near.'

Luciffen kept a firm grip on his staff.

'I can shield us for now, but this is going to be dangerous. Our only advantage is that Terra will not anticipate this move. She will expect us to be preparing the defences at Stormshadow Citadel.'

Vigoran did not look convinced but he said nothing more as the ship descended through the turbulent skies, rocking more violently in the winds as Herric guided the helmsman through the worst of the weather.

The lightning and thunder raged around them, brilliant forks of light slashing the darkness, and then Ayla noticed halos of light glowing amid the ship's masts. She pointed them out in surprise but Herric barely glanced at them.

'St Elmo's Fire,' he murmured in reply. 'The air is electrically charged, lots of energy floating around up here. Terra wields her sorcery well but even she can't control power like this. It's getting a life all of its own.'

The silence among the crew was infectious as the ship descended, the passengers sensing danger all around them. Ayla moved to the bulwarks and looked over the edge to see more clouds roiling thousands of feet below them, and then she saw something else flickering through the clouds and she felt a stab of alarm pierce her heart.

'There's something below us!'

Herric strode to the side of the ship and leaped up onto the bulwarks, his greatcoat fluttering like giant wings as he grabbed a rigging line and leaned dangerously out over the side of the ship.

'Emphysians,' he reported to the first mate, Jenson. 'Tell the men to man their posts and cover their eyes.'

Jenson hurried around the ship, yelling the order and preparing to cover his own scarred and tattooed head.

'What's an Emphysian?' Ayla asked, and Cyril replied.

'They're beautiful goddesses who haunt storms, with flaming hair and bodies that make them look as though they're made from burning metal. But they're lethal and will consume the flesh of men.'

Ayla raised her eyebrows as she saw all of the menfolk cover their eyes with low caps or blindfolds and grab hold of anything solid to steady themselves.

'What about women and girls?' Ayla asked, and Siren moved to stand beside her.

'Don't listen to them,' she warned. 'They will try to seduce you to become one of them. For women, it is their words and melodies that are dangerous, not their appearance. Cover your ears.'

Ayla covered her ears with her hands just in time as over the bulwarks of the Phoenix flew a dozen beautiful, shimmering beings. They looked to Ayla like mermaids of the air, their bodies glittering like gold and their hair literally aflame. They swarmed across the ship, searching the eyes of the crew, their long robes fluttering as they moved. She could see the glow from their bodies illuminating the decks in patches of shimmering light, the sailors' heads bowed and their eyes covered.

Ayla watched them, and suddenly she could hear their voices as sweet as those of young children, singing soft lullabies formed of spellbinding notes. To her surprise Ayla realised that she really wanted to hear the songs and she found herself lifting her hands away from her ears.

One of the Emphysians swung gracefully around and glided in toward Ayla, singing and smiling, her arms gently outstretched in a welcoming embrace. Her eyes were a stunning electric blue, her entire face glittering like jewels. Her smile was as inviting as anything Ayla had ever seen, more gorgeous and open and honest than any human being could possibly be. One of the Emphysian's hands lovingly cradled Ayla's cheek and she felt warmth flush her body at the contact, overpoweringly seductive.

Ayla's head jerked painfully as Siren jabbed her hand back over her ear with one free elbow. The haunting melody became muted again and Ayla blinked herself out of the Emphyisian's trance and pushed harder to block the sound of her voice.

The Emphysian scowled and turned away, fluttering across to the bow as Ayla turned and saw one of the crew drop to his knees as an Emphysian caressed his face and her hands slipped beneath his shirt. The man uncovered his eyes and looked up into her face, his mouth opening in awe and his eyes wide with desire, and like ravenous predators the Emphysians abandoned the other seamen and rushed in toward him. They swarmed around him in a glittering inferno and lifted the man off the deck, their smiles and singing mutating into grotesque screams of bloodlust and rage. The sailor began to scream but his voice was cut off as they flew away with his struggling body and vanished down into the turbulent clouds.

Siren took her hands off her ears. 'They're gone!'

Herric ripped his blindfold off. 'How many of the crew did we lose?'

'Just one,' Siren reported.

Herric raised an eyebrow in surprise and shrugged as he tossed the blindfold to one side. 'Not so bad. Maintain course, get us below the clouds before the storm breaks over us!'

Before the crew could respond, a sailor yelled a warning. 'Draguns, port bow!'

Herric responded in an instant. 'It never rains... Hard to starboard, head for the squalls!'

The Phoenix heeled over and sailed toward veils of falling rain as Ayla saw two Draguns roaring in from the left of the ship, their glowing black and orange bodies pulsing with each wing beat as they intercepted the Phoenix.

The Phoenix plunged into a dense rain squall and the Dragun's veered off as the downpour drenched the ship's decks. Ayla dashed into the cover of the wheelhouse with Luciffen and the others as the ship turned this way and that to maintain the cover of the rain and the clouds.

The Draguns wheeled about below them but then vanished as the ship entered a dense cloud bank.

'This is where it gets interesting,' Herric said through a grim smile. 'We're about as close as I can get you, old man. Any further in and we'll have an entire army attacking us.'

Luciffen nodded and peered out into the dense clouds. 'Can you set us down?'

'I'll do what I can, but you're on your own after that.'

'The deal was for a ride in *and* out,' Tygrin rumbled as he fingered the handle of his axe. 'I'd hate us to have a dispute about that.'

'I can wait,' Herric replied, unintimidated, 'as long as Terra's storms hold we have somewhere to hide. But there's no way I can sail any closer without Terra knowing you're coming so it's your call, mastermind.'

Tygrin said nothing as the Phoenix descended through the cloud layers, the winds ever more violent. Ayla touched Luciffen's arm.

'The source of the evil,' she said, 'it's as close as it's ever been. I can almost taste it.'

Beside her, the huge first mate Jenson peered at her with his dark eyes.

'You see the evil,' he rumbled, 'but you don't know its purpose.'

Just then veils of cloud rushed past the ship and it dropped out of the cloud layer and into a stormy, bleak wasteland of black rock and forests of thin, twisted trees devoid of leaves. The entire region looked as though it had been scoured of life.

In the distance, miles away, Ayla could see a soaring fortress of black against the horizon, surrounded by a lake of molten rock.

'The Towers of Vipera,' Luciffen said, gripping his staff firmly in one hand.

'End of the road!' Herric hollered as the Phoenix drifted down toward the barren landscape and two of the crew hurled an anchor over the bow.

The anchor plummeted down and slammed into the black rocks, and the Phoenix heeled over as she turned about in the wind, coming to rest fifty feet above the ground with the anchor cable pulled taut. Vigoran, Tygrin and Agry prepared their weapons as Siren and Cyril pulled their collars tighter about their necks against the cold.

Ayla stood with Jake and felt somewhat bereft as the Phoenix sank to within a few feet of the ground and Herric waved them off the deck.

'Get out of here and into cover before those damned Dragun's track us down!'

Ayla followed Luciffen down off the deck of the Phoenix and onto a short plank that had been extended over the side. One after the other, they jumped and landed below the ship. Ayla turned after they were all off and saw the Phoenix withdraw both the plank and the anchor cable and rise up into the air.

'You'd better be here when we get back!' Tygrin roared up at the ship.

Herric looked down at them but said nothing in reply, and then the ship climbed away and was lost amid the tumultuous clouds scudding by in the darkness overhead.

\*\*\*

## Thirty

A sepulchral silence enveloped the land around them as the last living things were finally overcome by the darkness entombing Chaoria. A frigid wind gusted into their faces as they walked, rumbling over the bleak landscape, and she could see Luciffen looking anxious.

'We must stop,' he said.

Vigoran brought them to a halt, the sky above laden with heavy clouds that looked fit to burst with rain. The wind buffeted them as Luciffen brought out his staff and began whispering in a dialect that Ayla did not recognise. The words sounded something like Latin mixed with Arabic, the same sort of words as Cyril had used to expose the Well of Memories. Luciffen mumbled with his eyes closed and his knuckles white as he gripped the staff.

'Mala ab oculis shield.'

Ayla saw the tip of Luciffen's staff begin to glow like a new–born star, and suddenly she could no longer feel the cold wind assaulting them nor hear its lonely song. Tygrin spoke softly from behind her.

'He is protecting us with a spell that ensures we cannot be seen. I've never liked this one, 'cause you never know whether it's worked or not until you stumble on something that can see you. Or can't see you, if you know what I mean?'

Luciffen lowered his staff and turned to Vigoran. The warrior drew his sword and then began to lead them on across the bleak landscape.

They walked for another hour, the lifeless soil beneath their boots changing to bare rock, a few scant weeds surviving in the wastelands. The sky above darkened further and Ayla recalled the flight with Ellegen out of the Mines of Poisor, the entire land enshrouded in the gloom that was the hallmark of Terra's domain. She scanned the skies for any sign of Draguns but could see nothing, and with a start she realised that she could feel and hear nothing either. Luciffen's spell may have made them invisible to everything else, but it also seemed to block Ayla's ability to sense the evil around them.

The hills and valleys were black as though forged from obsidian and coal, and she could see veils of rain pouring down from the turbulent clouds as flashes of lighting forked through the sky above them. She could not hear the crashes of thunder that must accompany the storm due to Luciffen's spell, but she could see the shape now of two or three Draguns arcing through the skies over the immense fortress carved into the side of a towering mountain.

The Towers of Vipera soared into the heavens, black spires and walls that shone with a malice and cruelty all of their own. Shaped like gigantic knife blades slicing the sky, there was not a curve in sight, everything jagged edges and severe lines.

Ayla could see some glowing windows here and there but the rest of the gargantuan monolith was silent and black.

'Jeez,' Agry muttered, 'no wonder she lives alone.'

'The spell's working,' Cyril noted. 'The Draguns would have seen us by now.'

'It will not hold once we get closer to the Towers of Vipera,' Luciffen reminded them. 'I grow weaker with each and every step. We must seek shelter as soon as we can.'

Ayla stayed close to Tygrin, the big warrior always as close to the front of the pack as he could be, although he stayed behind Vigoran out of respect. Ayla realised that she knew nothing of Vigoran or of how his Riders of Spiris came to be. The warriors all seemed so different and yet united in their determination to rid the realm of Terra.

'Vigoran is the son of the King of Stormshadow,' Luciffen replied when she asked him about the Riders of Spiris. 'Like all royalty, he was required to work as an ordinary citizen until he was old enough to take his father's throne, to learn how to live as a man and not a prince. He made his living as a blacksmith and crafted swords for the great knights that once roamed this land. One of those knights attacked a coven of wytches, injuring them severely. The wytches killed the knight and went in search of the man who forged the sword that had done them so much harm. They cursed Vigoran with a dark magic that even I could not undo. Vigoran is literally a shadow of a man, so that his father could no longer gaze upon him. He was outcast from Stormshadow as nobody could be sure who he really was, and was abandoned until he found solace among the Riders of Spiris.'

'And his father, the King?' Ayla asked.

'The King fell at the Battle of Stormshadow, defending the great mirror. He was consumed by the Dragun that now resides there.'

Ayla reflected for a moment on the tragedy that had befallen Vigoran.

'What about Tygrin?' she asked, interested.

'Tygrin is the son of a chieftain of the Savagen Tribe who live in the mountains,' Luciffen replied. 'He is here by choice, as was his father. He fights, although many of his tribe will not stand against Terra. Agry is also the son of a chieftain, but Terra's hordes overran his lands many years ago and with it his inheritance and his title. Agry is driven by anger and the need to avenge his losses.'

Ayla eyed Agry as they walked, the warrior listening she was sure to every word that was said. She still could not be sure that he had not seen Cyril and her following him into the woods the previous night, but he seemed to remain close to her at all times since as though he was preventing her from speaking about what had happened to anyone.

'Jake, I know about,' she said. 'What about Cyril, and Siren?'

Luciffen smiled. 'Cyril is a gentle soul whose family and tribe also suffered greatly when Terra expanded her control over the realm. They were farmers, all of whom perished when Terra's Draguns set aflame their land. Cyril was gifted naturally in the art of sorcery and I took him under my wing to ensure that he did not fall from grace and become an ally of Terra. It turns out that he couldn't be more good in his soul if he tried, and will become a great sage one day.'

Luciffen looked at Siren, who stared straight ahead as she walked, her eyes fixed upon the Towers of Vipera and the line of her mouth tight. She kept pace with Vigoran no matter how tough the terrain.

'Siren is the daughter of a farmer also, and her entire family was wiped out by Terra's Urk hordes.'

'Urk hordes?' Ayla asked.

'The Urks are a kind of goblin, born of the earth itself in great numbers and driven by a lust for blood and battle,' Luciffen explained. 'They come from the dark soul of the realm, a place of shadows and misery, and they draw their strength from the darkness and from our own fears. Terra has amassed an army of tens of thousands, all of them hell–bent on battle and pain. Siren escaped the massacre and joined us, and her determination worries me for one so young. She lives only to avenge her family's passing by killing Terra herself, and she is loyal only to Vigoran and Agry.'

'Agry?' Ayla asked. 'Why him?'

'Agry and Vigoran are both warriors by blood, and both have lost dearly to Terra's campaign of war. They both know what they stand to gain from defeating her – Vigoran his kingdom and Agry his lands, and will stop at nothing to be the first to drive their sword through her black heart.'

Ayla thought for a moment. 'And Terra herself?'

Luciffen sighed and shook his head.

'For another time, perhaps.'

Ayla was about to protest but Vigoran raised his hand to bring them to a halt near a river of stale water that smelled awful. As Ayla looked down she realised why Vigoran had stopped.

She could see her reflection in the water, which meant that Luciffen's spell had worn off and they could be seen by all.

\*\*\*

## Thirty-One

Ayla crouched down and hid beneath an overhang of rock as the rest of the riders tucked in around her to hide themselves from view.

They were within a hundred metres of the walls of the immense fortress, but Ayla could see that the rocky terrain between themselves and the Towers of Vipera offered little in the way of cover. Ayla looked up at the towering walls, which were surrounded by a moat of what looked like molten lava that shimmered with heat and clouds of toxic gas. A massive set of gates towered over them on the far side of the moat, blending in to the towers and battlements atop the huge fortress. Three Draguns where wheeling through the skies far above the highest towers, their dark wings flapping lazily as they circled on the thermals rising up from the moat.

'There's no way we can get across that moat,' Vigoran said, 'and even if we did we'd never get through those gates.'

Luciffen nodded, but his reply was as calm and certain as it had ever been.

'Terra intends to advance on the realm, and to do so she must lower the drawbridge to allow her armies to march out. If we can get close enough, we could sneak past them.'

'Past ten thousand Urks all baying for our blood?' Agry snapped in disgust. 'What kind of madness is that? What do you think they'll be looking at while we casually saunter past?'

'I didn't say that we would walk in at all,' Luciffen replied. 'There are others ways in, if we use our good senses.'

Ayla frowned and then looked again at the huge gates of the fortress as a violent boom echoed across the realm. They watched as chunks of ice were shaken loose as the gates began to move, rolling open to the left and right.

'Now,' Luciffen urged, 'get close to the doors before the army marches out.'

'The Draguns,' Siren warned, 'they're looking this way.'

Luciffen closed his eyes, his grip tightening on his staff, and he grit his teeth as he tried to generate the power needed to conceal them this close to the Towers of Vipera. His body shook and Ayla saw the tip of his staff glow with a blue–white light as he trembled and gasped.

'Go, now, stay close to each other, it won't last long!'

Vigoran leaped out and hurried along the jagged rocks toward the moat, Ayla right behind him with Cyril, Tygrin and Siren. Luciffen struggled along behind them while muttering spells and chants to himself. Ayla could sense the magic surrounding them but it was vague, fluttering in and out of existence like a light bulb that had reached the end of its life.

The moat cast heat out into the wilderness in the form of a rippling, billowing haze as they hurried toward it. The lava churned and spat plumes of glowing molten rock into the air that hissed and crackled as Ayla reached the edge and looked down into the hellish depths.

The huge gates rumbled open, Ayla able to feel the earth trembling beneath her feet with their movement. Each was as tall as a ten–storey building, and as soon as they were fully open so an enormous drawbridge began to lower from within. She could see immensely thick ropes supporting it and a latticework of braces on its underside.

'There,' Vigoran said as he saw the complex of metal braces beneath the drawbridge, designed to bear the load of armies marching in and out of the fortress. 'We can get inside by going beneath the drawbridge until the army has marched out.'

Ayla looked at the churning mass of lava roiling below them and wondered whether any of those gaseous blasts would reach the underside of the drawbridge.

'That's insane,' Agry spat. 'It's suicide and you know it, and the small matter of getting out again once the drawbridge is closed?'

Nobody answered and the warrior cursed and glanced over his shoulder, back the way they had come. 'There has to be a better way.'

'There is no other way,' Luciffen replied weakly, 'unless you intend to go up to Terra and politely ask for Gallentia's freedom and the Mirror of Souls.'

'More chance of me surviving that than…'

'Silence,' Vigoran snapped as the drawbridge slammed down onto their side of the moat with a deafening crash. 'Go, everyone, now!'

They dashed the last few metres to the edge of the moat and clambered down the rock face to a point just below the drawbridge. Vigoran led them beneath it, but Ayla turned back and helped Luciffen along. The old man was weakening fast, the effort required for his sorcery to conceal them from view draining him. He smiled his gratitude as he crept beneath the drawbridge and out of sight.

Ayla was about to follow him when she saw movement at the gates of the towers.

The entrance was a gaping maw of darkness, and within she saw countless points of light flickering as thousands of figures marched out of the fortress and into the gloom, flaming torches in their grasp. Ayla felt her stomach clench as she saw them, the hordes that Luciffen and the others had mentioned, marching in time toward her.

The Urks were bizarre, muscular creatures but their limbs were all at awkward angles, more like the twisted roots of a tree. Their skin was like bark and the colour of coal, their faces forged from stone and soil and their eyes glowing with a soulless light. They were armed with jagged, metallic weapons of all kinds; maces, swords, axes, slingshots and bows that caught the light of the moat beneath them and the flaming torches that they carried.

The Urks lurched, ambled and limped out of the Towers of Vipera in ranks fifty across, their flaming torches illuminating their gruesome features.

'Ayla!'

Vigoran called to her and she ducked out of sight beneath the drawbridge as the army began to march across it, the huge wooden boards shuddering with countless footfalls as the ranks of Urks passed by over their heads.

'This way.'

Vigoran led the way across the underside of the bridge, clambering from one support to another. Ayla followed, and looked down to see the lava moat beneath her spitting flames and blasting plumes of gas. The heat was intense, but she was relieved to see that the drawbridge was high enough to prevent them from being sprayed with lethal clouds of molten debris.

Vigoran reached the far side, the drawbridge still vibrating as the army passed by overhead. Ayla could see huge cogs and drive chains at the base of the drawbridge, the mechanism that allowed it to be lowered and raised. Vigoran pointed to gaps in the base of the bridge and Ayla nodded and headed for them.

She reached an immense tree trunk that had been shaped into a hinge, and she crouched down and peered up through a gap to see the Urks marching past in their thousands, oblivious to her presence.

Vigoran joined her, his voice a whisper.

'As soon as they're all out, the drawbridge will lift. We'll slip through then, and inside the Towers.'

Luciffen moved alongside Ayla, Tygrin with him, Cyril and Siren just behind. Ayla waited with them for several minutes until, finally, the last of the Urks trudged by and the sound of their marching rumbled away across the drawbridge. There was a long silence as they crouched in the darkness, and then a deafening creaking sound and the huge cogs either side of the drawbridge began to turn.

'Go,' Vigoran said.

The huge hinge was turning as Ayla crawled onto it and let its motion carry her over the other side. Vigoran helped Luciffen up as Tygrin squeezed his immense bulk through the gap and landed heavily on the other side. Ayla saw that they were in a vast entrance hall lined with towering statues of what looked like Greek Gods, handsome and majestic, but their stone faces had been shattered, leaving them horrifically disfigured.

The drawbridge rose up and then closed with a deep boom that echoed away through the fortress as they stood alongside each other and stared into the oblivion of the Towers of Vipera. Cyril looked around them, and then he frowned.

'Where's Agry?'

They looked around but the warrior was nowhere to be seen.

'Did he fall into the moat?'

'I was at the back,' Luciffen said, 'he wasn't there.'

'The *coward*,' Jake growled. 'I knew he'd run!'

Siren glared at Jake, one hand moving to her sword. 'He's no coward.'

'We cannot change what is,' Luciffen said. 'We must press on without him.'

Vigoran turned to Ayla.

'It's down to you, now,' he said simply.

Ayla sighed softly and with a reluctant gait she set off toward a distant, feeble sense of Gallentia's presence that shone within an immense darkness that surrounded them all.

\*\*\*

## Thirty–Two

The interior of the towers had been forged it seemed from seams of coal, but the walls were as hard as steel and cold to the touch.

'Obsidian,' Luciffen noted as they moved through the hall, his voice echoing into the darkness. 'It's a volcanic rock, very sharp and brittle. The entire fortress is built from it and strengthened with the magic that Terra wields.'

They moved through the darkness, the ranks of statues looking down upon them with their gruesome faces warped and deranged as though in the grip of unspeakable madness. Ayla looked up at them one after the other, and then from the gloom ahead she saw a wide flight of steps ascending into the interior of the fortress.

She led the way, focussing on the distant aura of misery that she knew must be coming from Gallentia. Her tortured cries were becoming steadily louder, clearer, chanting and baying their hymn of sorrow. Ayla knew that she was not crying out physically, but in her mind.

'We are closer,' Luciffen said, sensing the same presence that Ayla did.

Ayla thought it strange that she could not sense any of the evil that she knew must reside in this immense monument to Terra's power. Of course, the great wytch could be with her army which had just left the towers. Still, Ayla would have expected to sense Hell Hounds perhaps, the fearsome Cerberus that she had seen in the Mines of Poisor, or some other hideous guardians that the wytch might have left behind.

The flight of stairs carried them upward, splitting left and right and repeatedly doubling back on itself as they ascended higher into the towers. Ayla was conscious that they were also getting deeper and deeper into Terra's lair, with an ever longer flight to escape again. She had no idea how they were going to get out of here if they did manage to liberate Gallentia, and Luciffen seemed too drained to perform the kind of magic needed to spirit them invisibly beyond the great walls. She could only assume that Gallentia herself, once liberated, would lead them to safety.

The stairs finally reached an end and Ayla paused as she heard the screams more vividly than ever. Then, finally, she felt the evil that she had been waiting for, the cold and the darkness looming invisibly somewhere ahead of them.

'We're close,' she whispered.

Vigoran moved to stand beside her and drew his sword. Tygrin hauled his massive axe from his back as Siren prepared her slingshot and sword. Jake slid his sword from its sheath and his shield from his back. Ayla, feeling somewhat self-conscious, slipped her bow from her back and into her hands.

'Nice and slow,' Vigoran murmured.

They edged forward, spreading out into a wide line to avoid making an easy single target of themselves. Ahead, down a long and ornate hall, Ayla could see an archway that opened onto some sort of chamber that was vast and well lit. She could see more stairs ahead of them inside the chamber, and something was glowing brightly just out of sight.

She felt the bow humming in her grasp, and was surprised to see that the quiver of Griffon hair was now glowing with pure light, like lightning caught between the top and bottom of the slender, elegant weapon. She glanced at Luciffen.

'Now you know how it works,' he said, 'don't be afraid to use it.'

The bow responded to the presence of evil, Ayla realised, drew power somehow to become active only when needed for defence. She raised the bow, the quiver humming before her and looking every bit like something that would give her a nasty shock if she touched it. Carefully, she curled her fingers around the quiver and with a flash of light an arrow of shimmering energy pulsed into view, crackling softly in the darkness with a fiery orange glow.

The towering archway passed overhead as they entered an enormous chamber, the roof so high that it was barely visible. Before them was another flight of stairs and at the top, bathed in light that seemed to come from everywhere and yet nowhere at the same time, was a jagged pillar of glossy black rock that jutted from the steps like the ragged blade of a giant knife. It was as tall as Tygrin, and bound to the rock was a woman.

'Gallentia,' Luciffen gasped.

Before anyone could move toward the trapped white wytch, they heard a strange hissing sound. Ayla whirled as she felt a frigid chill fall like snow upon her skin and she saw a huge form slithering into the chamber behind them.

Ayla did not consciously think about her reaction. On pure impulse, she turned and aimed her bow at the huge twin-headed snake that rushed toward them, its slithering body as wide as a car. She pulled the bow back and launched the arrow straight at the snake's cruel left head as it reared up to strike.

The arrow seethed as it rocketed with the speed of a meteor and crashed into the snake's face, blasting it backward as the creature roiled in agony.

'Vipera!' Luciffen yelled the warning.

The group scattered as Ayla stepped back and drew another arrow, firing again at the twin heads. The arrow smashed into them in a burst of light and energy that crackled the air. The Vipera reeled, but then it slung one of its heads at Ayla and a stream of scalding acid sprayed toward her.

Ayla hurled herself to one side and the acid splattered across the stone flags where she had been standing a moment before. The stones cracked, hissed and popped as the acid ate into them and they collapsed into bubbling pools.

'Take the high ground!' Vigoran yelled.

Ayla hit the steps at a run as Luciffen and the others regrouped. Ayla turned and fired two more shots at the Vipera, holding it at bay amid blossoming explosions of energy that echoed back and forth through the huge hall as the Riders of Spiris backed up the steps.

The Vipera hissed and fired a stream of acid at them, but Vigoran leaped into the front of the group and his shield flared as it deflected the acid to either side. Clouds of toxic smoke billowed into the air as the acid landed on the steps and dissolved the solid stone flags in an instant.

Luciffen held his staff aloft and cried out in his strange dialect, the staff bursting with bright light that drove the Vipera back.

'Vipera et abierunt!'

The huge snake reared up, its heads shying away from the light, and Ayla backed up further and fired twice again. The arrows pounded the Vipera and to Ayla's amazement she saw the creature's vast bulk diminished, as though the onslaught were physically shrinking it.

'Siren!' Vigoran yelled.

Siren vaulted up onto the walls either side of the steps and swinging her slingshot above her head. The empty leather cups glowed with four crackling balls of energy and she hurled all of them at the Vipera. The four balls of light fanned out as they hurtled toward the giant snake, joined by thin and writhing streams of lightning, and they clashed with the Vipera's heads and wrapped themselves tightly, drawing together with immense force.

The Vipera screeched and reared up again, its heads butted together as it tried to aim at them to fire more acid. Both of the jaws opened wide, revealing huge fangs that glistened with acidic venom. Ayla aimed and fired directly into one of the open mouths. The arrow flashed straight and true across the hall and plunged directly into the snake's mouth. Ayla saw explosions of energy rip into the Vipera's heads and down its body, the beast shuddering with the blows.

The Vipera screeched and writhed in pain as the energy seethed through its sinewy body and burned the acid coursing through it. Ayla smelled a terrible scent of scorched flesh as the Vipera's great heads slammed down onto the stone flags and the light faded from its cruel eyes.

They stood for several moments and watched the immense snake's body twitch sporadically, but then it stopped moving and Ayla knew that it was dead when she saw the quiver on her bow fade away. She sighed in relief as she lowered the weapon, and she saw Vigoran glance up at her with those glowing blue eyes and nod once in admiration.

'Nice shootin',' Jake grinned at her, and then at Siren. 'You too.'

Siren flipped her slingshot over her shoulder and walked up the steps past Ayla. 'Not bad, for a Hybrin.'

Her tone was dismissive, but there was a tiny smile on her face as she passed by. Ayla felt a warmth wash over her, something that she had not felt in a long time, a sense of inclusion and belonging that she had sought for years and not even realised.

'Didn't even get to use my axe,' Tygrin grumbled as he shoved it back into place on his back.

Ayla turned, and now she could clearly see the woman bound to the rock above them. Gallentia was an older woman, but not as old as Luciffen. She had long dark hair that spilled like shiny oil over her white dress, one that was long enough to be draped part way down the steps. Her head hung limp from her neck as though she were sleeping, her arms aloft and pinned by her wrists to the rock.

'I'm not sure I want to know what Terra's done to her,' Jake said as he climbed the steps with them.

Ayla walked with Vigoran to the top of the steps, but Luciffen hurried up ahead of them and rushed to Gallentia's side.

'My love, what has she done to you?' he gasped.

Ayla watched as the woman lifted her head wearily to reveal a lovely, kind face drawn with pain and suffering. A pair of green eyes focussed on Luciffen's and she suddenly smiled and wept openly.

'Father, I knew you would come.'

Ayla moved quietly closer, understanding now why Luciffen had been so desperate to be reunited with the White Wytch. Ayla should have realised that blood tied as strongly in the realm as it did back home, and she recalled that it was her own mother's suffering that had driven her to come back here.

'Luciffen,' Vigoran whispered, 'we must leave, quickly.'

Luciffen nodded and turned to look at Ayla. For a moment Ayla did not understand, and then she remembered the knife in her pocket and she quickly reached up and cut the bonds holding Gallentia in place. The woman slumped and was caught by Vigoran, the warrior lifting her into his arms.

'Good, let's get out of here,' Siren snapped.

Ayla was about to turn and lead the way out of the chamber when she felt something twist her stomach with fear. A cold dread descended around her and her skin crawled as though ghosts were caressing it. She looked at Luciffen and saw a shock and realisation dawn in his paling features.

Ayla's bow hummed into life, but it was already too late. Hundreds of Urks poured into the hall, their faces shining with malice and the wicked blades of their weapons glittering as they chanted and bellowed at Ayla and her companions.

'It's a trap!' Siren growled.

A moment later, they all heard the same sound. A deep, cruel, manic laughter that echoed it seemed through the entire chamber. Ayla turned as she heard the laughter surround them with a doom–laden aura of fury and hatred.

'Herric,' Cyril uttered with contempt. 'He must have sold us out!'

And then, finally, they saw the great wytch, Terra, appear.

## Thirty–Three

From the darkness on the far side of the temple Ayla saw a cloud of white light suddenly blossom into existence, with what looked like black fumes spilling from it. Unlike the other sorcery that Ayla had seen in the realm, this light was not warm but was more like the fierce white fury of lightning, dangerous and fast. Instantly, Luciffen moved to stand in front of them as the twisting vortex of light and oily shadows spiralled up into the vault of the chamber.

To Ayla, it seemed to overwhelm them with its size and power, and she felt only darkness and rage within it, cold and filled with dread as it began to descend. The light and smoke formed three distinct shapes that settled on the far side of the platform. Ayla watched as two Cerberus landed, their heads growling as they strained at leashes of flame still connected to the central cloud of light.

The cloud condensed before them, but even before it had formed its final shape Ayla saw movement from the corner of her eye. Two more Vipera slid into the chamber, their scaled bodies shimmering, and two huge ogres lumbered up the steps to flank Terra.

Terra's forces had filled the chamber below, far too many for them to even think about fighting their way out. To her horror, among them she saw a troll being dragged by several Urks, his shoulders slumped and his eyes filled with sorrow. Ellegen looked up at the Riders of Spiris and his shoulders sank further, as though his entire body were weighed down by the chains and manacles that entrapped him. Somehow, he had been caught by Terra's minions, and Ayla was sure she knew how.

Agry must also have betrayed them, for he had snuck out of their camp and met with the gargoyle that Ayla now felt sure had come from Chaoria.

Vigoran set Gallentia's limp body down on the stones at his feet and placed one hand on his sword, ready to defend her at any cost, and he moved position to stand between Terra and Ayla.

The fiery orb of light settled before them, and Terra's features became clearer as she materialised, standing no more than ten metres away. Ayla could feel a chill in the air as she got her first good look at the most powerful wytch in the Mirrorealm.

To say that Terra was beautiful was an understatement. Her face was porcelain smooth with high cheekbones and full, sculptured lips. Her eyes were green and as deep as eternity as they glared upon Luciffen and his companions, and her hair was ravenously long and spilled down her shoulders as black as oil. She would have been even more beautiful were it not for the pair of vipers slithering through her long black hair, watching them and hissing occasionally as Terra approached.

She walked with long, graceful strides, her hips swaying and her legs long beneath her black robes. Ayla thought that she looked like a cross between a supermodel and Dracula, and one small horn poked through her hair on the right side of her skull to complete her ghoulish appearance. When she spoke, her voice was both seductive and barbed with malice.

'Luciffen,' she purred, 'you come here now in such a weakened state? Do you no longer wish to live?'

The old sage smiled, apparently unafraid. 'I wouldn't wish to live through any reign of yours.'

'Good,' Terra replied, 'for that's what will come to pass.'

She reached out to touch the sage's face and Vigoran swung his blade into action. The weapon flashed like lighting as it plunged down toward Terra. The wytch barely moved, her eyes flicking to the right to look at the warrior as one of her huge ogres lunged with his club to deflect the attack.

Tygrin whirled and thrust his great axe out, the weapon smashing the ogre's club aside as Vigoran ducked beneath the weapon. His sword clanged against the club with a metallic ringing sound but was smashed aside. Ayla's breath caught in her throat as the ogre leaned in and with one great shove threw a stunned Vigoran down to the ground and placed one heavy boot on the warrior's chest.

Siren yelled in horror as she rushed to Vigoran's aid.

The ogre turned and glared at Siren as with one giant arm he swung at her. The blow caught Siren across the chest and hurled her to the ground. Jake shouted a war cry and drove his sword at Terra's chest in one smooth motion that was so fast that Ayla barely had time to realise what he had done.

Terra lifted one hand and wafted it toward the lethal blade, a metal bracelet on her wrist deflecting the weapon with ease. Jakes's sword flew from his grasp and clattered down the steps of the platform. Terra turned as Tygrin raised his axe to attack her, and with a ferocious snarl she threw one hand up and a brilliant flare of lighting blasted out and crashed into Tygrin's chest. The huge man sank to his knees as he was consumed by the blast, his face contorted with pain. A deafening crack of thunder reverberated around the chamber and suddenly the brilliant light and Tygrin vanished from view.

Ayla stared in disbelief as the ogre lifted the great club to bring it down upon Vigoran's head.

'Belay!' Terra snapped. The huge ogre held the club aloft above his head, his eyes ablaze with the need for blood, but he controlled himself and stepped back as Terra looked down upon the fallen king. 'I have use for them yet, when we attack their citadel.'

The Cerberus growled and snarled, straining against their leashes, but Terra did not release them as Ayla had expected she might. Instead, she waved her Urks forward.

The Urks rushed up the last few steps and swarmed among the Riders of Spiris. Ayla felt her bow ripped from her grasp, the Urks searching them for any weapons before they bound their wrists with rope and slammed them to their knees. Ayla kept the invisible knife clenched between her forefinger and thumb, and the Urks did not notice it. Terra walked up and down once they were kneeling before her in a row, gazing upon them with what might even have been pity.

'What fool would think that their feeble magic could allow them to sneak in the Towers of Vipera and steal my prize, the supposedly all–powerful White Wytch?' she asked rhetorically. 'What thick–fingered ape would believe that they could deceive Terra, Queen of Wytches?'

Terra glared at Luciffen and the snakes in her hair hissed and writhed.

'Your arrogance is your weakness,' Luciffen murmured as he knelt alongside Ayla. 'It will be your undoing.'

'Your undoing is already here,' Terra chuckled as she paced back and forth. 'I knew of your plan long before you put it into action. I knew that you would come for Gallentia, and I knew precisely how you would attempt to do it. That's *your* weakness, Luciffen. You believe that with unity and faith in others, in strangers, anything is possible, when so obviously you're already defeated and cannot win this battle or any other.'

'The battle is not yet fought,' Luciffen pointed out.

'And nor will it be,' Terra replied. 'Your Centaur was captured long before he could reach many of the tribes, and his fellow trolls in the mines are all on their way to the slaughterhouses because of his treachery.'

Ellegen's head hung low in shame and despair.

'I guided you here,' Terra hissed at them, 'I brought you all here on your pathetic little quest so that any army you managed to raise would be leaderless. The Mirror of Souls and Stormshadow Citadel will be mine and there is nothing that you can do about it.'

'I wouldn't bet on that,' Ayla said.

Terra turned and her cold gaze locked on to Ayla's.

'Ayla Fox,' she purred, 'such a heroine to have taken up such a challenge. I feared that you would not return after deciding to leave the realm, but then you surprised me. You have fulfilled your role well.'

'Leave her be,' Vigoran growled.

Ayla frowned in confusion. 'I chose to remain here.'

'You chose *nothing!* Terra snarled. 'The only reason you're here is because of me! The realm may have chosen you but I have directed your every step to this moment! How many other people do you know of who got struck by lightning twice in one day, fool?!'

Ayla's heart began to sink as she realised the depth of Terra's deception.

'Yes,' Terra murmured softly, 'you believe with all your heart that you are strong enough now, brave enough now, that you have come so far and that you can do anything. But, my dear, I did not pick you for those qualities. You see, Ayla, I needed somebody stupid enough to feel that someday they could become someone important.'

Terra's words pierced Ayla's heart like a lance.

'Yes, Ayla,' the wytch whispered. 'You were not chosen to be here because of your courage or your spirit. I hope that your mother is feeling better – I thought that her illness might prompt you to reconsider after you ran away like a whipped dog!' Ayla's heart felt as though it was being crushed by shame and guilt as the wytch sneered at her. 'I was able to ensure that you would return because you were *weak*.'

Terra glided closer, her eyes burrowing into Ayla's, her voice filling the chamber and the snakes in her hair hissing and writhing as they too locked their eyes on her.

'You are afraid to stand up for yourself. You are victimised by some and ignored by the rest. You hide behind your mother at the slightest provocation and even your own father walked away from your miserable little world!'

Ayla felt tears well up in her eyes as Terra leaned in close.

'You're not special, Ayla. I chose you because you are *nothing*, and you'll *never* be anything else.'

Ayla stared into those evil green eyes and all at once she felt the pain and the humiliation and sorrow of her entire life well up in one awful, overwhelming black tide of grief that spilled as bitter tears from her eyes.

Terra laughed, a mouth wide–open laugh that reminded Ayla of Tamsin's bullying at school, of Schwarz's casual cruelty and of all the suffering such people caused, and all at once she felt rage burn through her soul. It crashed through her grief and pain and regret and sorrow in a tidal wave of fury. Ayla turned the invisible knife in her fingers and sliced through the bonds that held her wrists as the rage bolted through her legs and she leaped to her feet.

Ayla swung the invisible blade with all of her fury into Terra's face before the wytch could react. Those beautiful, fearsome green eyes had time only to register a brief moment of panic before she was struck.

In slow motion Ayla saw the blade plunge down and Terra's flesh burst open with a flare of blinding light that seared Ayla's vision, the weapon slicing through the wytch's perfect skin. Ayla smelled a revolting gust of putrid, rotting flesh as the blade slashed Terra open and the great wytch's laughter mutated into a scream of agony as she reared back from the strike.

Ayla stepped back as Terra held her face with one hand, her scream echoing through the chamber, and then she let the hand fall away in horror. Her left cheek was an open, festering wound of dead flesh as old as the realm itself.

The chamber was filled with a horrified silence, even the Cerberus apparently shocked by what had happened.

Then, in an instant, Terra's shock turned to outrage. She shrieked, a piercing din like the cry of a bird of prey that filled the hall as she lunged with one hand at Ayla. A brilliant flare of fearsome white energy blasted out and crashed into Ayla's chest and hurled her off the platform with tremendous force, Vigoran's horrified cry following her.

'Ayla?!'

Ayla hurtled through the air over the heads of the Urks. Her chest heaved and she felt her consciousness waver as she plummeted down and then crashed through the huge windows on the far side of the chamber amid a shower of sparkling glass fragments.

Ayla tumbled out into the cold darkness and spiralled down toward the glowing molten moat far below as her vision darkened and she lost consciousness. She never felt the hard, muscular form that caught her in mid–air.

\*\*\*

## Thirty-Four

Ayla awoke to the sensation of warmth beneath her and a chill above, and her body felt as though it was moving through the air. It seemed as though she were adrift on a turbulent, dark ocean and she forced herself to open her eyes.

The dark sky above tumbled with black clouds and flashed with lightning, and far below the wilderness was forged from black rocks, the forests wilting. Ayla looked down and gasped in shock as she realised that she was riding on the back of a gargoyle, the same winged beast that she had seen Agry meet with the previous night. The creature seemed to realise that she was conscious and screeched, its cry echoing across the bleak wilderness below as if flew, its wings beating the air.

Ayla could hardly jump to her freedom so she hung on to the gargoyle's back as it soared through the frigid night toward a thin strip of light in the distance. Ayla looked behind her and saw the Towers of Vipera in the far distance and, far below them, a marching army of flickering torches and tens of thousands of Urks.

The gargoyle flew on and slowly they reached the light, Ayla suddenly acutely aware of just how much the darkness had grown even since the previous day. Valleys that had been lush and green the day before were now barren and bleak, and the drifting rainbow shafts of light were weaker and paler than before.

The gargoyle flew into the light and slowed, gliding now as it soared above forests that stretched as far as the eye could see. It travelled for perhaps half an hour before Ayla saw something emerging from the mists ahead.

The mountains framed a huge citadel that was forged in white stone and shone brilliantly whenever the light struck it. Ayla could see that it was surrounded by a moat rather like the Towers of Vipera, but this moat was of water that glittered in the light. The citadel was surrounded by open fields and forests, only a few tracks leading to and from it, and by its sheer size and grandeur she knew that this was the place that Luciffen and the others had mentioned so often: Stormshadow Citadel.

The gargoyle turned away from the huge fortress and descended, and Ayla became aware of a large encampment among the nearby forests, hundreds of tents and smoking camp fires. The gargoyle glided down, and Ayla could see archers and other warriors aiming their weapons up at the beast until they apparently recognised it.

The gargoyle headed for one of the larger tents, and Ayla hung on as it flared its wings and flapped them hard as the ground rushed up, then landed at a trotting pace and came to a stop before a large tent where a group of men were arguing. Each of them were wearing what looked like armour and tribal colours, leather and metal everywhere; huge beards, fearsome gazes and immense weapons strapped to their bodies.

'We cannot stop her with the forces we have!' said a large man with one eye missing and only two fingers on his right hand. 'We will be crushed and we cannot fall back on the citadel because of the damned Dragun inside it!'

The gargoyle walked toward them and the men turned to look at her. Ayla stared back at them and then she saw Agry, pouring over a map.

'You!' she snapped.

Ayla vaulted off the gargoyle's back and stormed across to the map table. Agry looked up and then at the gargoyle in disappointment.

'You only brought *her* back?'

'You betrayed us!' Ayla snapped as she clenched her fist and swung a punch at Agry's miserable face.

The warrior blocked the blow easily, twisting Ayla's wrist and pinning it against her back as he growled at her.

'How did you get out?'

'I flew out of a bloody window!' Ayla shrieked as she pushed herself away from him.

'What about the others?'

'Captured by Terra, she knew we were coming,' Ayla snapped, 'no thanks to you! You sent that Gargoyle to warn Terra!'

The other warriors all began shaking their heads and muttering at the news that Luciffen and Vigoran were now prisoners of Terra, but they did not react to the news that Agry was apparently a traitor.

'With the great Wizzerd and Vigoran gone, we'll stand no chance against those hordes,' said one.

'She'll crush us within the hour,' said another.

'My men won't stay on the field let alone fight,' said a third. 'Especially if Gallentia remains imprisoned in the Towers.'

'We must stand together!' Agry yelled and slammed a bunched fist down on the table.

Ayla stared at the warriors in confusion as she pointed at Agry. 'He betrayed us!'

Agry glared at her sideways. 'I've been using that gargoyle to keep an eye on the Towers of Vipera for weeks! It's provided valuable intelligence, and I felt sure that they were walking into a trap. Turns out I was right. I asked it to watch out for us, and it brought me back here when you and the rest of the loons entered the Towers. I take it that Herric didn't return to help, because he sure wasn't there when I would have needed him!'

'There were Draguns,' Ayla said defensively, 'maybe he couldn't wait any…'

'Maybe *he* betrayed you all,' Agry snapped, 'and yet you come all the way back here to accuse me of doing so!'

'What are you doing here? Why did you run?'

'I didn't run,' Agry snapped back. 'I knew Luciffen's plan wouldn't work. It was suicide. If they failed and I got caught with them there would be nobody left to organise the armies of Stormshadow, and I wouldn't trust a buccaneer like Herric as far as I could throw him. I came back here and found three tribes that Ellegen managed to contact before he was captured. Two more are on their way, but there's no time to reach the others. We have to make our stand here because if we don't, nobody will *ever* be able to make a stand anywhere again!'

Ayla began to wonder if she'd misjudged Agry, and she looked round at the gargoyle.

'You met that creature in the woods when we were at camp,' she said, still angry but no longer accusing.

Agry raised an eyebrow again, this time in surprise.

'The gargoyle was one I found as an injured infant that was abandoned or lost by its parents,' he explained. 'I nurtured it to health and it's served me well ever since. They look like stone carvings when they're still, so I used it to stake out Terra's towers in case I could learn of anything. I told it to keep an eye out for all of you after I came back here. It must have recognised you, although it's only been gone an hour so you were lucky it found you at all. How did you end up flying out of a window?'

Ayla swallowed her pride.

'I cut Terra's face and she hurled me through a window.'

The warriors around the table all looked up at that, stunned into a momentary silence.

'You cut her *face*?' one of them finally uttered in disbelief.

Ayla nodded. The warriors all exchanged glances.

'Terra's going to be right displeased about that.'

'This is going to make everything a lot worse.'

'Her *face*?' Agry uttered in astonishment. 'How did you even get close enough?'

Ayla hesitated, unsure of how much she wanted to say about Feeher's accusations. 'She made me very angry.'

The warriors all regarded her for a moment in awestruck silence, but then Agry waved her aside. 'Get out of here, we have work to do.'

'Terra has Luciffen and the Riders of Spiris captive,' Ayla snapped. 'You're going to sit here and just wait for her to show up with her army? What about that Dragun up there in the citadel. If we can find a mirror that…'

'That *what*?' Agry shouted. 'A mystical mirror against a hundred–foot Dragun, one of the most powerful beasts in the realm? Are you going to head up there and face it? And where the hell would you find a mirror forged by a dragon in the next couple of hours? I'm done with spells and mystics and wizzerds, they've achieved nothing but to allow Terra to become more powerful and create Draguns like that one up there! You might as well throw stones at it!'

'There's no other way,' Ayla insisted. 'This army doesn't stand a chance against Terra's hordes and…'

'What the hell would you know about any of it?' Agry roared. 'You've never fought in battle! You're just a Hybrin and not a very good one at that. You said that Terra led you to the towers and doing so got everyone caught, except you of course, the *golden* girl, the *chosen* one. You helped lead them to their deaths!'

Ayla felt the same crippling shame well up inside her that she had felt in front of Terra, but this time she was not being confronted by an enemy and the rage did not follow. Retorts filled her mind but she could not move, as though her humiliation had frozen her to the spot.

'No more wizzerds, sorcery or Hybrins! You're done here!' Agry snapped with a wave of contempt and he turned his back to her and went back to poring over the battle map.

Ayla felt tears in her eyes again and she wiped them angrily away and turned from Agry and the chieftains. None of them seemed interested in her now, more concerned with the imperilled future of their respective fiefdoms.

Ayla saw nothing but the army assembling before her, with no place for a Hybrin whom everyone now seemed to consider to be bad luck. She saw the gargoyle waiting patiently nearby, and she was suddenly struck with the need to get away, far away. Suddenly she hated Agry and the army whom she had tried so hard to support only to be rejected and alone. Just like she had been at school.

Ayla leaped onto the gargoyle's back, and the animal reared up and swivelled one eye around to look at her. She reached out and stroked its head, spoke to it in a soft voice.

'Just take me away from here would you, please?'

The gargoyle watched her for a moment, and then it turned and beat its wings and took off in powerful gusts that blew grass and debris over the map table.

'Oi!' Agry yelled. 'That's *my* gargoyle!'

***

## Thirty–Five

Ayla did not know in which direction the gargoyle was taking her except that they were travelling away from the darkness, and beyond that she didn't much care. They flew across the wilderness, low clouds drifting and tumbling as golden sunbeams pierced them and cast moving light across the landscape.

The freedom that had been so exhilarating to Ayla before now felt barren. She was alone amid a vast and untamed land, but she might just as well have been wandering the streets of her hometown, free–running through the estates to clear her mind.

The gargoyle flew on and she stroked its head a few times, the creature seeming to enjoy the affection as it nuzzled its head back against her hand like a cat, purring. She guessed that Agry was unable to show the creature anything approaching true kindness, the animal merely a means to an end.

Ayla saw a huge valley open up before her, a river weaving its way between forests and open glades, and with a start she realised that she was back where she had been when she had first arrived in Mirrorealm.

Ayla looked around and she saw the clearing where old Agnis' cabin had been, and sure enough she saw a patch of scorched earth where the Dragun had burned the cabin to ashes. She guided the gargoyle down into the clearing, and it landed obediently with great beats of its powerful wings that rippled the tall grass beneath them.

Ayla climbed off its back and wrapped her arms around its neck, hugging it for a moment. Its big, brown eyes looked fondly back at her and it made soft clicking noises in its throat as it rubbed its head against her chest.

Ayla walked across to the remains of the cabin and stared down at them, the gargoyle ambling after her. She could smell the scent of the ash but the cabin's remains were cold now. She had arrived here in this realm confused and alone, and now she was back where she started.

'I haven't achieved much, have I?' she murmured as she looked at the gargoyle and rubbed its head again. 'I should have stayed at home. I wouldn't have screwed everything up if I'd just stayed out of it.'

Terra had been right. She was a stranger in a strange land, and her presence had done nothing but get Luciffen and the others caught right at the moment they were needed the most. If she had stayed where she was, then they would have been preparing to fight Terra and the tribes might have gathered in greater numbers. Now, they faced certain defeat.

Ayla sank to her knees in front of the charred timbers of the cabin.

'I wish I was home.'

'But yee are, lassie.'

Ayla jumped in fright as Agnis shimmered into view before her, hovering over the ashes of her home with her hands clasped before her. Her apparition was even weaker now than before, and Ayla sensed somehow that Agnis was no longer as vibrant as she had been when they had first met.

'The darkness,' Agnis said, recognising the look on Ayla's face, 'it overpowers us all. I canny stay for long.'

Ayla looked over her shoulder and saw the darkened clouds looming ever closer. They would probably reach Stormshadow Citadel within the hour, and Terra's forces would charge upon Agry's army and crush them.

'Without the mirrors, the light fades,' Agnis said sadly, 'and with the light goes all that we are, even wee little Agnis.'

Ayla's shoulders sank. 'I should have stayed out of this. Terra used me to capture Luciffen and the riders.'

'Pah!' Agnis waved Ayla's shame away with a waft of her hand. 'That's the great wytch talking. She always seeks to make people feel at their worst, that's how she controls them. I know a thing or two young lassie, and I'd wager she said yee were nothing, useless, right?'

Ayla nodded. Agnis drifted closer to her, but Ayla could barely see Agnis's apparition now, her voice distant and distorted.

'That's what all bullies do, when they're afraid.'

'I haven't helped,' Ayla insisted, 'and I'm as alone now as I was when I first came here.'

Agnis sighed and shook her head.

'You should try being a spectre for a while, lassie, then you'll know the meaning of alone. But do you see wee Agnis belly aching about her lot? Nee, I get up and I get on with it. Look at my home, there's nothing left of it but ashes. But home is not where we live, it's whom we live *with*. I have friends, and so do yee. They're all around yee, if yee'd only see them.'

'They don't want me.'

'They do,' Agnis insisted, 'it's just easy to feel that they don't when things seem to go wrong. Do you hate other people and not want to be with them?'

'Not really, hardly anyone.'

'But some might feel that way and you wouldn't even know it. Good people always assume the worst about how others feel about them, while arrogant people always think they're loved by all. You're a good person, Ayla, I know it and deep down so do yee.'

'I can't help them,' Ayla said, 'and Agry doesn't want me there.'

'You're running away,' Agnis replied, 'and since when does Agry tell yee what to do? Yee have to pull yeeself together and understand that everything yee need is right here in front of you're eyes.'

Agnis's apparition flickered and faded from sight.

'Don't leave, Agnis,' Ayla pleaded as she saw her vanish. 'Not again.'

'It's you who should not be leaving,' Agnis whispered from oblivion. 'Yee are who yee are, Ayla, and the answers yee seek are right in front of yee…'

'Agnis?'

A soft wind whispered through the trees but she could not hear Agnis and she felt more bereft than ever. She sank back onto her knees and stared down at the cabin. She had failed, that much was obvious, and Agnis was just trying to make her feel better. There were no answers right before her eyes, only the shattered and scorched remnants of Agnis's cabin. Ayla couldn't even get up and go home again, the mirror in Agnis's cabin shattered after she arrived, and then the whole lot had been torched by that damned Dragun and…

Ayla stared for a moment at the ashes and then a sudden rush of thoughts blazed through her mind. *The answers yee seek are right in front of yee.* Agnis's mirror had been here among the debris when the Dragun had set the cabin aflame. It had been scattered across the floor, and Ayla had passed through it minutes before it was destroyed. She recalled Ellegen's mirror, in the labyrinth, of how it had glowed magically after she had passed through it.

Ayla crept forward and began shoving piles of ash and brittle black wood aside, and something caught the light. She picked up a shard of mirror, and her heart quickened as she saw it glinting with a faint blue light around its edges. Quickly, she found another matching piece and she pushed them together. The two pieces of the mirror forged into one with a little flash of light.

'Oh, Agnis,' Ayla whispered as sudden hope blossomed like rays of warm sunshine beaming through her heart.

She hunted through the debris, the gargoyle watching with interest as she rooted out piece after piece of the mirror and placed them back together. With each successive fragment added the flashes of light grew brighter, and she began to feel the mirror hum in her hands with an unseen energy. It took her almost an hour to find all of the pieces, the mirror drawing the smallest fragments out of the ash of its own accord as it grew stronger. Finally, she stood up and held the completed mirror in her hands. It was no larger than her torso, but it was complete and solid and as magical as anything she had yet encountered in the realm.

And then she thought of home.

She could sit here right now, stare into the mirror and focus on home just like Luciffen had told her, and be back in her room. It had taken only moments the last time, and she was sure a mirror like this one would be capable of it.

Then she recalled Luciffen's words; *a Dragun of that size can only be truly defeated by itself, its attack reflected back at it from a mirror forged in the fiery breath of another Dragun.*

'Do you know what this means?' she gasped to the gargoyle.

The creature did not respond as she stared at the mirror in her hands. She could run or she could fight. Go large, or go home. Herric had run away from them. She herself had fled the realm once before. Her father had run away from her life, vanished and abandoned her and her mother to face life and its challenges on their own. She recalled how that had made her feel.

Ayla wrapped the mirror inside Jake's blanket and hefted it onto her back. Then, she climbed up onto the gargoyle's back and turned the animal around, thinking hard. She could fly back to the citadel right now and attempt to take on the Dragun with the mirror, but that would still leave the army below to face Terra's hordes alone if she failed. They wouldn't last long against ten thousand Urks. There was only one way to defeat Terra, and that was with Gallentia liberated, the Dragun slain and the army trapped within the Mirror of Souls at their side.

She realised that what she was contemplating was near–suicidal, but then she also realised that Agnis had been right. She *was* worth something and she *could* do this, if for no other reason than to show the rest of the world that Ayla Fox could do something important enough to change things. To change everything. Ayla was determined that she would not abandon those who needed her.

But she would need help, and she knew precisely where she had to go.

'Fly!' she cried to the gargoyle as it opened its wings. 'To the Mines of Poisor!'

The gargoyle launched itself into the air and Ayla gripped the reins, determined to look Terra in the eye once again with the great wytch in defeat.

\*\*\*

## Thirty–Six

The darkness was moving swiftly across the land, and as the gargoyle flew back toward it so Ayla could see in the distance a line of light and flame as though the realm's forests were burning. It was only as she got closer that she realised that the vast sea of flame was in fact the countless tens of thousands of torches born aloft by the Urk army as it marched ever closer to Stormshadow Citadel.

The citadel itself was still bathed in light far to the west, but the darkness was almost upon it now. Ayla could see that the tumbling clouds above were unable to dim its beacon–like brightness. She could tell that there was little time remaining now before Terra's hordes charged upon the little army standing somewhere between it and the citadel. The Valley of Maryn Tiell, Vigoran had said to Ellegen before he had departed for the tribes. She remembered that someone had to have betrayed them for Ellegen to have been caught and for Terra to have been ready with her trap at the Towers of Vipera, but it could not have been Agry. She thought of the Riders of Spiris and went through their number one by one, but she could think of none who would have sided with Terra in this war, none who stood anything to gain from an alliance with the great wytch save one. Herric. If he had sold her the Griffons…

Ayla guided the gargoyle down into the blackened canyons of Chaoria as the wind chilled her and rain spilled from the turbulent skies. Below, she could see once healthy trees crumbling and turning black, their leaves falling from their branches in great torrents that were picked up by the wind and swirled in great funnels into the bleak distance. The gargoyle shifted this way and that in the turbulent air, balancing Ayla on its back as it flew down into the depths. Ayla could see the huge waterfall from which she had plunged from the mines with Ellegen, and she guided the gargoyle up in a gentle climb as she kept a careful eye open for any Draguns flying nearby.

She spotted the building above the waterfall and the gargoyle flew to a ledge and landed smoothly near the broken windows through which Ellegen had so heroically dove to save her life. Ayla leaped from its back and could see that the animal would not be able to make it far into the tunnels, too cumbersome on its legs to follow her far.

Ayla took what little dried meat she had left and gave it to the gargoyle, the creature gobbling the small meal while making soft clicking noises of delight. It fed from her hand without hesitation, and when it finished it nuzzled her neck and purred softly.

'Stay here,' she said, wondering if the creature understood.

She pointed at the ground at their feet, and the gargoyle looked at the spot and moved to it. Then it made a puffing sound and sat down, watching her expectantly.

Ayla rubbed its head and then turned and hurried into the tunnel. She had only made it half a dozen paces when she heard a whining noise and turned back.

The gargoyle's soppy big eyes were watching her, bereft, over the bottom edge of the windows.

'I'll be back soon, okay?' she promised. 'Stay there, and keep out of sight.'

Ayla saw the gargoyle curl its legs up beneath it and rest its chin on the stony ground, whining softly in despair. Its big eyes watched her with a forlorn gaze as she turned and hurried through the darkness.

The halls were as much of a maze as she recalled, the chandelier still laying on the floor and shattered into pieces. She slipped through the shadows and down the huge hall until she saw the entrance to the prison cells. The ogres were still at their posts and she waited for the right moment to slip past and squeeze through the bars and into the prison. Every step was laden with the fear that a Cerberus would cross her path, but soon she spotted in the distance the faint glow from torches lining the cells where the Centaurs were imprisoned. She hurried down the sloping tunnels into the heart of the mountain and slowed as she approached the cells.

Many of them were empty, the Centaurs either working in the mines or perhaps having been exiled or punished in some way by Terra. She crept through the tunnels and saw several trolls locked in their cells. As she approached, they saw her and their eyes widened in horror as they turned their backs to her.

Ayla hurried to the cell of the nearest troll and rattled the gate.

'You need to come with me,' she urged.

The troll kept his back turned. 'You're not there.'

'I *am* here, and I'm not going away!'

'We don't want you here,' the troll grumbled. 'You've caused enough trouble already!'

Ayla looked over her shoulder to see other trolls watching. They all averted their gazes immediately, not wanting to catch her eye.

'If you don't get out of here soon, you'll never leave!'

'If you don't get out of here soon, we'll not survive the day!' the troll shot back, his back still turned. 'Do you know what happened to Ellegen's family when you forced him out of here?'

Ayla's heart missed a beat and she felt latent fear well up in her soul. 'No.'

'They hanged them in the mines as a warning to others,' the troll replied. 'They're still there now, above the flames. They won't last more than a couple of days like that.'

Ayla felt rage pour through her, scalding her veins like fire.

'And yet you stand here with your faces turned to the walls, pretending that there's nothing that you can do about it!'

The trolls did not move, and Ayla spoke loudly enough that her voice echoed down the tunnels around her.

'I did not hang Ellegen's family, Terra did. I did not imprison you in these mines, Terra did. The only person in this realm responsible for all your suffering is her, and unless you stand up to her you'll be here forever!'

'We already did stand up to her!' another of the trolls bellowed. 'Look where it got us! If one rebels, then another is punished for it! We cannot stand for fear of bringing down others, and Ellegen thought of nothing but his own freedom when he fled with you!'

'Ellegen thought of nothing but his family!' Ayla shot back. 'He is no traitor, he's the only one who risked everything to save my life, someone he did not even know. *That* is who the Centaurs are to me!'

Ayla saw one or two of the trolls turn to look at Ayla as she stood in the tunnel.

'Terra gains power over people by turning them against themselves, by convincing them that they are less than they are, powerless, defeated. But none of you are defeated! You're here, now, alive! You say that if you rebel then others will suffer, but that only works if some do not rebel with you! Unity is the only thing that Terra is afraid of! It's the only thing that all dictators are afraid of. We are nothing when we are divided, but we are *everything* when we are united!'

The trolls began appearing at their gates of their cells, holding the bars and listening as Ayla marched up and down.

'If you accept that you are all trolls and not Centaurs, then Terra has won! She has defeated you. Out there, near Stormshadow Citadel, is a tiny army preparing to battle Terra's Urk hordes, for all of you and for every living thing in this realm! They're outnumbered and facing certain defeat, because nobody will stand to help them. Is that what Centaurs have become?'

'No,' growled a troll from nearby.

'Then stand up, all of you!' Ayla yelled.

To her amazement, almost every troll in the cells got to their feet and lumbered to their door as Ayla spoke her last, her fists clenched.

'Terra is now so powerful that if she wins this battle, both the realm and other worlds will be conquered and there will be no stopping her. If you do not stand now there will never be another chance! Terra doesn't know you're coming. The army of Stormshadow doesn't know you're coming! This is your chance to go into battle and show Terra that just when she thought you were defeated, you fought back the hardest! Are you going to stay here in your cells, or are you going to ride out there and show the realm who the Centaurs really are?' She looked at the nearest prisoner. 'Are you trolls, or are you Centaurs?'

'We are Centaurs.'

Another troll stepped to the gate of his cell. 'We are Centaurs!'

Another voice joined in, then another, then dozens more and then hundreds of others from other cell blocks until the tunnels filled with the roar of their voices.

*'We are Centaurs!'*

The Centaurs rocked their cell gates back and forth and bayed for their release. Ayla pulled the invisible blade and slashed through the giant padlock holding the nearest cell gate closed. The padlock fell to the ground and the troll inside lumbered out.

'There are others, in the mines,' he rumbled.

Ayla looked him in the eye as she began slashing other cells open to thunderous cheers. 'We leave nobody,' she insisted. 'If the Centaurs are to ride again, there can be none left for Terra to harm.'

The troll nodded and Ayla dashed away down the tunnel, the invisible blade in her hand slashing through metal padlocks, the tunnels echoing to the sound of falling metal and enraged trolls roaring and beating their chests.

\*\*\*

## Thirty–Seven

Ayla ran with the trolls behind her and they thundered into the mines in an immense flood of muscle and rage. The vast vertical shaft was filled with trolls labouring at the rock faces, massive ogre guards watching over them, the entire shaft flickering in the light from hundreds of flaming torches.

Ayla ducked to one side as she saw a huge ogre guard in surprise to see the prisoners rushing toward it. The ogre lifted its club but before it could swing the weapon the prisoners crashed into its legs and toppled the great beast. The guard hit the ground on its back and the trolls swarmed over it, beating it with their fists and pick axes.

The prisoners working in the mines saw the commotion and instantly they realised that a full–blown riot was in progress. Ayla had feared that they would sit down and do nothing, hoping to avoid Terra's wrath, but the sheer numbers of prisoners flooding into the mine was so great that she saw them leap up and smash their own manacles off with their tools as they heard the chants of the rioting trolls.

'We are Centaurs! We are Centaurs!'

The great ogre guards roared and swung their clubs at the rampaging prisoners, but they were overwhelmed and brought down one by one in clouds of dust as the trolls took their tools to them in frenzied clouds of blows. Ayla watched as throughout the mines the ogres were toppled to cheers from the enraged trolls, then she turned and descended through the mine as she sought some sign of the captive family of Ellegen. She found them within minutes, at the very bottom of the mine.

They were no longer under the curse that Terra had placed upon them, their troll forms gone and their graceful equine bodies bright white in the glow of the lava that flowed below them in the depths of the mine, but that was where their glory ended. Their wings were pinned to their bodies with thick ropes and metal chains, and they were suspended over a lake of fire by taut wires, trussed up like the victims of some horrendous spider waiting to devour them. Their manes were lank and their eyes closed, their bodies drenched in sweat that glistened in the glow from the flames below. She could see a male, a female and a foal that was barely conscious.

Ayla leaped onto the rock face and clambered along the ropes that held them in place, climbing high above the churning molten rock below. Her movements alerted them to her presence, as did the commotion in the mines around them, and they opened their eyes and watched her as she approached.

Ayla had the knife between her teeth, giving her features an unusual grimace as she reached the first of three Centaurs trapped in the ropes. She cut through the thick ropes with ease and they frayed and parted enough for the Centaur to struggle free. The male turned and dropped from its bonds, its wings spreading enough for it to glide to safety and land on one side of the shaft.

Ayla methodically cut the female free, her long blonde hair damp with sweat, but as she hung inverted from the tangle of ropes the Centaur begged Ayla:

'Not me, my child first!'

Ayla turned and saw the young foal, and she scrambled over the mother and began cutting the youngster free. She knew that it would not be able to fly itself to safety and she turned in time to see the male lift off again and fly up toward them. Ayla cut the foal free and it fell into the male's arms to be carried to safety.

Ayla turned and saw the female Centaur smile at her weakly as the frayed ropes holding it aloft spun apart.

'No!'

The ropes holding the Centaur failed, snapping all around Ayla, and she saw the female plummet from the ropes toward the lake of fire below. Ayla screamed in horror as the graceful animal plunged toward certain death, and then she saw the gantries to her right topple. The huge assembly collapsed across the shaft as the trolls deliberately cut through its legs, and the entire gantry smashed down above the lake of fire.

The Centaur landed heavily on the maze of scaffolding, the gantry sagging beneath its weight, and then the male Centaur rushed back in, its huge wings beating as it hovered above the fallen Centaur and lifted her clear of danger.

Ayla turned and clambered back to the ground as the rescued Centaurs were tended to by their brethren. The commotion above had died down and she saw the body of an ogre plunge down from the heights and crash into the molten lava, the burning corpse sinking amid vicious flames.

'What now?' one of the trolls demanded, his face sheened with sweat and drool. 'As soon as we leave, Terra will come for us.'

'Terra is otherwise engaged,' Ayla replied, 'and the last thing she expects is for us to come charging at her. We leave this place and make sure it can never again hold prisoners like this. Then, you'll get your chance to take revenge on Terra for all that she has done.'

Ayla stepped to one side and looked up through the towering catacomb of the mine, where now hundreds of liberated trolls lined the walkways and looked down at her expectantly. Ayla called up to them at the top of her lungs, letting the enormous mine amplify her voice as it echoed up and down.

'Take all of the pieces of the mirror that you've found and cast them into this lake of fire, so that Terra can never use them! She'll be outraged and she'll seek to destroy each and every one of you, so nothing's changed except that you're now free to take the fight to her! Are you all ready for a war?!'

A deafening crash of cheers soared down from the heights, and Ayla saw a billion fragments of the ancient star sparkle down through the mine shaft and plummet into the molten lava at its base. Mirrors from the prison cells flashed as they rushed down and plunged into the molten rock to melt into the liquid, lost forever. Ayla turned to the trolls nearest to her.

'Let's go.'

One of the freed Centaurs, the female with the flowing blonde mane, stepped forward and lowered her forelegs in an invitation for Ayla to climb onto her back.

'Are you sure?' Ayla asked, concerned that the Centaur would have been weakened by her captivity.

'You freed us,' she replied, the young foal by her side, a girl of perhaps seven or eight years of age. 'Now let us do the same for you.'

Ayla didn't hesitate any longer and she climbed aboard the Centaur. The Centaur turned and flexed her wings in the heat, and then with a mighty leap and beating of her wings she soared upward through the mine. Ayla held on as they climbed steeply, circling as they went and riding the thermal updrafts from the lake of lava. The other two freed Centaurs flew with them, and to either side Ayla could see countless trolls lumbering up the gantries toward freedom, still entrapped in their gruesome bodies but yearning now to be free as they tossed their weapons into the pit of fire far below and flooded toward the exits.

With the weapons, Ayla saw thousands more fragments of mirrors tumble like sparkling dust into the lake of fire to the cheers of hundreds of trolls.

The Centaurs flew to the upper tiers of the mine, where hundreds of their brethren were battering their way through the gates of the prison. As they flew toward the huge gates, Ayla sensed the evil just the other side and she saw a pair of Cerberus snarling at the escaping prisoners. The huge gates creaked and strained as the trolls battered them with their tools and weapons and suddenly the locks and hinges failed and the gates crashed inward.

The trolls charged over the fallen gates in their hundreds and the Hell Hounds suddenly turned and fled as they were overwhelmed by the sheer number of escaping prisoners. Ayla squealed in delight as the Centaur she was riding flew through the gates and soared around to the right, following the same route as she had done in escaping the mine.

The amassed trolls beneath them suddenly were consumed in a shimmering halo of bright orange embers of light that spilled in torrents from their bodies as they ran. Ayla watched in amazement as one by one they broke free of Terra's magic and the flood of lumbering, awkward trolls became a tremendous wave of light barrelling toward the exit.

Ayla ducked as her Centaur dived down and flew into the hall, and almost at once Ayla saw the gargoyle awaiting them by the smashed windows. The animal got to its feet and seemed about to flee when it spotted Ayla on the back of the nearest Centaur.

'Time to leave!' she yelled ahead.

The gargoyle spread its wings and leaped from the ledge as Ayla's Centaur reared up. She clawed at the air with her hooves and shattered the windows in a cloud of glass fragments. Ayla yelped in delight as the Centaur soared free of the darkness and out over the plunging valley, clouds of glass falling around them. Ayla looked behind her and saw hundreds of trolls pour from the hall and plummet into the canyon outside as countless windows shattered. Their troll forms vanished and they spread their hundreds of wings in a deafening boom as they became a flock of white-winged Centaurs pouring from the mines. They soared and wheeled over the canyon and climbed to follow Ayla into the tumultuous skies.

'Where is Ellegen?' the Centaur beneath her asked.

'A prisoner of Terra,' Ayla replied. 'They're heading for Stormshadow Citadel!'

The Centaur needed no prompting and turned for the west at once, and in the far distance Ayla could see beneath the darkened clouds a faint beacon of light, like a defiant star shining alone in an immense darkness. The gargoyle flew alongside them, and on an impulse Ayla stood up and leaped across onto the gargoyle's back and ruffled its feathers

She looked over her shoulder once again and her breath was taken away by the sight of the huge black canyon behind them, and against it hundreds and hundreds of white Centaurs flocking into the sky.

\*\*\*

## Thirty-Eight

The army of the Queen of Wytches marched toward the beacon of light that was Stormshadow Citadel, trudging endlessly on to the mournful hymns of the Urks in their tens of thousands behind them.

Luciffen had never felt so weak. His staff, along with all of their weapons, was in Terra's possession now and without it his already fading power was severely depleted. That would have been bad enough, but the darkness around them was now so powerful, so overwhelming that he felt physically drained, each step taking a little more out of him on the long and arduous journey.

Terra had placed them at the front of the army, forcing them to walk as a human shield against any frontal attack that the tribes might attempt. Luciffen knew that the tribes, if they had gathered at all, would not open fire from a distance for fear of hitting either himself or the Riders of Spiris. Of course, if Agry had made it back and was now commanding the defence of Stormshadow Citadel, then it was possible that he might direct his attack just the same and to hell with the consequences.

To his right, Gallentia was still chained to the shard of ragged rock, her head up now but her power likewise heavily drained. To see his daughter in such dire straits caused his heart to ache in his chest, knowing that he was powerless to help her. Beside him, Vigoran and the Riders of Spiris likewise were manacled and forced to walk at the head of the army. Even the younger members such as Siren and Cyril were there, Jake between them. With both Agry and Tygrin gone, they seemed as adrift and broken as Luciffen felt.

Luciffen knew in his heart of hearts that they were out of options now. They could not prevent Terra from expanding her reign to the entire realm and beyond. There was little that could be done in Ayla's world to combat the spread of the evil now dominating the realm. It had been the perfect deception, using Ayla, an unwitting and unexpected Hybrin, as a means to draw them all into her trap.

His last hope would have been to have sent Vigoran back into Ayla's realm to attempt to change things there and perhaps tip the balance in their favour, but now his magic was too weak to even think about attempting such a feat. Besides, both he and Vigoran knew what had happened the last time they had risked such a venture.

'There is an army waiting,' Vigoran said.

Luciffen could not see well enough, but he trusted the King's vision better than his own. As they walked, gradually he began to see a faint cloud of dislodged dust in front of the vast citadel dominating the horizon before them. As they crested the top of a slope, they were afforded a panoramic vista of the valley ahead and Stormshadow Citadel.

The citadel itself looked just as he remembered it, grand and imposing, the home of all the world that he had known and everything he had held dear. The light seemed to shine from it like a beacon that was both bright and yet welcoming, and even the darkness surrounding it in all directions was not strong enough to weaken its glow.

Near the citadel, in the valley, he could see an army arrayed in multiple units, ragged banners flying in the wind. Weapons of cold, bright metal glinted in the light, and although he reckoned there to be two thousand men and horses before them, he knew Terra's army to be ten times that number of Urks even without the Draguns and ogres accompanying them.

Across the sky beams of light drifted across the landscape, weaker now than they had ever been. Terra's victory was within her grasp. Luciffen looked up to the heights of the citadel, and there he could see a faint haze of smoke and flame wherein the great Dragun guarded the Mirror of Souls.

Vigoran was silent as he surveyed the army. Luciffen knew that he would be assessing its strength and position, but even as a non–warrior he could tell that they would be crushed within the hour. Agry, who whomever commanded them, had chosen to abandon the high ground because of the presence of the Draguns. Forced to hold the low ground near the river, Terra's charge would smash them and they would easily be flanked.

'They should retreat,' Luciffen said finally. 'There's nothing more that they can do here.'

But Vigoran's response surprised him.

'Agry is leading them,' he said, 'look, you can see his standard at the centre.'

Luciffen squinted and recognised the House of Draye colours fluttering in the cold wind.

'But if *he* did not betray us…?' Luciffen said, confused.

Vigoran shrugged, uncertain himself of what to think, but Terra broke across all their thoughts as she called down to them.

'Any last words for your friends before they're slaughtered by my Draguns?'

Luciffen turned and looked behind him at the Great Wytch. She stood on a chariot of flames, one hand holding the reins of a team of Cerberus that stomped and snorted, excited by the tension in the air and the promise of blood and battle.

Luciffen was about to reply, but then he saw something from the corner of his eye and he smiled softly. He did not dignify Terra with a response and he simply turned his back to her. Terra's cry echoed out across the lonely battlefield like that of a bird of prey.

'Destroy them!'

Luciffen heard a terrible screech as over their heads flew four Draguns, their bat–like wings beating the air and their tails swishing behind them as they accelerated toward the army in the valley below.

\*

'She's sending in the Draguns!'

The cry went up from the front line and Agry saw the four creatures fly over the enemy forces and plunge down toward them.

'Water bearers at the ready!' he yelled. 'Snares ready!'

The warriors at the front line yelled their responses as one. The river at their back was part of Agry's plan, manned pumps sucking water out of the river under pressure. Hoses were held by teams who now aimed them at the onrushing Draguns while others swirled weighted snares in the air in the hope of bringing the savage beasts crashing to the ground. Agry knew that it was dangerous to surrender the high ground so early in the battle to Terra's forces, but without the water the small army would be defeated by the Draguns alone long before the Urks charged.

The Draguns rushed out of the sky and their great mouths opened, streams of fire tearing across the front lines. The terrible flames crashed into the army, billowing and raging through their ranks. Rows of soldiers crouched behind their shields as snares were hurled high into the air and flames washed over the men in a hellish blast of heat.

'Hoses, now!' Agry yelled.

The hoses were opened up and water jets blasted the Draguns as they soared overhead and wheeled around in the turbulent skies. Clouds of steam burst from the animal's bodies as they flew through the streams of water. Two of the snares caught a Dragun's wing but it beat the wing hard as it climbed and the snares burned through. The other three dragons trailed clouds of steam behind them as they climbed away, but the water quickly boiled off their scalding bodies and they turned back.

Agry saw the Draguns dive down again, and this time the water hoses were not ready and he could see there was no way to defend against the charge. A thick plume of lethal flame seared the front ranks of the army and Agry saw dozens of soldiers writhing in flames as the Draguns criss–crossed the ranks.

'Fall back!' one of the chieftains yelled. 'Fall back to the water!'

Agry saw a Dragun rush toward them and it opened its mouth to blast them with lethal flame. The army's ranks broke in panic as the tribes' courage failed them.

'Hold firm!' Agry yelled.

The Dragun opened its fearsome jaws and blasted the soldiers as they fled, flame ripping through them. Agry staggered backwards and the Dragun landed within ten metres of him and glared with cruel eyes as he drew his sword and shield. The Dragun opened its jaws and plunged toward him.

And then a cloud of nets dropped from the heavens and tangled themselves around the Dragun, pinning it to the ground. Agry looked up in surprise into the tumbling clouds as he heard a great cheer rise up from the army.

***

## Thirty-Nine

'Charge!'

Ayla's cry carried far and wide on the gusting wind as the Centaurs plunged out from the cloud cover and thundered down toward Terra's massive army. Ayla and the leading Centaurs all headed directly for the Draguns soaring over the heads of Agry's forces, and she could see the strips of fearsome flame sweeping like a scythe through the ranks as she plunged down.

Ayla picked out one of the Draguns as it landed amid the carnage and she hauled a trapping net from her waist and swung it around over her head. The gargoyle beneath her charged bravely down, and Ayla pulled up at the last moment as she hurled the weighted net at the Dragun.

The huge net expanded out as the weights pulled it open, and as she rushed overhead she saw the net slam down around the beast and tangle in its wings and its neck. The gargoyle pulled up into a steep climb, and Ayla looked over her shoulder to see the Centaurs raining flaming arrows down on the Urks, forcing them to crouch and take cover beneath their shields. Deep among their front ranks she could see Vigoran, Luciffen and the others all manacled together, held at the front as human shields, with Gallentia still chained to the rock and Ellegen still in his troll form. The Centaurs were charging in but the defensive ring around the captives was deep and well-armed.

Ayla hauled the gargoyle around and dove in toward them. She could see Terra's glowing chariot further back from the front line, the great wytch screaming at the Urks as she directed their defence against the unexpected aerial bombardment.

'Crush them! Crush them all!'

The Urk army let out a blood chilling howl of battle lust that echoed across the valley as they broke ranks and charged Agry's forces, pouring down the hillside like a black wave filled with flashing swords, spears, axes and pikes.

Ayla dropped low over the Urks as the Centaurs pulled up from their attack, and she reached for the blade that had served her so well. She gripped the weapon in one hand as she dove down and aimed directly at Vigoran and Luciffen, who were trapped amid the Urks rushing past them.

The Urks came up from behind their shields, screaming in rage at the Centaurs. They didn't see the gargoyle rushing in from their side until the last moment. The animal beat its wings to slow down and then ploughed straight through the Urks, hurling them to either side like a meteor crashing through a forest as it landed directly behind Vigoran and Luciffen.

Ayla slashed the bonds that held the king and the sage, the metal chains clattering to the ground as two huge ogres whirled and charged in. Vigoran and

Jake turned to face them, and Ayla grabbed another net and hurled it at the closest of the Urk ranks as they swarmed between the legs of the ogres. The net unfolded and crashed down around them, pinning at least a dozen of them to the ground.

Vigoran moved with tremendous speed and ferocity. He rushed past her and disarmed an Urk of his sword at the first encounter and then drove it straight through the heart of the next Urk before it could bring its weapon to bear. Ayla saw Jake smash two Urks aside with his fists, and he grabbed a scythe from one of them and twirled it in a hurricane of flashing metal.

An ogre charged at Ayla, his face filled with murderous rage, and he swung his club at her head.

Ayla barely had time to react and she threw herself from the gargoyle's back. The club swept through the air just above the gargoyle, missing her by inches. She hit the ground hard, rolling over to get away, but the impact had winded her and her vision blurred as she tried to get to her feet.

'Ayla?!'

Luciffen staggered back from the giant's advance, his own features filled with horror as the ogre raised the club once again and bought it crashing down toward them.

The gargoyle hurtled in from the side and ploughed into the ogre, hurling the creature onto its hairy, hunched back. Ayla scrambled to her feet as the ogre swung its club into the gargoyle's side and the animal squealed in pain and staggered sideways.

Ayla dashed forward as the ogre got to its feet and growled as he swung the club at her, seeking to take off her head with one mighty blow. Ayla ducked, and she held up the tiny knife in her hand. The huge club swung through the air and the wooden shaft passed through the blade. It sliced through as cleanly as a hot knife through butter and half of the club spun away through the air to crash into the ranks of Urks charging past them in the confusion.

The ogre roared in fury and lunged toward her, his massive hands outstretched for her throat. Ayla danced backwards out of his reach and sought an escape route, but they were surrounded by running Urks and there was nowhere to run. The ogre yanked a sword from the dead hands of an Urk and with a roar he plunged the weapon down toward her.

A flash of metal flickered before Ayla's eyes and she saw the ogre's blow deflected by another sword. She turned, and saw Vigoran's cold blue eyes glaring from beneath the hood as he parried the blow and stepped in, one elbow jabbing into the ogre's face as he drove the big creature backwards.

Vigoran's blade flashed in the light, his moves far too fast for the ogre to counter. Vigoran moved with cold precision, stepping left and countering the ogre's clumsy attack while driving a boot into the big creature's ankle and thrusting the edge of his blade at the ogre's neck. The ogre leaned back to avoid the blow, and Vigoran swept the blade downward as he turned a full circle and sliced through the back of the ogre's leg. The creature let out a roar of pain as its leg collapsed beneath it and it fell to one knee.

Vigoran whirled as the ogre tried one last time to cut him down, the blade flashing as it swung around for Vigoran's belly. Vigoran twisted aside from the blow and then stepped inside the ogre's weapon and thrust his blade straight through the ogre's massive heart.

Ayla's own heart missed a beat in horror, but then the ogre's eyes lit up with hellish flames and she saw his huge form mutate in an oily black cloud. The huge ogre breathed its last before it fell onto its back, its body decaying rapidly into soil and stone before their very eyes. Vigoran's blade slipped from its body and the warrior king hurried to Ayla's side.

'Are you all right?'

Ayla got to her feet, confused but unhurt. 'I'm okay.'

To one side, she saw Jake cut Gallentia down from the rock as beside her Ellegen was suddenly consumed once more by brilliant halos of light. His troll form vanished and from the halo of light Ellegen burst forth, his wings spreading as he reared up and his hooves crashed down on the charging Urks, trampling them.

'Ellegen!'

The Centaur responded to Vigoran's call and galloped to his side as the warrior heaved Gallentia's weary body onto his back.

'Take her to safety!'

Ellegen whirled and his great wings beat the air as he launched himself away from them and flew up into the turbulent sky, joining the hundreds of Centaurs that were battling to hold the Draguns back.

'Riders, on me!' Vigoran yelled.

Around them, the Riders of Spiris began regrouping and rallying on Vigoran. Ayla hurried to the gargoyle and saw it get to its feet, a ragged red gash down its flank where the ogre had struck it. She hugged it closely and the animal purred into her ear as she stood back and held its great head in her hands.

'Can you fly?' she asked it, as though it could understand.

The gargoyle's tail swished enthusiastically and Ayla leaped onto its back.

'Ayla!' Luciffen called. 'Where are you going?'

Ayla pointed to Agry's forces down the valley, where the Urk army was charging toward their front line.

'I can't help here, but there is one thing that I can do to bring Terra's army down! He needs more reinforcements!'

Luciffen knew instantly what she was planning because he shook his head vigorously.

'It's too dangerous Ayla, you can't do it alone!'

Vigoran saw her and cried out above the din of battle. 'Ayla no, I can't protect you if you leave! Stay here!'

Ayla did not listen to him as she turned the gargoyle and it lifted off and climbed above the battlefield. She saw below the Urks charge toward Agry's army and collide with its front line, could hear their hellish screams and the clattering of metal against metal as they crashed into one another. They mixed like a lake of seething oil filled with razor blades, weapons flashing in the rapidly fading light.

Ayla turned the gargoyle and headed directly for Stormshadow Citadel.

\*\*\*

## Forty

Against the turbulent sky Jake saw hundreds of Centaurs soar overhead, their graceful white forms soaring like angels above the sea of hell. The remaining Draguns wheeled around to face them but swathes of nets fell down around them, threatening to trap their wings and bring them down to the ground. A torrent of arrows swept across the Urk forces as the Centaurs opened fire. Three of Terra's Draguns crashed down onto the ground, trails of scalded grass behind them as their wings were entrapped amid the burning nets.

'Slay them, before they can rise!' Agry yelled, his voice audible even above the din of battle.

The army charged forward and soldiers hurled spears and axes into the grounded beasts, killing them where they lay. Vigoran fought his way to Jake's side and cut their bonds, freeing Cyril and Siren at the same time as Luciffen handed them their weapons.

'There isn't much time,' Vigoran snapped. 'We must help Agry hold the line! Protect Cyril, we'll need him! I'll stay with Luciffen!'

Jake ran in pursuit of the King with Cyril close behind him, but the Draguns were already dead and the Urks were bearing down upon the army in a wave of screams and flashing weapons.

'Get behind me, stay close!' Jake said to Cyril as they ran in pursuit, cutting Urks down to either side.

Cyril moved close behind Jake's right shoulder, but he stayed clear enough that he would not crowd the soldier's movement. Jake looked up and saw a gargoyle climbing high into the sky. He squinted and saw Ayla still on its back, urging the creature on as her hair flew in the wind.

'Where's she going?' Jake uttered.

Cyril looked up and saw where the gargoyle was flying to, and he knew in his heart of hearts that there was only one reason she would be flying directly toward Stormshadow Citadel.

'She's going to take on the Dragun,' he replied.

'She's going to *what?*'

Cyril had no time to reply as the Urks crashed into the army's lines and smashed their way through the front ranks with the momentum of their charge. Jake saw Urks being hurled up into the air by the shields of the front rank, their ungainly limbs clawing the air, only to come crashing down on the heads of soldiers further back.

An Urk charged direction and swung a mace at Jake's head. The young soldier ducked beneath the blow and drove his sword straight through the Urk's chest.

Jake yanked the weapon free again and spun to one side, turning through a half–circle and swinging his sword to slice the head off another Urk alongside the first, who had dropped to his knees clutching his fractured heart.

Hundreds of the ungainly creatures flooded toward them, far too many for Jake to confront all at once, and Cyril closed his eyes and murmured in ancient Realmic.

'Aquam ad restinguendum ferret malum ortum!'

From the ground beneath the Urks water suddenly swelled in thick pools that bubbled and churned around their boots. The soil turned to mud and slush across the battle line and as one the entire Urk charge slowed, their thick legs mired in the gloopy mud as Cyril held them at bay.

'Forward!' Agry yelled as he saw the charge falter, and spurred his horse into motion.

Agry's cavalry lunged through the ranks and galloped onto the field, blasting through the ranks of sluggish Urks with their swords swinging this way and that, cutting down the Urks by the dozen.

Jake turned and looked toward Stormshadow Citadel, and there he saw the gargoyle land on the fields near the base of the fortress.

'She's down!' he said to Cyril. 'The gargoyle must be injured. She needs our help!'

He turned to look at Cyril, but the young sage was wafting his hands this way and that, wandering around with his eyes closed. Wherever he directed his hands, the legs of Urks were snatched from beneath them and they toppled into the mud, writhing as the blades of tribal warriors killed them where they lay.

Jake dashed through the battle, swinging at Urks as he passed by. He had no idea what Ayla thought she was doing, but he knew that she could not single–handedly take on a fully grown Dragun and hope to win.

*

Ayla climbed off the gargoyle's back, and she could see right away that the poor creature could go no further. The gash in its side was wide and deep and leaking blood, and its chest was heaving with the effort of flying.

'You've done your best, my brave little gargoyle,' she whispered in its ear as she pointed to a nearby glade that flanked the river. 'Go there and rest, there's no more that you can do for me now.'

The gargoyle looked at the river and trotted wearily off toward the promise of water and rest as Ayla turned and looked at the ancient white walls towering over her. They rose up to immense heights, and their spires and towers rose up even further, capped by the dirty cloud of fumes and smoke that was the Dragun's lair.

Ayla ran to the moat and picked the narrowest spot before she slipped into the water and swam for the far side. It only crossed her mind half–way across that there might be some horrible creature or other stalking the moat, another deterrent against an attack by Terra's forces, but she reached the other side without encountering anything.

The walls rose up almost sheer before her, but they were built from huge panels of rock that were filled with fissures and imperfections. In fact they looked just like the gaps in the buildings she had used to climb and free–run across the estates back home. She dashed forward, her eyes scanning the walls for the best way up, and leaped into a crevice. She clambered upward, lithe and quick, climbing farther up the walls. She scrambled from gap to gap, her limbs aching and her lungs burning but her determination undiminished as she scaled the heights.

The sounds of battle became fainter as she climbed, replaced by the cold howl of the winds and then by something else, the sound of countless souls crying out for release from their suffering. The Mirror of Souls was somewhere above her in the towers and she could hear the cries of those entrapped within. Ayla could not help but feel disturbed at the nature of their suffering, as though they were entrapped in a world where nothing made sense, where cause did not precede effect and where time did not flow as it should.

Ayla reached a parapet far above the ground and she gratefully clambered inside and landed within a small chamber that seemed to be some kind of storage room, filled with barrels and boxes. She turned and looked out over the battlefield and her heart sank as she saw Agry's army surrounded on three sides and being driven back toward the river. Centaurs dived and rose again like birds of prey feasting on the black hordes of Urks, but they and Agry's forces were hopelessly outnumbered. She knew that if they were pinned against the water they would be slaughtered, and she could see that the Centaurs were struggling to prevent Terra's forces from spreading out either side of the army and crossing the river. If the defending forces were flanked, it would be over and the Urks, ogres and Terra would reach the fortress.

A face popped up in the opening and she almost screamed as Jake lurched into view from below.

'Get out of the way!' he gasped. Ayla jumped back as Jake crawled through the parapet and collapsed onto the stone floor, his chest heaving and his brow sheened with sweat. 'Jeez, Ayla, since when were you Spiderwoman?'

Ayla shook herself from her amazement and helped Jake to his feet.

'I can defeat the Dragun,' she said.

'How?'

'I'll tell you later, but we need to hurry or Agry's going to be overrun.'

Together they hurried to the storage room's door, but it was locked. Jake heaved on it and shoved it with his shoulder, but he couldn't make it budge.

'Damn it, we climb a hundred feet okay but we can't get through a single door,' Ayla uttered.

Jake looked at the base of her neck. She looked down, and saw the Dragun's tooth there that Agry had so reluctantly given to her. Ayla took it off and pressed it against the wooden door, and immediately a patch in the centre of the door burst into flames. Thick smoke billowed from the blaze as it spread and they stepped back, crouching down to stay below the smoke until Jake was sure the door had weakened. He got up and hurled himself at it and the door blasted outward in a billowing cloud of smoke and embers.

Jake tumbled out into a stone corridor and Ayla followed, stamping out the flames as Jake got to his feet. They were standing in a hallway that smelled musty, as though nobody had walked here in many years. Ayla could see dust on the stone flags and cobwebs draped upon walls and light fixtures.

Through the halls she could hear the voices crying out, echoing through the darkness. One voice in particular called out to her, more familiar than the others, and she finally realised who she could hear.

'Tygrin,' she whispered. 'He's imprisoned in the Mirror of Souls.'

'Gotta feel sorry for the rest of them stuck in there with him, if you ask me.'

Jake stood alongside her, his sword drawn and ready, and Ayla turned and walked along the hall toward the relentless cries.

\*\*\*

## Forty-One

'Hold the line!'

Agry leaped from the saddle of his horse and twisted aside from an Urk's savage thrust with a pike, then pinned the pike against the ground with his boot as he yanked his sword up with all of his strength and severed the Urk's head clean off its shoulders.

He whirled and drove the same sword through another Urk's chest as he saw Siren twirling her staff over her head as she danced through the battlefield, lithe as a cat. The blurring staff flipped and smashed an Urk's head aside and then Siren turned on one heel and drove the wickedly tipped blade on the end of the staff through another Urk's throat.

Agry leaped to her support and together they battered the advancing hordes aside around them, the Urks like a river swirling around two rocks. Agry saw Vigoran through the dense battlefield, Luciffen at his side casting spells this way and that to hold the more numerous Urks at bay. The Riders of Spiris were forming a ring, side by side in the centre of the battlefield, and holding back countless hundreds of Urks.

'They're being surrounded!' Siren yelled as she spotted Vigoran and his men close by.

Agry did not reply but he could see that it was not only the Riders of Spiris that were being encircled. The entire army was being driven back toward the river, and even with the Centaurs in support their flanks were in danger of being turned.

Two more Draguns appeared above the battlefield and began sweeping in for their attacks, flames blazing from their mouths and slashing through the tribal army. Smoke and flame billowed in a trembling heat haze above the battle, and behind the advancing Urk hordes Agry could see Terra astride her hellish flaming chariot. The vipers in her hair hissed and spat as she advanced with a grin of malicious delight shining on her face.

Agry felt his blood boil at the sight of her and he looked up at the Draguns. One of them wheeled through the sky to the right of the army and turned, coming back in for another pass.

Agry whirled and grabbed the first horse that he could find, leaped up into the saddle and rode hard toward the Dragun. He gripped the handle of his sword as tightly as he could and galloped into the path of the charging Dragun as it swooped down and opened its mouth to breathe deadly fire upon the fighting tribesmen.

Agry ducked down in the saddle and dodged the horse left and right past his fellow soldiers as the Dragun opened its mouth and a stream of fire and heat blazed down upon the battlefield.

Agry's horse turned hard right to avoid the rushing flames, and as it did so Agry leaped up in his saddle, one foot in the centre of it as the Dragun roared toward him. With a roar of fury Agry hurled himself up into the air. He flew upward from the fleeing horse, the Dragun's wings sweeping past above as he brought his sword over his head in a double–handed blow.

The thick blade slashed through the Dragun's wing and tore it off near the root, the entire wing folding back on itself with a deep boom as the Dragun screeched in pain and plunged down into the sea of fighting soldiers and Urks. It ploughed through them like a burning ship crashing into a port, then tumbled to a halt amid a roiling cloud of smoke and flame.

Agry landed hard and rolled to absorb some of the shock, coming up on his knees. He looked over his shoulder to see the Dragun writhing on the ground as it tried to right itself. Agry hauled himself to his feet and ran to the animal as soldiers struggled to get clear of its toxic breath and the streams of agonised flame blasting from its mouth.

He sprinted to the animal's side as it got to its feet, and with one great thrust he plunged his sword into the side of its chest and it sank to the hilt into the scalding flesh. The Dragun's back arched and flames shot from its mouth as the fatal wound tore into its body, and Agry could feel that great hot heart throbbing through the chest wall and down the length of his sword. The Dragun shuddered and its legs folded beneath it as it slumped dead on the ground, the earth beneath them smouldering as the grass burned.

Agry hauled the sword from inside the animal, its surface smeared with the Dragun's hot blood. He turned and his eyes locked onto Terra's chariot as she led her Urks ever closer to Stormshadow Citadel, toward the power and victory she craved but which had never been hers to hold.

Agry prepared to charge the great wytch, when a hellish screech split the air right by his side.

A second Dragun charged toward him, and Agry realised that his horse was long gone and there was nowhere left to run. The huge animal opened its mouth to blast him with flame, pursued by a dozen Centaurs who couldn't hope to catch it. Agry hurled his gloved hands uselessly in front of his face to protect it from the blast as he dropped to his knees.

Suddenly a shower of brilliant white fireballs slammed into the Dragun from one side and it lurched off course and crashed into the ground. The flames from its mouth broke up and missed Agry where he crouched on the ground.

A ragged cheer went up and Agry turned in amazement to see a ship descend out of the clouds, her hull booming as cannons fired blasts of blue–white fire that hammered the Draguns. The ship's sails rumbled in the winds and her crew cheered and threw themselves over the side and into the fight as the ship sailed low over the battlefield. Agry saw the name Phoenix upon her bows, and her cocky captain waved at him as he leaned over the bulwark and called down with customary bravado.

'Anyone fancy a fight?!'

Herric launched himself off the deck and onto the back of a huge Griffon, and the animal screeched as it took off and dove straight for the nearest Dragun, which shrieked and fled at the sight of the beast. From behind Herric another dozen or so Griffons launched themselves off the deck of the Phoenix, their hunter's eyes locking on to Terra's Draguns.

Agry grinned with savage delight as he turned and drove his sword into the dead Dragun's burning heart once more, Luciffen's words echoing in his mind. *Only a sword burning with the heat of a Dragun's blood could perhaps kill Terra.*

Agry hauled the sword out of the body, the blade dripping with what looked for all the world like molten metal as he turned and yelled at the top of his voice.

'For the House of Dray!'

His sword still smouldering from the heat of the Dragun's body and smeared with its molten blood, Agry charged through the battle and headed straight for Terra. Urks rushed to stop him but were cut down with the blade now glowing with heat and untold power as Agry forged his way toward her.

Terra saw him coming and her Cerberus whirled, flames snorting from their nostrils as they clawed at the earth. Terra cracked a whip of flaming light and the Cerberus charged, Urks hurled from their path as Agry ran at full sprint toward them.

'Agry, no!' Siren screamed as she realised what he was doing.

Agry barely heard her as he ran, saw Terra's malicious smile over the Cerberus' heads as she charged him. He waited until the last moment, and then he turned aside as the Cerberus raced past and he swung the sword at their muscular legs. The fiery blade cut the nearest of the savage beasts down with a single blow as Agry turned with the speed and grace of the veteran warrior and swung the lethal sword at Terra's head.

The great wytch leaped to the far side of her chariot and threw her head back, the glowing blade flashing past an inch from her face, and Agry saw a thick scar marring her savage beauty where he realised Ayla must have stabbed the wytch. Agry saw his blade miss and turned to try again as the chariot wheeled around.

Siren leaped through the battlefield as she tried to fight her way to Agry, Urks lurching toward her with weapons flying and flashing in the light. She ducked and weaved, stabbed and parried her way forwards, and she broke free of a ring of them to see Terra in the center and charging toward Agry, who was on his feet with his sword held double handed before him.

Siren sprinted into the clearing and she hurled her slingshot not at Terra but at the remaining Cerberus, the weighted snares unfolding and crashing into its legs. The snares tangled and tightened in an instant and the Cerberus howled as it tumbled to the ground.

Agry darted to one side as the chariot swerved out of control. Terra leaped from the chariot as it was suddenly overturned and came crashing down on its back. The great wytch glided on darkened wings that unfolded like black smoke from her robes and she drew two swords, each with a blade of polished obsidian, as black as night.

Terra landed right in front of Agry and her blades struck in a blur of motion. Agry staggered backward beneath the weight of the attack as he struggled to fend the wytch off, and Siren ran to intervene.

'Agry!'

Terra lunged with both swords, the weapons both far heavier than Agry's, and the chieftain was hurled backwards to the edge of the ring of Urks. Even as he backed up to them, Siren saw two of them pull their arms back to drive their swords into him from behind.

'Agry, enemy rear!' she screamed.

Agry turned and his wild parry smashed the Urks' weapons aside.

Even as he did so, Terra lunged.

Agry turned full circle and deflected the first of the wytch's glossy black blades, but the force of its strike pushed his sword downward, and Siren screamed as the second sword thrust straight and true and pierced Agry's chest. It passed all the way through and out of his back, his body hanging from the blade as his glowing sword fell from his grasp.

'No!'

Siren's shriek soared above the din of the battlefield and she hurled her slingshot at Terra's head. The weighted weapon collided with the wytch and wrapped tightly around her head and throat, pinning the snakes in her hair against her head.

The wytch hauled the sword from Agry's body and the warrior slumped to his knees as Terra glared at Siren. The slingshot wire around her skull burst into flames and flew apart as the wytch charged toward her, fury radiating from her body and her hair trailing flame as she raised her swords and brought them crashing down toward the girl's skull.

***

## Forty-Two

Siren ducked and rolled under the blow, the huge swords slamming into the earth in a cloud of flames and embers as Terra whirled and swung the swords again. Siren leaped backwards to avoid the lethal blades and she stumbled backwards over the body of a dead Urk and fell onto her back.

Terra lunged in and lifted the swords over her head ready to bring them down upon Siren, and Siren threw her hands up uselessly to defend herself. Terra's face twisted in malicious joy and she swung the swords over her head. The blades flashed as lightning tore across the heavens above her, and then Siren saw a huge blast of energy smash into Terra and knock her off balance.

The great wytch staggered to one side and the swords slammed clumsily into the ground as she was hit by blast after blast. Siren leaped to her feet and hurled a snare at the wytch's legs, the weighted snare wrapping around Terra's ankles. The blasts smashed into her and the great wytch toppled and crashed down as Siren dashed clear and turned to see where the surprise attack had come from.

From the turbulent heavens above she saw a swarm of Griffons soar down, their golden coats and broad wings shimmering as blasts of energy rocketed from their beaks and smashed into Terra, pinning her to the ground. Siren saw Herric riding the leading Griffon, hauling the beast from its suicidal dive and swooping low over the battlefield as he led his cavalry into a climb to attack the Draguns still soaring over the battle.

Siren dashed clear of Terra as the wytch's fury burned through the snares and she leaped to her feet and climbed aboard her chariot once more. Rage emanated from her in a halo of dark, smoky shadows that writhed this way and that as she raised her swords and her cry echoed across the battlefield.

'Forward! Crush them all!'

From the earth itself a train of flaming stallions materialised in front of the chariot, Siren gasping at the hellish sight of the Valkyries that clawed at the earth with flaming hooves as Terra launched herself at the citadel with the rest of her army in pursuit.

Siren fought her way to where Vigoran and Luciffen were holding the line, the great sage holding a sword in one hand while casting spells with the other. Siren could see him looking up at the Griffons and smiling as he saw them swarming around the Draguns.

'We're still outnumbered!' Vigoran shouted. 'Even with the Griffons and the Centaurs we can't hold back a force this large!'

'Where's Ayla and Jake?' Siren yelled above the din.

Luciffen gestured to the citadel. 'I believe they were leading an attempt to open the Mirror of Souls.'

Siren glanced at the nearby citadel, and then at Terra. The great wytch had picked up Agry's body and pinned it with one ferocious blow from her black swords to the front of her chariot. The Urk hordes around her cheered, their combined voices shaking the ground beneath them as they roared their approval and surged forward. Terra looked across the army and she saw Luciffen and Vigoran. Her eyes flared with a hatred cold and pure and she pointed one sword at Luciffen as she turned her chariot and charged.

'Go!' Luciffen snapped at Siren. 'Find Ayla. Without the mirror of souls opened, this battle will be over in minutes!'

Siren sprinted away through the battle toward the army's rear ranks, and she wondered how the hell she was going to get all the way up onto that citadel in the space of a few minutes, or open the Mirror of Souls. Then she saw Cyril, casting spells that tripped Urks or filled their boots with mud and sharp stones, causing them to hop about in pain, and she had an idea.

*

Ayla hurried along a large corridor that led toward the grand chamber, Jake close behind her.

'It's just ahead, through those doors.'

They could see before them a huge archway, two huge doors ajar, and as they jogged along so Ayla caught the first acrid stench of burning. She slowed down, the smell of sulphur thick in the air and smoke drifting in veils from somewhere within the great hall.

'The Dragun's in there,' Jake said.

'D'ya think?' she whispered.

Jake shrugged as they eased up to the doors. Both were made of thick wood standing thirty feet high and both were scorched black and warm to the touch. Ayla listened intently for a moment and then she peeked through the gap between the doors.

The interior of the great hall was enshrouded in darkness and smoke. She looked up and could see far above them a glass dome through which pale light from the stormy skies filtered down into the hall, but the smoke was too thick for it to penetrate far.

Ayla crept into the hall, trying not to cough as she got down into a low crouch and slipped beneath the coiling veils of smoke. Jake followed, both of them creeping one pace at a time toward a distant altar. In the pale light of the glass dome, Ayla could at last see a mirror mounted in an ornate frame before them. It looked to be as tall as a barn and was facing away from them into the darkness at the rear of the hall.

'There it is,' Jake whispered.

'Y'know, I'm really glad you came.'

'Stop it,' Jake smirked.

Ayla was about to reply when a deep rumble filled the hall, as though someone were dragging boulders across the ground. Ayla froze and peered into the drifting veils of smoke ahead but she could see nothing.

There was a long pause as the rumble faded away. Ayla could hear the distant sounds of battle ongoing far below on the plain outside, the muted cries and screams coming from the Mirror of Souls, and her own heart thumping against her chest.

The darkness deepened before them as something moved.

Then, amid the black, she saw two cruel eyes the size of dinner plates glow into life and look directly at them. The ground trembled as something massive stood up, blocking the view of the mirror, and two huge wings spread wide enough to fill half the hall.

The huge Dragun's form suddenly burst into light and life as it breathed in and molten rock surged between its scales. Ayla gasped as she realised the sheer size of the creature. The Dragun was three times as large as any she had seen yet, twin horns on its head pointing forwards as it rose up to confront them. Heat shimmered from its enormous bulk and she felt a waft of hot air from it.

Jake swallowed, his eyes fixed on the immense beast.

'Can you run?' he asked.

'Oh yeah!' Ayla replied frantically as the Dragun sucked in a huge rush of air and its huge body glowed more brightly. 'Scatter!'

Ayla dashed left and Jake sprinted right as the Dragun blasted a fearsome pillar of flame that crashed into the hall doors and slammed them shut. Flames burst outward from the impact like a blossoming flower and illuminated the entire hall as Ayla ran around the edge of it, trying to get behind the altar.

The hall was circular, with towering walls and pillars around the altar in the centre beneath the glass dome. The light from the Dragun's attack flickered around her and she saw that the steps leading up to the altar were also circular and that the Dragun's nest was along the front edge.

The huge animal turned, its tail swishing through the air. Ayla ducked and rolled as the tail swept by over her head with a rush of hot air. She came up on her feet and dashed up the steps toward the Mirror of Souls, climbing hard, her arms and legs flying and her heart hammering in her chest.

'Ayla, get down!'

Ayla turned at Jake's warning and saw the Dragun turn its massive head and spray flames at her, too quickly for her to reach the mirror. She threw herself down on her belly against the far side of the steps and the flames roared past just inches above her. The heat scorched the back of her neck and singed her hair as she tried to make herself as flat as possible.

***

## Forty–Three

The flames subsided and Ayla felt the steps tremble as the Dragun lumbered in pursuit. She jumped to her feet and her heart fluttered in her chest as she saw the huge animal looming above her, the gigantic head on the long, thick neck rising up and the beast's mouth opening to reveal rows of sharp, glowing teeth.

'Over here!'

Jake shouted across the hall and the Dragun turned just in time to see Jake thrust his sword into the animal's tail.

'Jake, no!'

The Dragun shrieked in pain as the weapon plunged hilt–deep into its smouldering flesh and it whirled to face Jake. Its great tail yanked the sword from Jake's hand with enough force to pull him off the ground and hurl him across the hall. Ayla saw Jake fly through the air and crash onto the stone flags on the far side of the hall. He rolled to a stop, his body motionless as the Dragun lumbered toward him.

The animal's huge tail moved over Ayla's head and she saw the sword embedded in its flank. Ayla sprinted across the steps and with a deft leap up onto the side of the Dragun's tail she grabbed the sword handle and yanked down on it as she twisted the blade sideways.

The Dragun howled and turned back to face her as Ayla let go of the sword and backed up the steps, hauling her backpack off her shoulders and ripping it open. The Dragun stalked up the steps, Jake's body forgotten as it drew its great breath. The coals of its body brightened and it reared its head up high and then brought it crashing down as searing flames tore from its mouth and filled Ayla's vision.

Ayla threw herself clear and the flames blasted the steps beside her, scorching the stone as she scrambled to one side. Her backpack with the mirror inside it was still on the steps on the far side of the Dragun and she knew she would not be fast enough to dash to it without the Dragun intercepting her.

The beast advanced and Ayla backed up, not sure of where she could run to. She stumbled backwards down the far side of the steps. The Dragun reared up behind the mirror and looked over the top at Ayla, and then it descended toward her. Ayla retreated past the pillars and her back hit the outer wall of the hall, and she knew that there was nowhere left to run. The beast approached, its head four times as large as her body. Smoke drifted from its nostrils, each as big as a dinner plate as it moved in for a closer look, and she could see those immense fangs smouldering like hot coals. Its terrible eyes glowed with an unnatural light, that of evil incarnate, and she felt the heat blazing from its black skin and smelled the sulphur from its breath.

The Dragun's belly shuddered, a rattling sound as deep as the earth itself, and then it opened its mouth to bite into her.

Three powerful blasts smashed into the Dragun from behind and it reared up and away from Ayla. She looked up and saw four Griffons crash through the entrance and soar through the hall. Herric was guiding one of them and shouted at her, Siren sitting behind him.

'Somebody said you'd need a lift?'

Ayla's heart leaped for joy as Herric's Griffon screeched and fired a ball of white energy that smashed the Dragun straight in the face. Its body writhed with fury and it fired a stream of flame that the Griffon barely avoided as it twisted aside. Another Griffon carrying Cyril likewise jerked away from the fearsome blast.

The hall was too small for them to fly properly and the Griffons were forced to land as Ayla sprinted past the Dragun toward her backpack. The Dragun sprayed seething streams of fire this way and that, the Griffons scrambling to stay out of the way as they encircled the great beast. Ayla crouched down and hauled Agnis's mirror from her backpack, then ran out toward the Griffons as the Dragun stood on the altar beside the Mirror of Souls and confronted them.

It reared its great head back once again as Herric raised his arms and waved to get its attention. Ayla ran as hard as she could with the mirror in her grasp, and she dashed in front of Herric's Griffon as the Dragun hurled its fiery breath. Ayla stood her ground and held the mirror up to the scorching flames as they filled her vision, and she screamed as they hit the mirror in a blossoming fireball. Ayla felt unbearable heat blast all around her and the mirror shook in her grasp, shining with a bright blue light.

Ayla felt herself pushed backwards by the force of the blast and she dropped to her knees, heat billowing past her and the Dragun's scalding breath staining the air and making her eyes water as she fought back. The mirror trembled and then suddenly it seemed to respond to the blast.

The mirror flared and the flames blasted back directly at the Dragun as though coming from within the mirror itself. Ayla stood with the mirror in both hands and watched as the fearsome flames changed to a brilliant stream of blue light that crashed like a wave into the huge Dragun. Its immense head vanished in a cloud of steam and smoke as it thrashed sideways and staggered down off the altar, its keening cries soaring through the hall.

The mirror's vibrant glow faded, and Ayla saw the blast subside as the Dragun staggered weakly away, its head a smouldering mess of blackened coal that began to harden with a crackling sound. The glowing lines of molten rock faded away amid coils of writhing smoke that consumed the beast's great head. Ayla watched in amazement as the Dragun's head turned to stone before her and the huge beast slumped onto its belly, the glowing coals of its body fading to a dull black, the entire animal enshrouded in a cloud of smoke and steam.

Ayla stood for a moment, exhausted, and then she heard the mournful cries of the thousands trapped in the Mirror of Souls. She turned and ran up the steps with Agnis's mirror still in her grasp. Nearby, Herric dismounted from his Griffon and followed her with a casual gait.

'You're welcome, and all that.'

Ayla ignored him and moved to the front of the mirror. She looked into its awful depths as Herric moved to stand alongside her.

Ayla's stomach flipped as she saw the great mirror reflecting nothing of the hall around her, instead showing an endless sea of faces that were imprisoned within a blackness that seemed as deep as eternity. They were distorted, warped, twisted and grotesque, riven with suffering as their cries suddenly became deafeningly loud in her ears. Among them she heard a voice that was deeper than the others, and she recognised Tygrin's melodious wailing, the faces in the mirror filling it with the misery suffered by those entrapped within.

Herric peered into the mirror and frowned.

'You think we can charge them for getting them out? A shekel a head's not so much?'

Cyril and Siren moved to join them in front of the great mirror, its blackness so intense that it gave Ayla a sense of vertigo just looking at it. *The dead core of a sun*, Luciffen had said, that's what this thing was made of, something so massive compressed into a sliver of material that could achieve the impossible, and yet also conjure the greatest evils she had ever encountered.

'What do I do?' she asked Cyril.

Cyril gestured to the mirror she was holding. 'Let them see themselves, let them see the light again.'

Ayla glanced up at the glass dome above them and the faint light beaming down through it, the last remnants of light remaining in the realm. She aimed Agnis's mirror at the light, and then turned the mirror so that it reflected the light beam straight into the Mirror of Souls.

The weak light from above hit the surface of the mirror. For a moment it was reflected back at her in the normal way, but then she saw the glow begin to creep into the darkness, as though afraid to take each step. The surface of the mirror seemed to change its shape, no longer something solid before her but something with immense depth and distance.

Suddenly Agnis's mirror flared and then so did the Mirror of Souls. An intense, fearsome orb of light surged out and Ayla turned her head to one side and squinted against it.

The brilliant glow faded and through the mirror she saw the sea of suffering faces turn to look out at her as though suddenly realising that she was there. The screams of mourning suddenly changed note and became even louder, as though they were rushing toward her. One by one Ayla, Herric and the others began to step back from the huge mirror as it suddenly changed form and became a portal, no longer flat but with intense depth as though she were staring into a blackened abyss with no end. The souls within became solid and as one they rushed from out of the mirror with brilliant flashes of light.

Ayla, Cyril, Siren, and Herric hurried clear as hundreds of people flooded out of the mirror and poured into the hall. Ayla stared in amazement as she saw archers, swordsmen, cavalry and their horses, Griffons, Centaurs, Unicorns and countless innocent people stagger out, squinting and peering about them as others rushed out from behind them.

A young man of perhaps fifteen dressed in old–fashioned clothes staggered, blinking, into the light and looked straight at Ayla. Despite being bedraggled, weary and having been imprisoned for centuries, he bowed deeply before her.

'Percival Longbottom, at your service. My gratitude ma'am, for thy efforts!'

Ayla didn't know quite what to say, but before she could think of anything a fresh commotion broke out. From the masses a giant lumbered into view, his great thick beard and twinkling eyes standing out like a sore thumb as he shouldered his way through the crowd toward her.

'Tygrin!'

Ayla set Agnis's mirror against a nearby pillar, still directing the light into the Mirror of Souls as Tygrin rushed in and scooped her up into his great arms. She felt as though she was being squeezed to death as he held her.

'I knew you would come,' he said in his thick, heavy accent. 'I knew you would.'

Tygrin set her down and looked at them all fondly as hundreds more warriors poured out behind him, and then he frowned.

'Where are Vigoran and the riders?'

Ayla pointed out the windows of the citadel. 'They're up against Terra's hordes,' she said. 'Their line is weakening and we don't have much time.'

Tygrin looked over his shoulder at the huge windows, and then he saw the dead body of the Dragun lying nearby. He looked at her appraisingly.

'I had help,' Ayla replied, and looked about at the countless warriors milling around them, 'and we could do with some more out there.'

Herric shouldered his way toward them with some of his own riders, the magnificent Griffons following, and with them they carried Ayla's bow and shield, Tygrin's axe, along with Vigoran's sword and Luciffen's staff. Tygrin took the axe from Herric with a nod and he looked at Ayla.

'Leave them to me,' he said with a wink.

Then, before them, the Mirror of Souls began to glow with an ever–brightening light. They began to back away from it, the Griffons screeching and tossing their heads.

'Time for us to make ourselves scarce?' Percival Longbottom said.

'Let's get out of here,' Herric urged as he leaped onto his Griffon. Ayla was about to join him when she saw the gargoyle trot happily to her side.

She jumped onto its back and turned it.

'Time to fight back,' she said, and the gargoyle launched itself into flight.

\*\*\*

## Forty-four

Luciffen saw Terra charge in on her flaming chariot, the Valkyries snorting flame as they galloped toward him. The great wytch's swords flared as she aimed them at Luciffen and blasts of searing fire zipped across the battlefield toward him.

The sage staggered backwards as he threw his hands up to deflect the blasts, but without his staff he was severely disadvantaged and he knew that he could not defend himself for long. The blasts hit him one after the other and he fell to his knees, his hands held before him and a weakening sphere of blue light the only thing between himself and Terra's rage.

The wytch thundered overhead and soared up into the sky, wheeling her chariot around as her army of Urks pushed the defending forces back to the river. The tribes crashed into the water and began floundering, their swords clumsy now as they struggled to stay upright in the chaos. The *Phoenix* cruised along in front of them, her guns pounding the Urk hordes and cutting down hundreds with each salvo, but their numbers were so vast that nothing could stop their advance.

'Hold the line!'

Vigoran stood tall before the rushing sea of Urks, his sword flashing as he turned and parried and struck and thrust the weapon, cutting Urks down one after another but hopelessly outnumbered by the sheer size of Terra's forces.

'We cannot!' Luciffen shouted wearily.

Terra dove down once more, her eyes aflame with delight and malice as she saw Luciffen on his knees, weakened and defeated, and realised that her victory was at hand. She raised her right sword and with a hellish scream of vengeance she launched a stream of fire at the kneeling sage.

Luciffen raised his hands slowly to deflect the sheer force of her attack, as though he knew that he could not hope to survive it, and then suddenly the blast was deflected by a blaze of white light that soared in from one side. Luciffen turned in amazement as he saw Cyril standing with Luciffen's staff in one hand and determination writ large upon his face, his features flushed with exhaustion from what looked like a long run. The staff shook and shuddered with restrained power as the stream of energy turned and blasted toward Terra and her chariot.

The wytch roared with fury and smashed straight into the beam, blasting it back. Cyril tumbled backwards as the shockwave hit him and he fell onto his back in the mud as Terra's chariot landed right in front of them all and her screech echoed across the battlefield.

'They are beaten!' she cried, and the Urks roared their approval in their thousands. 'Kill them! Kill them all!'

Vigoran and the Riders of Spiris formed a protective ring around Luciffen, cutting down Urks as they rushed toward them in their hundreds, but it was no use and they were pushed back toward the sage in their centre.

Luciffen called out to Terra. 'You've won, spare the rest!'

Terra glared at him, pure evil radiating from her. 'As you spared me and mine?' she screeched.

Luciffen said nothing but he saw the confusion on Cyril's face, the concern on Vigoran's as Terra pointed her swords at them all. Behind the great wytch advanced thousands more Urks, all hungry for victory.

'Take them apart!' she yelled, 'and the citadel will be ours!'

The Urks roared, their thousands of voices and cheers deafening and seeming to shake the very ground as they rushed in. Luciffen stood with his hands clasped calmly before him and his eyes closed, accepting the fate that the realm had chosen for him.

Above the roar of battle a new sound soared across the realm, and this one sounded like nothing that any of them had ever heard before. The low and mournful wail of a great horn echoed out across the battlefield and away into the distance, overpowering the sounds of battle enough that humans and Urks alike turned toward the source of the sound. There was a moment's pause, and then from the deep darkness of the battlefield a blinding light blazed from the citadel's highest towers like a lighthouse beam slicing through the rain and darkness of a storm.

Luciffen whirled, as did Vigoran, Terra and every warrior and Urk on the field.

From Stormshadow Citadel's heights blazed what looked like a new born star, a piercing blue and white light that drove back the tumbling clouds and revealed the eggshell blue sky far above. The tumult of battle fell silent for what felt like the first time in hours, Luciffen squinting into the light now spreading outward like a blossoming flower from the citadel.

The light hit the field and swept across it like an unstoppable wave, and it hit Gallentia where she was pinned to the rock. Her white dress flared brilliantly in the glow and she threw her head back, her eyes wide open and her hair rippling in a wind that only she could feel. Terra staggered away from the prisoner, one arm shielding her eyes against the intense blaze.

From the great heights Luciffen saw something tumble into view. As he stared, squinting, he saw a huge form plummet from the citadel and crash into the ground beneath the walls, a plume of oily brown smoke spiralling from its remains. For a moment he could not believe what he was seeing, but then he recognised it as the dead body of a huge Dragun, the huge beast turned to solid stone.

A tremendous cheer went up from the army as they realised that the citadel was theirs once again, but Luciffen thought he saw further movement amid the source of the light. It seemed as though the upper towers of the citadel were falling and rushing toward them, and then the light faded enough for him to see what it had been concealing and his heart leaped with joy.

From the brilliant light soared Herric's Griffons. The animals dove down almost vertically from the great heights of the citadel and spread their wings, pulling out of their suicidal dives and rocketing across the battlefield, streams of blue and white fire blasting from their beaks to hammer the Urk hordes. Luciffen saw their salvos crash into the ranks of ungainly creatures and drive them back from the edge of the river.

Herric led the Griffons, a cutlass in one hand and a shield in the other, and flying right next to him on a gargoyle Luciffen saw Ayla Fox, her hair flying in the wind as they rushed over the battlefield.

Another penetratingly loud horn sounded, and to Luciffen's amazement he saw the great drawbridge to the citadel open. The immense bridge crashed down and from the darkness within he heard a howl of thousands of liberated souls echo across the battlefield. Terra's Urk hordes faltered in their advance, staring at the citadel, consternation writ large on their unnatural features. There was a moments' silence, and then an entire army burst forth into the light.

Hundreds of cavalry, archers, pikemen and swordsmen charged at a full run and gallop across the drawbridge, their hooves and boots thundering like a wave as they plunged onto the battlefield.

Luciffen looked at Vigoran, the great warrior as surprised as he, and then Vigoran raised his sword above his head, the blade flashing in the new light.

'The battle is not yet lost, *forward!*'

The tribes cheered in joy as the ten thousand warriors once trapped in Terra's Mirror of Souls crashed past them and ploughed into the Urks' front line. Their massed weapons clattered and rang in a bloody hymn of battle that battered the Urks back from the river, the army fuelled by an insatiable lust for vengeance. Luciffen saw Terra screaming in rage, and the wytch turned and rushed toward Cyril.

Cyril saw her coming, but he also saw Luciffen struggling to get to his feet. He called out as loud as he could.

'Luciffen!'

The sage's heart plunged into his stomach as he saw Cyril ignore the wytch and hurl the staff toward Luciffen.

The staff flew it seemed in slow motion across the battlefield, even as he saw Terra launch a blast of flame at Cyril. Luciffen leaped to his feet and ran at a speed he had not achieved since he had been a young man, many hundreds of years before. The staff plunged down toward him and he caught it in mid–flight as he flipped it over and hurled with all of his might every last ounce of magical power he could muster.

The staff radiated a blast that stopped Luciffen in his tracks and hurled him onto his backside in the mud, blinking at the shock of it. He looked up and saw

Terra thrown aside by the blow, her attack missing Cyril by inches as the young sage ducked down and threw his hands over his head.

'Luciffen!' Terra screamed and charged toward him, her shimmering black swords sweeping in.

Luciffen smiled and closed his eyes, his strength gone now and his staff's power spent in that final blast of energy. There was no need to resist. His time had come, and now there were others who would stand in his stead, their youth and vigour far more valuable than his weakening skills.

He heard rather than saw Terra's wicked black blades slice through the air toward him, whispering of death's final embrace.

\*\*\*

## Forty-Five

Ayla ducked down and dove for the ground as she saw the old sage hurled onto his back by the force of the blast that had saved Cyril. The gargoyle rocketed down toward the chaotic turmoil of the battle below, and then pulled out at the last moment, it's wings flaring as Ayla leaped from its back and landed like a cat in front of Luciffen.

Terra's black swords smashed down as Ayla crouched and threw her shield up. The weapons clashed against the shield and bounced off it as though they were made of rubber, but the blow hurled Ayla onto her back alongside Luciffen.

Terra shrieked in rage and lunged at Ayla, who rolled aside as the thick, ragged black blade plunged into the earth alongside her

'You!' the great wytch hissed. 'You of *all* people!'

Terra swung the other blade and Ayla ducked beneath it, the wicked black weapon flashing past above her head as she danced backwards. The wytch lunged again, advancing on Ayla, her fearsome features twisted with rage and the black swords flashing this way and that in a blur of motion. Ayla hurled her shield up, deflecting the blows one after another, but Terra was too fast and too powerful and Ayla's arms ached and began to slow.

Terra saw her tire and she suddenly rushed forward and brought both of the blades crashing down in an overhead blow. Ayla could not hope to leap clear and she held the shield aloft above her and took the full force of the attack. The swords smashed her down to her knees as her arms buckled and went numb, and the shield tilted to one side, thrown off balance by the force of the strike.

Terra slid one blade beneath the shield and Ayla felt the jagged edge touch the side of her neck as with the other sword Terra pried the shield away from her. The wytch leaned in close, the wretched scar on her cheek glowing like a tattoo of lava as she sneered at Ayla.

'Die,' she hissed, the vipers in her thick black hair squirming at her.

'Not today!' a huge voice boomed.

Then the ground beneath them shook and Ayla heard a roar of fury from behind her. She turned her head and saw Tygrin's immense form loom up, the great axe high above his huge head as he brought it crashing down onto the ground beside her. The weapon slammed into the mud and split the earth with a thunderous crack as the living rock was split asunder.

Terra staggered sideways and Ayla rolled clear of the swords. The earth crackled and rumbled as the great wytch's entire army was split into two, the immense crevice swallowing hundreds of Urks that fell to their doom within its shadowy depths. Ayla scrambled back from the precipitous abyss, and then the gargoyle swooped down and screeched at her as it thumped down by her side. Moments later, they leaped into the air, the gargoyle's wings beating the air as it climbed away from certain death.

Vigoran sprinted to the rock where Gallentia was still chained and with a slash of his sword he cut her bonds. The white wytch collapsed to her knees and then in a brilliant flash of light she disappeared. Luciffen and the king stared in shock at the spot where his daughter had been moments before, unsure of what had happened.

As the earth trembled beneath Tygrin's blow so the light from Stormshadow Citadel grew brighter and Luciffen turned to see atop the lofty heights of the fortress Gallentia, her arms spread wide and the warmth of the suns of countless worlds beaming outward from the citadel.

Terra threw her arms up and screamed as the light hit her again, and her army tumbled backwards and away from the powerful sorcery as Gallentia looked down upon them all. Almost immediately, Luciffen saw Agnis pop into existence next to him as though coming awake from a deep sleep.

'Oh, here I am!' she chortled, and adjusted her petticoat and collar. 'Now, Luciffen, what *have* you been up to?'

Herric's Griffons soared overhead, this time accompanied by hundreds of Centaurs and the Army of Stormshadow, and Terra's Urks turned and began fleeing in their thousands. Ayla saw the infuriated wytch blasting them in disgust as they retreated in terror, but now she was facing GAllentia, Luciffen, Cyril, Siren, Herric's Griffons and the Phoenix along with around ten thousand warriors all desperate for revenge for being incarcerated inside the Mirror of Souls.

Terra leaped aboard her flaming chariot and turned, casting one last furious glare at Ayla. Slowly, her eyes radiating hate, she pointed at Ayla with one long finger and whispered something that Ayla could just about make out as she circled above them.

*I will find you.*

Then, she took off and flew away from Stormshadow Citadel toward the rapidly receding black clouds of Chaoria.

A great cheer went up from the army around them as the Urks turned and fled, and above them the turbulent black clouds rolled back to reveal a blue sky and bright veils of gorgeous ghostly light beaming down across the land.

Agnis dusted off her hands and folded her arms across her chest, the brilliant light glowing behind her atop the citadel.

'Wee Agnis shows up and they run with their tails between their legs! Let that be a lesson to yee, Terra!'

Luciffen stared in wonder, unable to appreciate the sheer magnitude of what had just occurred. The Centaurs and the Griffons wheeled and swept across the skies above them and the cold winds of the realm suddenly faded away along with the banks of black cloud now retreating to the east. He closed his eyes as he felt the warmth of distant suns upon his skin and felt life rejuvenating him, tears flowing freely down his cheeks and into his beard.

A voice whispered into his ear.

'Now don't yee forget, Luciffen, that lassie is *my* Hybrin.'

He smiled as he opened his eyes and saw Agnis hovering alongside him, her hands on her hips and a stern look on her face. All around them among the living, the spectres of the past began returning, their faces alive with joy.

'That she is,' Luciffen said as he looked up into the bright sky and saw Ayla riding the gargoyle and ruffling its neck as Herric's Griffon flew protectively alongside them. 'That she is.'

\*\*\*

## Forty–Six

Ayla landed the gargoyle in the centre of the battlefield in time for Tygrin to stride across to her and lift her up in a great bear hug that seemed to squeeze half of the breath out of her lungs once again. The big man set her down as Luciffen made his way across the battlefield toward her, limping slightly and using his staff to balance himself. On his other arm, Cyril helped him along.

'Ayla,' Luciffen greeted her.

Ayla threw her arms around the sage, feeling something for the old man that seemed warmer than anything she had ever experienced before. It was like how she felt when she saw her mother after a long absence, or when she thought of her grandparents or friends long gone.

Cyril was beaming all over his face and staring at his hands, wonder in his eyes. 'Terra attacked me and it just blew past like it was nothing. I can't believe my sorcery has grown so strong.'

Ayla looked up at Luciffen, who winked but said nothing. All around them the battlefield was strewn with thousands of fallen Urks, their weapons scattered on the muddy, churned ground. The army was hurrying about helping the injured, but despite all that had happened Ayla could feel the change in the air. The sky was blue and the dark storm clouds were receding into the distance almost as quickly as Terra's Urks. The air was warm and although there was no sun in the sky she could feel the warmth being radiated out by the great mirror high in Stormshadow Citadel.

Vigoran strode into view, his blue eyes glowing amid the darkness of his hood and although Ayla knew that he had no face she could sense in his gait the joy surging through him. The warrior moved to stand before her for a long moment before he spoke.

'All Mirrorealm owes you a great debt, as do I.'

'As do we all,' Luciffen added before Ayla could say anything.

Then, quite suddenly, she saw Vigoran, Luciffen and the others slowly get down on one knee before her.

Ayla felt embarrassment brush like warm tingling fingers all across her shoulders and the skin on her face flushed red as hardened warriors got down onto one knee in their hundreds, and thousands all around her.

'All life comes from a woman,' Luciffen said, 'and we are indebted every day of our lives to how strong you can all be. But you, Ayla, are like no Hybrin that has ever walked this land. Like no woman that has ever walked this land.'

'I'm just a girl,' Ayla managed to utter, appalled by her own sense of insignificance.

'Ayla,' Luciffen said softly, 'there is no such thing as *just* a girl.'

'And the lassie's all mine!' said a broad Scottish accent, and Agnis zipped to Ayla's side and hugged her, her arms passing through her neck. 'You should be ashamed of yeeself, Luciffen, for putting a wee lass in such danger!'

'Ayla put herself there, with great courage,' Luciffen smiled, not bridling at the ghost's admonishment. 'For which we are all very grateful.'

'C'mon,' drawled a voice from nearby, 'it's not like we all didn't have a part to play, right guys?'

Herric leaned against his Griffon's chest, his arms folded and that crooked smile on his face. Several of his crew were standing with him, and the Phoenix was landing on the moat nearby, Jenson and the rest of the crew frantically putting out fires on her deck and in her rigging.

'You were breeding Griffons to fight Draguns,' Cyril said. 'That's why you had one in your hold.'

'Keeping the eggs warm,' Herric replied as he ruffled the Griffon's neck. 'You can't win a war without air power, right?'

Ayla strode up to him, taken by a sudden confidence that she had never felt before in her life. She reached up on tip–toe and kissed the pirate captain on the cheek.

'I knew you'd come back,' she smiled. 'There's more to you than just money.'

Herric's cocky grin never slipped.

'He only got here when the battle was already won,' Jake interrupted, folding his arms across his chest and scowling as he joined them.

'Better late than never,' Herric replied, not taking his eyes off Ayla as he added more quietly. 'I didn't leave you all at the Towers, I went to get the rest of the Griffons. There was no way your little army would win a battle with Terra's Draguns unleashed on them. Seemed like the only way to make sure you got the upper hand.'

Ayla had so much that she wanted to say to Herric but somehow felt that she couldn't, and she didn't know why. Maybe it was because everyone else was there surrounding them and listening. Then she realised that one of the Riders of Spiris was missing, and she looked around for Siren. For a moment she could see her nowhere, until she spotted a small form kneeling among the bodies of Urks nearby.

'Agry,' she whispered as a sudden realisation dawned.

The army was reforming into its battalions around them, and as they turned to watch the young girl kneeling in the mud, so the countless Urk bodies around them began to dissolve. Ayla watched in fascination as the Urk corpses degenerated into soil and sand, salt and stones, collapsing and vanishing into the very earth beneath their feet.

'Back to where they came from,' Luciffen whispered, 'for they were never truly a part of our realm in the first place, only alive due to Terra's sorcery.'

Ayla saw the grass return, pushing up through the mud as though it were being fed by the decaying Urk's bodies. Warm light flooded the battlefield and it seemed as though before their very eyes the bloody remains of the battle were washed away to leave only Siren kneeling beside Agry's body.

Luciffen walked slowly over, the army gathering around them as Tygrin, Vigoran and others moved to stand protectively over Siren.

'We owe him our lives,' Luciffen said to Siren. 'He gave everything for all of us.'

Siren did not respond, but Ayla could tell that she was listening. The girl knelt for a moment longer, and then she got to her feet. Siren turned to face Luciffen, and for a moment it seemed as though the entire army were listening to her, the only other sound the rumble of the warm wind blowing away the smoke from the field.

'No more,' Siren said. 'No more standing by and letting Terra grow in power. No more waiting for things like this to happen, for our lives to be taken. We don't stand by and hope that others will stand in our stead to face evil. We don't wait for evil to come here at all. We stand and we face it together, all of us, as one.'

Siren hauled the sword from her back and she drove the blade into the ground at her feet.

'We fight back,' she snapped, '*all the way* back until we find Terra and we finish her for once and for all.'

A great cheer roared up from the army around them, and Ayla saw Tygrin raise his great muscular arms and beat his chest as he bellowed his approval, and the Centaurs beat their wings and the Griffons growled. Ayla felt caught up in the joy and the hope that seemed to fill the very air around them, but when she looked at Luciffen she saw him briefly close his eyes in what seemed almost like regret.

Ayla couldn't get his response out of her mind as she watched the Riders of Spiris lift Agry's body onto their shoulders and carry him off the battlefield and into Stormshadow Citadel. Behind them, the entire army marched with banners flying in the warm wind and smiles on thousands of faces as they followed them into the citadel and the great drawbridge closed safely behind them.

\*\*\*

## Forty–Seven

The great citadel was transformed without the presence of Terra's evil haunting the halls. Although Luciffen had once said that the citadel had been abandoned for many decades, it was clear to Ayla that much of its aura of disrepair had been down to sorcery and the demonic presences stalking the darkness.

The halls were now filled with flaming torches and bright light beaming in through tall glass windows cleaned of the grime that had accumulated over the years, and they were filled with both soldiers and ordinary people going about their daily business. In the days that had followed the battle, many of the tribes struggling to survive out in the wilderness had migrated back to the valley of Maryn Tiell and were now working the land nearby or helping repair the damage in the great hall.

In the centre of the great hall there were now two mirrors standing and radiating light out into the realm. The Mirror of Souls glowed on one side, and on the other stood the smaller fragment that belonged to Luciffen, which Vigoran and his riders had collected from the Well of Memories and brought back to its rightful place.

The corpse of the Dragun that Ayla had slain had turned to dust and stone, a bizarre statue of the once vibrant creature that had taken some time for the local people to break up and clear away. The head of the beast had been kept however, its stone tongue lolling from its fanged jaws, and was mounted above a plaque that Ayla now read as she walked into the great hall.

**A Dragun slain here in this hall, in battle, by Ayla Fox in the defence of the realm**

'Herric will have something to say about that,' Jake said as he moved to stand alongside her. 'He's been demanding a fee for his part in saving the day.'

'What would he do with it?'

'Land for his Griffons and riders,' Jake explained. 'Luciffen said he would think about it, but I can't stand the idea of a loon like Herric galavanting around with an army of Griffons. He'd tear up half the realm, and besides it's not like he's not making any money from those eggs he has. It's just as well he's leaving.'

Ayla felt the bottom drop out of her heart. 'He's what?'

'He's leaving,' Jake repeated. 'They're loading the Phoenix right now.'

Ayla hurried away from the gathering celebrations and rushed down to the lower levels of Stormshadow Citadel, where several vessels were moored near a large jetty. The biggest of the ships was the Phoenix, her crew working hard to repair the damage from the battle. She saw Herric directing them, moving up and down the ship as his precious cargo of Griffon eggs was unloaded.

Jenson, the first mate, saw her coming and noticed the look in her eye. One huge hand rested on her shoulder, and she was surprised at how gentle the big man's touch could be.

'Go easy,' Jenson said in his deep, melodious tone. 'He's got a lot on his mind.'

Ayla eased past the giant and confronted Herric.

'You're leaving,' she said.

Herric watched a crate containing one of the Griffon eggs being unloaded as he replied to her.

'People to see, places to go. Griffons eggs will be in high demand right now so there's trade to be had, especially in those hard to get to places.'

Ayla recalled Herric's meeting with the thugs at Port Ranken.

'Won't Dunfig be angry that you're not heading off to repay him?'

Herric turned and leaned against the mainmast of his ship.

'Dunfig is a thug, nothing more. He'll turn up sooner or later, but it's not him that I owe anything.'

'It's Terra, isn't it,' Ayla said, knowing somehow that she was right.

'She paid me to collect all these Griffon eggs, so that there would be no opposition to her Draguns when she launched her attack.' Herric rolled his eyes. 'Oops, butterfingers.'

'Terra is dangerous and powerful,' Ayla snapped at him, concerned. 'This isn't a game, Herric. If she catches you, she might kill you!'

'And that bothers you?'

Ayla reeled herself in a little. 'You're a good fighter and the army here could use your ship and these Griffons.'

Herric smiled broadly. 'That's not all of it.'

Ayla said nothing, holding back for reasons she herself could not understand. Herric pushed casually off the mainmast and stood before her, just inches away. The wind ruffled his mop of shaggy black hair but the mocking smile never slipped an inch.

'I've sold enough of these Griffon eggs to Stormshadow that any Dragun attack in this part of the realm will find itself facing serious resistance. Others will buy more from me, and I'll have doubled my money. If Terra wants to come after me it wouldn't be the first duel I've fought, if you know what I mean.'

Ayla nodded. 'And what happens if it's your last?'

The cavalier grin didn't slip as Herric's hand gently touched her cheek.

'Then my problems will be over. Take it easy, Ayla.'

'Sure', she replied as anger welled up inside her, 'look after yourself, Herric, it's what you're best at.'

Herric did not appear to hear her as he strode away across the deck of his ship.

Ayla guessed that Jake was right, and that as Herric worked for no flag nor master he could not be trusted enough not to show up later fighting for the other side. Ayla had a sneaky suspicion that Herric harboured a heart of gold somewhere beneath that leather greatcoat of his. Or maybe that was just what she was hoping for.

She turned and stormed off the deck with her hands shoved into her pockets.

Herric waited until she was out of sight, and then turned and watched her hurry away from the Phoenix. He realised that he was clenching his teeth and his fists, angry and yet he didn't really understand why.

'You should go to her.'

Jenson's deep tones broke him from his thoughts and he snapped over his shoulder. 'Since when do you give the orders? Get back to work!'

Jenson shrugged his big round shoulders, and Herric continued to watch Ayla until she disappeared in the throng.

'I know what I'm doing,' he added, and then wondered if he was just trying to convince himself.

\*

The great hall had been laid for a banquet, rows of tables set before the Mirror of Souls now shining brightly up into the sky through the great glass dome. At the head of the table Luciffen sat alongside Gallentia, who now positively radiated health and vitality. Ayla could not take her eyes off of her, more radiant than Terra's savage beauty perhaps because her appearance was real and not the result of sorcery.

Ayla sat down with the Riders of Spiris and marvelled at the array of rich, steaming food before them. Some things she recognised easily, but others looked alien and strange to her, and the smells coming from some others seemed positively lethal. Tygrin, it seemed, wanted all of it.

'Waste not, want not,' he said to her as he helped himself to his fourth plate of food. 'I'm a growing lad.'

'You grow any more,' Jake pointed out, 'you won't make it out of the hall.'

'You answer me back again lad, you won't make it through the evening.'

'You couldn't catch me, you're so full of Mowak meat!'

'And you, Jake, are full of sh…'

'Shall we raise a toast?' Luciffen interjected, as he raised his glass and stood at the head of the largest table.

The hundreds of people in the hall fell silent as the great sage spoke.

'There are those that say that over the past century or so our lives have become safer, and in some ways that is true. The worlds which we inhabit were far more dangerous in the past than they are now. And yet, in other ways, we have never been more vulnerable. What happened in the past was that magic was weak enough that only local damage could be done, only people in the immediate vicinity could be harmed. Nowadays, sorcery has become so powerful that a wytch like Terra can raise an army of ten thousand Urks and almost take control of the entire realm.'

The listening crowd rumbled their dislike of the great wytch.

'As it is here in the realm, so it is elsewhere in the other worlds that occasionally overlap with our own. And in one particular world, so close are the parallels that it has become clear that what affects one will affect the other. Our realm is much unexplored, and in the other world four fifths of the population live in poverty. While the remainder live in relative comfort, their lives are as vulnerable as our own here in the realm, interconnected, supported only by their cooperation and the desire to live in peace. The last time peace in that world collapsed into all–out war, Terra rose to power here in the realm.'

Ayla listened as more discontented grumbles filled the hall at the mention of the wytch's name.

'We fought back,' Luciffen said with one fist clenched by his head, to a low cheer, 'but although the battle has been won, the war is only just beginning. Terra and her legions will not stop. They will try again to conquer us, and the same is true in the other worlds. There is always good and there is always evil, just as there is always the light and the darkness here in the realm. But we cannot fight both wars, we cannot cross into the other worlds for we know well of the terrible calamities that such a breach can cause. Fortunately, we now have a new champion, and one who has in the space of just days slain not one but two Draguns, released ten thousand warriors from the Mirror of Souls and liberated Gallentia, my daughter, from captivity along with countless Centaurs. She has become the defender of this realm, and in being so, the defender of her own.'

Ayla felt the hairs rise up on the back of her neck as Luciffen raised his glass, staring right at her.

'To Ayla Fox.'

'*To Ayla Fox*,' said a thousand voices in reply as glasses were raised in her honour.

Ayla found herself looking at Vigoran, the hooded warrior watching her silently as Luciffen went on.

'We stand together, as must the people of Ayla's world. We cannot sit back and expect others to do our work for us, to make us safe and to find the answers to the problems that surround us. We cannot flee or hide, for to do so would be to abandon the homes and lives and friends that we all love. We must become *one*, of our own will, for together we are far more than we are apart. Alone, we are weak and vulnerable to the attacks of the cruel and the hateful. Together, we are invincible even to Terra and her legions! So, stand up and make yourself known to your neighbour, to everyone here with us tonight and everyone you meet in the future, for we are in this together and we will prevail against anything and anyone that would try to harm us!'

A great cheer went up and Ayla felt herself caught up in the celebrations. Musicians started playing music and men and women began dancing and laughing and talking and getting to know each other. Most of the people in the hall were eager to meet Ayla, and by the time the sun had long set and the moon was high in the sky Ayla felt as though she had met every single person in the realm. Her hand ached from being shaken by so many others, her arms throbbed from being hugged so many times and her mind was swimming with so many names and faces that she did not have a hope of recalling.

***

## Forty–Eight

Ayla managed to slip away from the throng onto a balcony that overlooked the Valley of Maryn Tiell, the night air warm now as though summer had arrived out of nowhere. She was looking up at the glistening stars when she heard someone approach and turned to see Jake Shaw watching her.

'Pressure of fame?' he asked with a smile.

Ayla shrugged and smiled back. 'Not used to the attention.'

Jake joined her on the balcony, a tankard in one hand as he looked out over the valley before them. 'You've created quite a name for yourself.'

'It was a team effort.'

'Are you kidding? We all just followed your lead.'

'I'm no leader.'

'No good leader ever thinks that they are.'

Ayla couldn't help but smile. Jake's hand rested on top of hers and she felt a buzz of what felt like electricity bolt up and down her spine.

'I've got your back, Ayla,' he said, his face inches from her. 'Herric and others like him, they're only out for themselves. We're not like that, are we?'

'I guess not,' Ayla whispered in return.

'You say you're not a leader, but you've got me following you about like a lost puppy, haven't you?'.

Ayla's voice caught in her throat, and she suddenly realised how close Jake was standing to her. She struggled to think of something cool to say, anything at all, but her mind had gone into meltdown. Jake moved a little closer still, his eyes looking deep into hers and…

'There she is!'

The doors to the hall burst open again and Ellegen strode through with his family around him, the Centaurs crowding onto the balcony as Jake released her hand and slipped away. Ayla gathered her wits from where they had tumbled to the floor around her and talked amiably to Ellegen for some time. It was then that they all saw the graceful shape of a vessel leaving the port below them and gliding silently into the moonlit night.

The Phoenix looked more lovely than ever, her rigging glowing with lights as she sailed away into the night sky. Ayla watched and felt something tug at her heart as the pirate ship climbed into broken clouds and was lost to the darkness.

'He'll be back, lassie,' Agnis promised as she hovered to Ayla's side. 'I don't think he's leaving because he wants to.'

Ayla smiled softly, but she didn't feel the same as Agnis. 'Then he shouldn't have left at all, should he?'

Ayla was exhausted, and although others were still partying into the night she felt herself flagging. Quietly, hoping that nobody would notice, she slipped away from the balcony and through the busy hall, then headed down the main corridor toward the sleeping quarters.

She was barely out of the hall when she saw Luciffen awaiting her. She offered him a weary smile, but as always the wise old sage knew what was on her mind.

'It is time for you to sleep,' he said, 'and sleep you will, most deeply tonight. When you awaken, you will be back in your world.'

Ayla's lethargy slipped away like an old skin as she felt something like panic rip through her.

'Home? But I only just got here?'

'And look at all that you have done,' Luciffen said. 'Terra will be at bay for a while now, and there is much that needs you at home. It may not look like the darkness of our realm, but evil has many faces. To not return home would be just as bad as not having faced the darkness here, as you did with so much courage.'

Ayla felt a sense of resignation as she realised that she could not avoid the reality of the world in which she grew up.

'Things aren't the same there,' she whispered as they walked.

'Then change them,' Luciffen replied. 'The world we have is what we make of it, Ayla. Surrender yourself not to apathy or faith, but apply yourself to hope and to acts. You can change anything you want to Ayla, and if you don't believe that then think about how much you've changed here. In comparison, at home the smallest acts of kindness can have the most dramatic effects.'

Ayla knew that Luciffen was right, and she was too tired to resist anyway. An image of Herric popped into her mind and she glanced out of the windows of the hall to the far horizon.

'And that young man is both a blessing and a concern,' Luciffen said as though reading her mind. 'Herric is a complex soul and it will take time for him to realise what is most important to him.'

'He doesn't care about anyone but himself,' Ayla said, and heard the bitterness in her own voice.

Luciffen slipped an arm around Ayla's shoulder and guided her to her quarters.

'That's not quite true,' he replied. 'Herric is a wild card and flies just as free. To him, any home is only ever temporary because he has known nothing else in life. He will learn, in time.'

The room into which Luciffen led her was dominated by a four–poster bed and lit with candles, hundreds of them all around the room. Ayla was so tired that she could barely make it to the bed, and she climbed gratefully in with her clothes still on and fell fast asleep within seconds.

Luciffen stood and looked down at her for a moment, and then he tucked the sheets over her and gently waved his hand over her face. A sprinkle of gently sparkling orbs drifted like starlight across her, and Luciffen smiled.

'Sleep well, Ayla. We will see you again soon.'

Luciffen turned to the shadowy figure standing in one corner of the room. A nearby mirror showed a reflection of Ayla's bedroom in her own world, far from the realm and yet sometimes it seemed so close. Luciffen often felt that it would be easier to combat the forces of darkness in a world devoid of magic, where technology was predictable, where there was a clear boundary it seemed between right and wrong. Then he looked down at Ayla's sleeping face and recalled how she had been unwilling to return home at all, much as Jake had been when he had arrived in the realm. The grass always seemed greener on the other side of the fence, he smiled ruefully to himself, but their problems were likely every bit as hard to solve as those in the Mirrorealm.

'You will watch over her?' Luciffen asked, still looking down at Ayla.

The shadowy figure stepped into the light. Vigoran nodded. 'I will. It's because of me that she is here.'

Luciffen nodded, pleased to hear Vigoran accept the responsibility that he had for Ayla, for her future, in this world or another.

'She has suffered, Vigoran, as has her mother.'

'For what I did,' Vigoran agreed. 'I allowed matters of the heart to cloud my mind.'

Luciffen placed a hand on the warrior's shoulder. 'No man should call love a crime,' he said, 'but you had to leave them.'

Vigoran nodded, his fists clenched by his side. 'To be seen as human again, for who I am, by Rachel. It was….'

The warrior stumbled on his words.

'Unforgettable,' Luciffen answered for him, and Vigoran nodded and fell silent once more. 'The sorcery of the wytches that plagues you here in the realm was impotent in Rachel and Ayla's world. What is done is done, and we both knew that Ayla would have to come here one day. We just didn't know it would be when she was so young.'

'We had no choice,' Vigoran said, 'Ayla is the one.'

Luciffen led him from the room and closed the door behind them.

'You will see them again,' he replied, 'as they will one day see you.'

\*\*\*

## Forty–Nine

Ayla awoke, and for a moment she did not know where she was.

The digital clock on her bedside table blinked silently before her, and read *8.04am.*

Ayla sat up in her bed and realised that she was fully dressed in her tunic and leather, which would have been an embarrassment to say the least had her mother been in the house. Ayla recalled that it was a Sunday and that her mother would still be in the hospital, but if she was feeling better then she could be discharged at any moment.

Ayla got out of bed, feeling strangely wistful for the Mirrorealm but also somewhat more contented than she had been before all of this had begun. It felt as though she had a purpose, something to aim for that had eluded her until now. There was more to her life than just school and exams and boys and music, something bigger, and she was a part of it all. Best of all, nobody else on the planet knew about it. A part of her wanted to shout it from the rooftops that she, Ayla Fox, was now a renowned Dragun slayer and had joined an epic war against the forces of darkness in a realm so fantastical that nobody could ever believe that it existed, much less that it could be found on the other side of a mirror. Which was the problem of course – nobody would believe her.

Ayla didn't shout it from the rooftops. She got dressed and had breakfast instead.

Her mother finally returned home just before lunch, Geraldine giving Rachel a lift home from the hospital. Ayla did everything she could to make her mother feel better, joining her to sit in the garden because the storms had finally stopped and the sun was shining again.

'We'll have to do something about that tree,' her mother said as they sat in the sunshine and looked at the blackened hulk.

Ayla watched the tree for a moment, and then she saw something on one of the branches. She got out of her seat and examined it.

'I think the tree will be just fine,' she replied.

'Are you kidding? It got deep fried, along with you!'

Ayla gestured to the buds growing on the branches, and Rachel got out of her seat and looked at them in amazement.

'How is that even possible?'

'Anything's possible,' Ayla replied.

They spent the rest of the day chilling out, enjoying the sunshine and generally lazing around, which is what all Sundays should be about. Although her mother seemed much happier now, Ayla could not help but feel a melancholy about not being in the Mirrorealm. Life outside of it just seemed so, so.., *ordinary.*

They went to bed early that evening, but Ayla could not sleep for several hours. Her mind was filled with Draguns and Terra, Luciffen and Vigoran, Jake and Herric. She wondered what they were doing now, and where the cavalier Herric had flown to with his Griffons aboard the Phoenix. She fell asleep with the image of his wonky smile and sparkling, roguish eyes filling her mind.

Her mother left for work early the next morning with something of a spring in her step, which was encouraging for Ayla. And for the first time, she realised that she was getting ready for school on a Monday morning without a care in the world.

That, of course, was until she opened her school bag and saw Tamsin's maths homework staring back at her. For a moment she considered dumping the book down a drain as she had originally considered, but then she had a better idea. She spent a few minutes calculating the answers, which were not exactly difficult anyway, but she spent some time getting them just right before she headed off to school.

The sun was out again in a cloudless sky and the air was warm as she walked happily along the pavement to the bus stop. She saw Rose coming the other way, staring at Ayla in wonder.

'You're the talk of the town! Everyone's still asking how you survived!'

Ayla had almost forgotten about the lightning strike, and the fact that most of the children in the school would have last heard about Ayla on the news. It all felt like it had happened years ago.

'Oh, it wasn't so bad,' Ayla replied with a smile.

'Wasn't so bad?!' Rose echoed in horror, and then stopped as she peered at Ayla. 'What's going on?'

'What do you mean?'

Rose looked Ayla up and down as though she had grown horns. 'You look, *different*.'

'It's the same uniform.'

'Yeah, but, I mean you. *You* look different.'

Ayla looked in a shop window as they passed by and she realised what Rose meant. Ayla was walking taller, more casually, almost with a swagger that had never, ever been there before.

'I just had a good weekend, that's all.'

'You got fried alive by lightning, twice, and you call *that* a good weekend? I'd hate to see you on a bad one!'

They laughed as they reached the bus stop where a large crowd of children were waiting for the bus. Rose's laughter was cut abruptly short as a harsh voice snapped out at them.

'Oh look, it's Ailing Sox!'

The crowd parted and Rose seemed to shrink in size as Tamsin and her crew shoved their way through to confront Ayla. For a moment Ayla's heart skipped a beat in panic, an old habit that was hard to break, but then she stood her ground.

'You got me grounded for the weekend when you didn't show up for school on Friday,' Tamsin snapped as she shrugged off her blazer and rolled up her sleeves. 'I'm gonna make that lightning strike look like a slap on the wrist, Wailer Fox.'

The crowd giggled and jostled each other for a better look.

Ayla glanced at them without interest, and then back at Tamsin. The girl who had seemed so dangerous and cruel before now looked like a spoilt, overweight brat.

'Go ahead, fatty,' Ayla uttered.

The crowd fell silent and it seemed as though they were all holding their breath. Tamsin peered at Ayla and then glanced at her friends for support. 'What did she call me?'

'What you are,' Ayla replied for them. 'An overweight bully, as thick as one short plank.'

The crowd stared in amazement as they waited to see what would happen next.

'Man, that lighting strike really screwed up your brain, Fox,' Tamsin sneered as she advanced, her fists balled.

'At least I've got one.'

The crowd chortled in delight, but Tamsin's face flushed with rage and she swung a punch with all of her might.

In the past, Ayla would have never seen it coming. Now, Tamsin might as well have sent a Letter of Intention to Strike. Ayla stepped toward and slightly to the left of the punch and Tamsin's fist sailed past her. Ayla stuck one foot out and Tamsin stumbled over it and fell flat on her face on the pavement with a loud crack.

Ayla let her school bag slip from her shoulder and handed it to Rose. 'Would you mind?' Rose, her jaw agape, took the bag with one hand and wide eyes as Ayla turned to where a furious Tamsin staggered to her feet and charged at Ayla with a scream.

Ayla waited until the last moment and then she ducked down as Tamsin threw a punch. Ayla slammed an elbow up into Tamsin's belly as she passed by. Tamsin's breath left her lungs in a foul gust of air as Ayla slid out from beneath her and turned.

Tamsin's face was twisted with pain as she struggled upright and tried to reach out for Ayla to grapple her to the ground. Ayla hopped back out of reach, light as a cat on her feet, and as Tamsin lunged clumsily for her again Ayla pushed her arms aside and jabbed two fingers into Tamsin's eyes.

Tamsin squealed in pain and then began to cry as Ayla shoved one foot behind the bigger girl's ankle and pushed her hard under her chin. Tamsin flipped backwards and crashed down onto her back, sobbing and unable to see properly.

The tears washed her mascara in thick black lines down her face. The rest of the children looked on as the bus rolled in behind them and the doors hissed open.

Ayla looked at the forty or so children watching in awe, and shook her head.

'Every single one of you has been pushed around by Tamsin, and never once have any of you ever stood together and fought back. Are you all telling me that Tamsin is worth forty of you?'

The crowd stared at her in amazement but nobody said a word.

'Stand together,' Ayla said to them as she glanced at Tamsin's crew, 'they're only strong because they pick on one person at a time when they're all together. Tamsin and her little minions are nothing compared to all of us. *Nothing.*'

Ayla saw the children all considering this, and then the crowd closed in around Tamsin and her three minions. Ayla saw the sudden panic on the faces of all four of them, and they cowered as the other children loomed over them in silence.

Ayla turned to Rose and silently took her bag back, and from it she pulled the maths book and dropped it onto Tamsin's bleating face. Ayla would have liked to have done more, but she thought of Luciffen, Vigoran and Ellegen and their dignity, so instead she slipped her bag back over her shoulder and looked down at the girl who had once seemed so threatening.

'It took me all of five minutes to finish that maths homework for you,' she said as she turned her back on Tamsin. 'A five–year old could have done it. Get a grip.'

Ayla smiled as the crowd of children parted for her, giggling at Tamsin's stupidity, and Ayla marched toward the bus at the head of the queue with nobody daring to oppose her. Gary Schwarz stood nearby with his arms folded and a smile on his face as he looked her up and down.

'That was pretty cool, Fox,' he said. 'Maybe you and I could get together and…'

'I'd rather date a chimpanzee,' Ayla interrupted as she breezed past him and grabbed Josh Ryan's arm. Whether he liked that or not she couldn't tell, but she tugged him with her and slipped her other arm through Rose's as they walked onto the bus.

For the first time in her life Ayla realised that it wasn't fear or intimidation itself that mattered, but how you dealt with them. She promised herself that she would never let herself be intimidated by anyone ever again, either here or in the Mirrorealm when she returned.

And she was definitely going to return there as soon as she possibly could. There was much to be done.

***

## Fifty

The Towers of Vipera stood immoveable against the violent storms, the rain lashing down across the blackened wasteland beyond the walls. Through the brutal gales trudged thousands of Urks, marching back toward the fortress, snarling and growling at one another.

From a hall high above the violent wilderness, Terra stood and watched as her hordes marched slowly back to the safety of the towers. The rain streamed down the glass, and the darkness beyond reflected her image. Her beautiful face was marred by a thin gash down her left cheek where the knife had slashed her face, and no amount of sorcery had removed the garish wound.

Fury boiled inside her and she both heard and felt the two snakes in her hair writhe and hiss, sensing her rage.

Terra turned away from the stormy spectacle and glided through the great chamber that she called home. A few scant torches flickered in their mounts against the walls, and two hulking ogres stood in silence near the door, guarding it as always. On the other side prowled a pair of Cerberus, sniffing and occasionally scratching at the door. They wanted to be inside with her, but she did not want their attention right now. Terra wanted to be alone.

'Get out,' she whispered.

The two ogres turned without a word and lumbered from the room, ushering the two hell hounds out of the way and closing the doors behind them with a dull boom that seemed to echo through the fortress and away into eternity. Terra ascended a flight of steps to an ornate throne that stood at one end of the chamber, crafted from the bones of enemies long gone. The seat cushion was crafted from the clothes that they had worn, and stuffed using their hair and skin. The back of the throne was forged from the steel of their swords and lined with precious stones that glittered in the torch light as Terra sat down.

She waited for a long time, not moving, her thoughts away with memories of centuries gone by, lost in a miasma from the past. She had sat for so long that she could not recall when she had actually arrived, and when she finally emerged from her thoughts she looked down and saw that the backs of her hands were wet.

When she reached up to her face, she realised that her cheeks were also damp. She swiped them dry with a hasty flourish, and then the sound of movement outside the windows of the towers alerted her to someone or something approaching, and she stood and walked back to the windows. There, against the storm clouds and lightning, she saw a shadowy form flicker like a dangerous thought from one shadow to the next.

Terra opened the nearest window and the demonic form fluttered inside, flying around the hall before it settled atop the statue of a long–dead warrior whose name Terra had long forgotten.

'What news?'

The reply came in a deep, murderous voice. 'I know where Luciffen hides the Well of Memories.'

Terra felt righteous rage soar within her and she clenched her fist. 'I knew it. I knew that they would not be able to hide it forever, and with it in my possession I will be able to master their sorcery as well as my own. They rallied to the girl's cause and now it's left them exposed. Where is it?'

The demon had no mouth, only glowing red eyes and a shadowy form, but Terra could sense the smirk on its face.

'All in good time,' it whispered.

Terra's clenched fist burst into light as a ball of fire ignited within it and she raised her arm. 'Tell me now or you'll be lost to damnation before this day is out!'

The demon tilted its head with interest, unafraid. Then it fluttered down from its perch and landed before her. Slowly, its shadowy form began to harden and it loomed taller than her, and its voice began to resemble something more human.

'If I do, you will charge in and lose your advantage, just as you did on the field of battle today. You have lost Gallentia, the Mirror of Souls and the new mirror you took so long to gather, which now boils in molten rock in the Mines of Poisor.'

'The Centaurs will pay for their treachery in their hundreds and I will find others to dig in the mines!' Terra shot back. 'The girl was lucky, nothing more, and she knows nothing of her powers!'

'But she will,' the demon replied, forming arms and legs as it stood before her, its voice fully human now along with its features. 'And when she does you must be ready, for she will oppose and destroy you.'

'Pah!' Terra snapped. 'What could a pathetic girl like Ayla Fox do to *me*?'

'Slash your face?' the demon uttered, grinning.

Terra hissed at the demon as it took its final form, the dashingly handsome face looking into hers. To her surprise, the demon reached up and gently touched the gash on her cheek.

'Such rage, that you cannot control.'

'Don't lecture me,' Terra snapped as she turned her head away from the demon's touch.

'You summoned me,' the demon reminded her. 'If you wish to control the realm, first you must learn to control yourself.'

'They could move the Well of Memories again,' Terra urged. 'We must strike while we can and…'

'They will surely move it if you attack now, and then you'll have nothing, just as you have nothing now from your efforts to take Stormshadow Citadel. Now is the time to wait, to listen and to learn, for there is something that you do not know about the one they call Ayla Fox.'

Terra touched the scar on her cheek at the mention of the name, and she leaned closer to the demon.

'What is it?' she asked. 'Why was she chosen as the next Hybrin? She seemed to be nothing, a nobody.'

The demon leaned in and whispered to Terra and her eyes widened in delight and malice as she realised what the demon had managed to discover.

'And they don't suspect that you know?'

'They suspect nothing,' came the reply, 'for now at least. I am in their trust, remember?'

Terra could barely contain her delight. Now that she knew the location of the Well of Memories she could start to think about destroying all that Luciffen and his forces stood for from the inside out. She had lost the battle and she had lost control of Gallentia, but she had gained so much more as a result.

'You are right,' Terra said finally, and this time it was she who reached out to touch the cheek of the other. 'I should have listened to you before now.'

'Yes, you should,' the demon agreed, 'but now I must leave before they suspect me. They will not sleep for long for they have much work to do, and as you pointed out, there should not be two Hybrins in the realm at the same time. They might begin to understand what has happened.'

'Go,' Terra said, 'and bring me good news as soon as you can!'

In the dim light from the torches, Terra watched as Jake Shaw's handsome features dissolved once more into demonic form and he fluttered away and vanished into the darkness of the night.

\*\*\*

Sign up to Dean Crawford's Book Club to get notification of new releases and special offers! You can find other books at Dean's website:

# www.deancrawfordbooks.com

## ABOUT THE AUTHOR

Dean Crawford is the author of almost thirty novels, including the internationally published series of thrillers featuring *Ethan Warner*, a former United States Marine now employed by a government agency tasked with investigating unusual phenomena. The novels have been *Sunday Times* paperback best–sellers and have gained the interest of major *Hollywood* production studios. He is also the enthusiastic author of many independently published novels under his own label, *Fictum Ltd*.

Printed in Great Britain
by Amazon